THE DEVIL'S DAUGHTER

THE DEVIL'S DAUGHTER

GORDON GREISMAN

BLACK
STONE
PUBLISHING

Copyright © 2024 by Gordon Greisman
Published in 2024 by Blackstone Publishing
Cover design by Bookfly

All rights reserved. This book or any portion
thereof may not be reproduced or used in any manner
whatsoever without the express written permission
of the publisher except for the use of brief quotations
in a book review.

Any historical figures and events referenced in this book
are depicted in a fictitious manner. All other characters
and events are products of the author's imagination, and
any similarity to real persons, living or dead, is coincidental.

Printed in the United States of America

First edition: 2024
ISBN 979-8-212-34257-5
Fiction / Mystery & Detective / Private Investigators

Version 1

Blackstone Publishing
31 Mistletoe Rd.
Ashland, OR 97520

www.BlackstonePublishing.com

For Elinor

CHAPTER ONE

2022
I can't hear a thing.

I have a hearing aid. It's in the utility drawer in the kitchen, I think, but there's an infernal buzzing whenever I wear it, like a mosquito circling over my bed in the dark on a summer night, so I never use it.

I can't really see either.

I have three pairs of glasses—three because I usually don't have the slightest idea where I put any one of them down. They have lenses as thick as double-glazed windows that make my eyes bulge like a cartoon character, but if I don't wear them, the world has all the clarity of a Haley's M-O commercial. Are there still commercials for Haley's M-O? Is there still Haley's M-O, for that matter? One of the many strange and disturbing things about living into your nineties is that the past has a way of collapsing in on itself. Something as trivial as an ad on TV that you're sure you saw just a couple of days ago hasn't actually aired in years. That collapse goes for people too, people who were once close friends, kids from the old neighborhood, guys I knew in the service, drinking buddies, mooks I took down or ones I put down, and—infinitely more distressing than all of them—women I once loved.

There weren't that many. I was never one for the errant lay, not one of those guys who took imbecilic pride in the notches on their belt. Does anyone still say that? Notches on your belt? Probably not. Anyway, like

I said, there weren't that many. I lost my virginity to Mary O'Callahan, a kindly local pro, when I was thirteen, which proved to be far more terrifying than exciting. There were a few assignations and brief affairs after that, but as it turns out, I have to feel something a little more nourishing than passing lust.

Some of those people do turn up at the oddest times though. I can be combing what's left of my hair when Edie Marx, an artsy girl I once had a fling with, suddenly appears in the bathroom mirror behind me, wearing nothing but one of my old white Oxford shirts and smoking an unfiltered Lucky. She blows a perfectly round smoke ring with a click of her jaw and asks if I want to go to the Vanguard later, Oscar's quartet is playing, and she thinks Bud might be there.

Or I can be walking over to Queensboro Wine and Spirits in Stockbridge—hobbling over, is more like it—when Carmine Rizzo falls into step with me. He says The Chin wants a sit-down. I ask when, and he says, "How 'bout right now? No time like the present, Jack."

I don't say anything. I know Carmine isn't really there. I know Edie isn't either. I may be blind as a bat and deaf as a post, but I'm still playing with a full deck even if the cards have gotten a little frayed. I still recognize John Coltrane's "Straight Street" from its first four notes, know that Gleyber Torres went three for four last night, and read Krugman's column when the *Times* posts it online. And almost every day now, I FaceTime with Sarah, though it took her the better part of a freezing January afternoon to teach me how.

Tracy doesn't appear as often as she used to, and that makes me sad. We were married for thirty-two years, and for months after she was gone, I would wake up in the morning not only expecting her to be curled up next to me but sure that she was. I felt her hand in mine and her cheek warm against my shoulder, and it wasn't until the fog of sleep and the haze of the two Klonopin I took the night before cleared from my head that I realized she wasn't actually there.

I loved Tracy, but she wasn't the love of my life, which I guess she knew. We were happy together but more comfortable than passionate. That not only annoyed the hell out of her, it hurt, and I'm still sorry about it. It's not that we never made love, and it was always good when we did, but I was in my forties when we married, not exactly in my sexual prime. Tracy was younger, not obscenely so, but young enough to expect more than a kiss and a friendly squeeze on her behind when she crawled into bed with the man she loved. She told me that more than once, often in tears. I felt bad, promised to do better, and would for a month or two before falling back into the old routine of dozing off watching *Johnny Carson* or an old black-and-white movie on *The Late Show*. But we were content. That sounds like pretty weak sauce, but it was more than that. We were close, talked and laughed, shared secrets, took showers together, and read the Sunday paper on a bench in Washington Square Park when the weather was decent. And she loved it whenever Monk stopped by on his way uptown, or we went out to dinner with Bud and his latest. Tracy was generous and kind, put up with my moods, which could turn sour for no apparent reason, and never complained when I went out on a job and didn't come home for a day or two. When I once asked her why she didn't think I was cheating on her, Tracy smiled and said having an affair took effort and deceit and that I was too lazy to sneak around.

I was gutted when cancer took her. That was nearly twenty years ago, and I still miss her. I closed up the house in West Stockbridge then, holed up in our apartment on Perry Street, and wept. Sarah and the girls came by every couple of days with their arms full of groceries from Balducci's and buzzed around the place chattering at me, hoping that would draw me out of my funk. And eventually it did. Like I said, I loved Tracy, but the truth is, she wasn't V.

CHAPTER TWO

1957
Richie Costello can't stop staring at V, which is not only embarrassing but pretty inappropriate, considering he's a priest. Actually, Richie is more than that. He's a monsignor and executive secretary to Cardinal Spellman, the archbishop of New York. He looks the part too: his fingernails are manicured, his hair razor-cut, and the cassock he's wearing is so expertly fitted that it could have been tailored on Savile Row. In fact, it probably was.

"Jack," Richie says, "His Eminence would consider it a personal favor if you would look into the matter for him." V's sitting across the kitchen table from him, and he finally manages to wrest his eyes from her to me, adding, "Louis Garrett has given generously to the church, despite not being a member of the flock. And from what I understand, his daughter is basically a good kid, a little confused maybe, but what teenager isn't?"

I know Richie from the old neighborhood. His family lived in a tenement on West Forty-Sixth near the corner of Eleventh Avenue. His father was a day laborer, and his mother went to noon mass at St. Malachy's most every afternoon, which probably explains why Richie ended up the way he did.

"How long has she been gone?" I ask.

"Just a few nights. There's probably a perfectly innocent explanation, but her father is very worried."

"Then why doesn't he call the police?"

"Mr. Garrett would rather keep it a private matter and only inform the authorities if it's absolutely necessary."

This kind of bullshit probably works for Richie most of the time, but if Garrett's kid just snuck out to spend a couple of nights with her boyfriend, her father wouldn't have sent an emissary from His Eminence the cardinal to have a guy like me find out what happened to her.

"Can I get you something a little stronger than that cup of coffee, Father?" V asks, getting up from my kitchen table. "You look like you could use it."

She doesn't wait for an answer. V goes to the sideboard, pours Richie three fingers of Irish over rocks, pours another three neat for herself, and flashes the monsignor a little cleavage when she sits back down. She's being a wiseass on purpose, not just because Richie hasn't been able to stop staring at her breasts, but because she's made him for a phony and an officious little jerk. Where V comes from, that's a mortal sin.

Thelonious Monk introduced us. There was an after-hours cutting contest at Minton's, and when Kenny Kersey took over from him, Monk escorted the most beautiful woman I had ever seen over to my table. When I finally managed to recover from the shock, he told me her name was Vicky, but I already knew that. I hadn't actually met Victoria Hemming before, but I'd seen her in ads in magazines and peeking seductively over a bare shoulder on billboards around town. Monk grinned and told me that I was going to spend the rest of my life with her, but I knew that wasn't true. So did V, but she sat down anyway and offered to buy me a drink.

When I asked, she said she was from Texas, that her father was an oil wildcatter and her mother was a Houston society doyenne. When she was sixteen, she took off with her boyfriend, crossed the state line into Louisiana, and married him. The marriage lasted a week. By the time she was eighteen, she was living in Paris and modeling for Christian Dior. He introduced her to a French count who V said was so handsome his looks nearly made her cry. He was twice her age, destitute, and lived off her, which she didn't really mind. What she did mind was that Monsieur

Le Compte was serially unfaithful, sleeping with every young model he could get his hands on before she finally threw him out. Her marriages may have failed, but her career was spectacularly successful. Now she's chased around town by movie stars, jet-setting playboys, scions of vast family fortunes and their fathers. What she sees in me is a mystery.

"I can't imagine this will take up too much of your time, Jack, and Mr. Garrett will pay handsomely for your services." Richie knocks back half his drink in a gulp to settle his nerves. V is still toying with him, and I shoot her a look telling her to cut it out, but she ignores me. "It would be a real blessing if you can help the poor man out," Richie says, rattling the ice in his glass. "It really would."

My dad was raised a Catholic, but then he became a radical Wobbly and never stepped foot inside a church again. My mother was Jewish, a piece of information that was best kept under wraps in our neighborhood. She came from a lot of money, but her family cut her off when she married a goy, so we never saw a penny of it. I was raised to be suspicious of anyone sanctimonious enough to wear a collar, but being that I'm nearly broke right at the moment, I tell Richie I'll do what I can.

"I can't make any promises, but I'll talk to this guy Garrett, if that's what you want."

"It's not what I want, Jack, it's what His Eminence wants."

"Well, in that case, how can I possibly refuse?"

CHAPTER THREE

I've been taking the subway by myself since I was five. I'd take it now, but V is done up for a job, so instead of grabbing the Seventh Avenue Express at Fourteenth Street, we walk to Sixth and hail a cab.

This requires virtually no effort. Looking like she does, all V has to do is stand on the sidewalk and lift a finger, and every cabbie in the vicinity makes a beeline for us. A Checker beats the others to the punch. We slide into the back seat, and when Moe Moskowitz—Moe's name and mug shot are on the taxi license pinned to his dashboard—finally stops gawking at V, we take off and head uptown.

Moe pulls to a stop in front of Avedon's studio on East Forty-Ninth Street. V gives me a smooch before she gets out; then I tell Moe to take me crosstown to the Beresford on Central Park West.

The Beresford's doorman, a human slab of cement in a Ruritanian uniform complete with gold brocade epaulets, accosts me the second I cross the building's threshold.

"Can I help you with something?" he says, looking like he'd rather help crush my skull than do me any favors.

"I'm here to see Louis Garrett."

"Is Mr. Garrett expecting you?"

"No, buddy, I'm the Fuller Brush man. Just call up to Garrett's apartment and tell him Jack Coffey's here."

In other circumstances, the slab would have busted my nose for a crack like that, but he's on duty and I might be somebody important, so he does what he's told.

Now, I'm not entirely unfamiliar with how the other half lives. For starters, V's apartment on Beekman Place is a very cushy prewar six. I don't know why she prefers spending her nights in my quasi dump on Perry Street, but she does. And I've worked for a few Park Avenue swells who had nasty secrets and habits that I kept out of the papers and off the police blotter. Their places were pretty impressive, but none of them hold a candle to Louis Garrett's sixteen-room luxury duplex. For one thing, the elevator goes right up into the apartment, which must be why the building's management employs a guy like the slab to patrol the lobby.

I'm greeted by Garrett's butler when the elevator doors open. He's friendly, not the doddering Englishman in livery that I'd expected. He introduces himself as Burton—I don't know whether that's his first name or last—and he takes my hat and coat.

"Mr. Garrett is on the phone," he says. "If you could just wait for him in the library." I follow Burton into a room with floor-to-ceiling mahogany bookcases and a panoramic view of the park. He asks if he can get me anything: a glass of water or a cup of coffee. I beg off and he says, "Mr. Garrett shouldn't be very long," before he leaves me alone.

There's an antique writing desk in the center of the room. On it are three photographs in sterling silver frames, all of them featuring a pretty teenage girl, who I assume is Garrett's daughter. One is formal, subtly lit, and obviously shot by a professional. Another is taken at a cotillion of some sort. The girl is wearing an evening gown, and she's on the arm of a West Point cadet in full dress uniform. The last one is a vacation snap. In it she's smiling for the camera and looks genuinely happy. I'm holding the picture when Garrett walks into the room.

"She's lovely, isn't she?" Garrett says. He's in his fifties and wearing an old cashmere sweater with a pinhole in one of the sleeves, a pair of baggy gray trousers, and bedroom slippers. He hasn't shaved in a couple of days and looks pale and drawn. "Thank you for coming on such short notice, Jack," he says, and we shake hands.

"Not a problem," I say. "Is this your daughter?" I show him the photograph.

"Yes. That's my Lucy, and I'm worried sick about her. Do you mind if I pour myself a drink?" It's ten o'clock in the morning, but the guy is upset, and I'm not going to begrudge him a little liquid fortitude. "Can I get you one?" he asks, but I shake my head. After he pours himself a jigger of scotch with a splash of soda, we take seats, Garrett behind the writing desk and me in a chair in front of it. Like I said, he looks like hell and I feel for the guy, but empathy isn't what he wants from me.

"Why don't you tell me what happened?" I say.

"Lucy was supposed to be spending the night with her friend Muffy."

"That would be Muffy . . . ?"

"Palmer. Muffy Palmer. Her parents have an apartment at 998 Fifth Avenue across from the museum. Lucy has slept over there before, but she's always home by noon the next day."

"What did Muffy say when you called?"

"That she had been there that first night but left in the morning, and Muffy hadn't seen or heard from her since."

Somebody could have grabbed Lucy crossing through the park on her way home. That's happened before. Some psycho could have raped and murdered her, then stashed her body behind a bush. I don't tell Garrett that because it seems unnecessarily cruel, and I don't know if it's true. It could also be that somebody knows exactly who Lucy and her father are and snatched her, counting on a king's ransom for her return. That's more likely, but I don't tell Garrett that either. The guy's rattled enough as it is.

"Talk to me about Lucy," I say instead. "What's she like?"

Garrett shuts his eyes and inhales like the thought of his missing daughter and what might have become of her is physically painful. I expect him to say that she's the light of his life and that he's terrified something terrible has happened to her, but he surprises me.

He says nothing. Maybe it's a lump in his throat, but I don't make Garrett for the type to burst into tears, so I'm not sure.

"Are you and Lucy close?" I ask.

"Yes, very," is all he can manage before bolting his drink, and now I think the guy really is doing his best to hold it together.

"What about Lucy's mother? She must be worried."

"She passed away years ago, I'm afraid—giving birth to Lucy."

Of course, this makes me feel like a first-class shit, and as if to prove that I am, Garrett rummages in one of his desk drawers, pulls out a photograph of his wife, and slides it across to me. Garrett's wife couldn't have been too much older than his daughter now when it was taken, and Lucy looks just like her.

"I've raised her on my own," Garrett says. "Fortunately, I've been able to give her the best of everything—which means I spoiled her, I guess. Look, I'm not going to lie to you, Jack, Lucy can be pretty wild. She's stubborn and used to getting what she wants. I don't always approve of her friends either."

"Friends like who?"

"Like Rex Halsey. A real bad egg, that one. I'm sure you know the type. Too smooth, too charming, and far too old for her. But I don't think Lucy's with him now though."

"Why's that?"

"Because I paid him a lot of money to go away."

I don't have the heart to tell Garrett that writing a check to a guy like the one he just described doesn't guarantee anything, not unless you hire a little muscle to back it up. But then, maybe that's what he did. Maybe the slab of cement in the lobby does more than carry packages and whistle for cabs.

"Mr. Garrett, I need you to level with me. Are you sure this isn't some stunt Lucy's pulling? I mean, is she annoyed with you for some reason? Forgive me, but rich kids are like that, and you said she's used to getting her own way. Muffy Palmer could be lying for her. Maybe Lucy has been with her the whole time."

Before Garrett has a chance to answer, a woman enters the room without bothering to knock. She looks about forty, wears a cream-colored blouse and an ankle-length tweed skirt, has tortoiseshell glasses propped on the top of her head, and her hair is in a bun held together by a yellow number-two pencil. "Mr. Garrett, your meeting downtown is in an hour, and I'm sure you'll want to shower and shave before you go. Then you have lunch at the Colony at one, the lawyers at three, and I called over to the Statler. Mario is happy to come by anytime you'd like to cut your hair."

"This is my secretary, Lillian Crouse," Garrett says by way of introduction. "Jack is helping me with Lucy."

I smile and nod, but Lillian doesn't acknowledge me in any way.

Instead, she says, "Your car is already waiting downstairs," turns, and leaves without another word.

"No, Jack. Believe me, this isn't a stunt," Garrett says, answering the question I asked before Lillian walked in. "Something's happened to Lucy, I'm sure of it, and I want you to find out what it is."

I'm happy to charge Garrett my usual fee, a hundred a day plus expenses, but before I can tell him that, he offers me ten grand as a retainer and another ten as a bonus if I bring Lucy home safe and sound. Before I accept, I gently broach the possibility that she might have been kidnapped. I say that if he gets a ransom demand, he needs to inform the police immediately, and that if he doesn't, I will. Kidnapping is a federal offense, and as much as I understand his desire to keep this whole business under wraps, I'm not about to get myself in hot water with the FBI at any price.

Riding down in the elevator with Garrett's check in my pocket, I'm thinking my first move is obvious. I'll go over to Muffy Palmer's apartment, and with any luck Lucy has holed herself up there just to torture her old man, making my bonus the easiest money I've ever made. The elevator reaches the lobby, the doors open, and there's a beefy guy in a suit and tie waiting for me to get off. I don't know who he is, but somehow he knows me.

"You must be Jack Coffey," he says, sticking out his hand. "I'm Bob Carson. I work with Lou Garrett."

I don't mind glad-handers like Carson. They're usually harmless and sometimes they're useful. If you want tickets to a fight or a show or dinner reservations at some place that doesn't know you from Adam, Bob Carson is your man.

"It's a shame about Lucy," he says. "She really is a sweet kid."

"Why is it a shame?"

"Just that she's taken off. It's not the first time either. Lou does the best that he can with her, but Lucy's a real handful."

"I'll keep that in mind," I say, and Carson steps onto the elevator as I step off, but before the doors close, he reaches into the breast pocket of his suit and hands me a business card. I glance down at his card. All it says is "Carson & Co." and a telephone number. I'm not sure what good it will do me, but I slip it into my jacket pocket before I leave.

"Give me a call if you need anything, Jack," he says. "I mean it. Anything at all." And he rides the elevator up and out of sight.

CHAPTER FOUR

"I'm sure Mr. Garrett is worried sick, so you need to tell this gentleman the truth, Muffin."

"But I promised, Mama."

"I don't care what you promised, young lady, you'll tell Mr. Coffey everything he needs to know and you'll do it right this minute!"

Muffin Palmer, known for obvious reasons as "Muffy," is a plain-looking sixteen-year-old girl with stringy blond hair and a pale complexion currently in the throes of a bout with acne. She's sitting on a couch in the family living room. The room is plush, full of antique furniture and neo-modern art, but feels cold like a high-end interior designer with an attitude has had at it. Her mother, a whippet-thin woman with a mean streak, is standing over her.

"Lucy wasn't really here at all, was she?" I ask gently.

When Muffy hesitates, her mother barks, "Answer Mr. Coffey!" loud enough to give the kid a start.

"Okay! Okay, I said she was here, but she wasn't. Lucy told me that if her father called, I should say she slept over, but she really didn't."

"You lied to Mr. Garrett!" A vein is pulsating in Mrs. Palmer's neck, but if she keeps browbeating her kid, I'm not going to be able to find out anything, so I take the woman aside and say that if she could just leave me and Muffy alone for a few minutes, I'll get her daughter to tell me what I need to know and get out of her hair.

"I won't tolerate lying, Mr. Coffey. I just won't."

"I get that, but why don't you give me a chance to find out what really went on? Can you do that for me?" I don't wait for an answer. Instead, I usher Mrs. Palmer out of the room and close the door behind her.

"How long have you and Lucy been friends?" I ask, pulling up a chair opposite Muffy.

"Since fifth grade," she says. "I mean, we haven't been friends the whole time or anything. Only since last year. She didn't talk to me very much before that."

"And this isn't the first time you lied to her dad, is it?" Muffy scratches at a nonexistent itch and stares into her lap. "Don't worry," I say, smiling as if we're about to share a secret. "I won't tell your mother. I don't want you to get in trouble, Muffy, but I do need to know the truth."

"It's not like she never slept over. I mean, she did once, but—"

"Do you know where Lucy is now?"

Muffy chews on a thumbnail and won't look me in the eye.

"Is she with Rex Halsey?"

"I don't know. Probably."

This poor kid is being played. Muffy is a little bit homely and more than a little bit lonely. Lucy Garrett is pretty and popular. A girl like that always has a factotum, someone to do her bidding, someone she can use when it suits her, then discard.

"Have you ever met Rex?"

"No, but Lucy told me all about him. He's like really handsome and older, so he can get her into all these cool places. Do you know the Blue Note?"

I've spent half my life in joints like the Blue Note, and when I nod, Muffy says, "Rex takes her there sometimes. And to Birdland. And Minton's Playhouse up in Harlem. I'd be too scared to go there, but Lucy is just so brave."

I'm thinking Monk probably knows this guy. If he's a regular at Minton's, Monk must. "Is that all they do together? Go to jazz clubs like Minton's?"

"They do other stuff too. Rex knows all these negro musicians.

You're going to think this is really bad and she made me promise not to tell anybody, but she says that she smokes marijuana with them. I don't know if I believe her, though. Lucy likes to make up stuff."

"Do you know if Rex ever takes her up to his apartment?"

"I don't think so. They go to a hotel sometimes, but please don't tell anybody that. I mean, if my mother or Mr. Garrett finds out . . . just don't say it was me, okay? Lucy will kill me."

"When was the last time you really did see her?"

"At school on Friday. She sits in front of me in bio."

"And you really don't know where she is now."

"No," Muffy says, blowing her nose into a lace handkerchief. "I'd tell you if I did. I swear I would."

Sweet little Lucy Garrett, the apple of her father's eye, is smoking weed and sleeping with Rex Halsey, a guy twice her age.

"Why doesn't that surprise me?" I ask V. We're taking a bath together. The tub is in my kitchen, a quirk of living in four rooms in the West Village.

"At least she's not dead," V says, examining my back for pustules and blackheads. I think it's disgusting, but V calls it primate grooming and gets a kick out of it.

"There's a cheery thought."

"Didn't you think she might be?"

"Yeah. I guess, Rex doesn't want to kill her, he's only after her money."

"Or maybe he just likes young girls."

"Or both. You know, it might be as simple as Lucy's gotten in over her head. A teenage kid rebelling against her father hooks up with a sleaze without knowing what she's in for. It happens all the time."

"Whoever this Halsey is sounds like a real bum to me."

V gets this word from Toots. Everybody's a bum as far as Toots Shor is concerned. But she's right about Halsey. He is a bum, though I'll bet he scares easy.

I'll dig him up, make a few not-so-veiled threats, and that should make him back off. Lucy will kick and scream, hollering about how much she hates her father and loves Rex, that they're going to run away together and there's nothing anybody can do about it. She might even take a swing at me. Maybe I'll bring my buddy Carmine along as muscle.

CHAPTER FIVE

I was fourteen the first time I snuck into Minton's Playhouse. Teddy Hill had put together a house band: Joe Guy on trumpet, Nick Fenton on bass, Kenny Clarke on drums, and Charlie Christian on guitar. When they wouldn't let me in the front door, I went around the back and slipped in through the kitchen when one of the busboys went out for a smoke. That Monday night was celebrity night. Dizzy and Bird were there. So were Don Byas, Coleman Hawkins, and Ben Webster. I got a slap from the old man when I crept back into the apartment at four in the morning, but I didn't care. And I kept going back.

When I got home from overseas, there were new faces: Dexter Gordon, Fats Navarro, Art Blakey, and Miles Davis, who was as young as I was. And there was always Monk. He was there that very first night and most every night after that, and I could have listened to him play forever. He would sit at the piano in a sharp suit, shades, and a fez and get so carried away by an aggressive attack or a wildly improvised melodic twist that he would suddenly stop, stand up, and dance around the piano before sitting back down to pick up where he left off.

Tonight when I walk into Minton's, Monk is at the piano inventing a riff with switch key releases, silences, and hesitations. I sit and soak it in until he finally takes a break and comes over to the table with a snifter of bourbon in his hand and a cigarette dangling from his lips.

"Where is she?" He means V.

"Every girl needs her beauty rest, Monk."

"That one doesn't. She could be up for a week and still turn every head in this joint. I still don't get what she sees in you, boyo." Monk likes to call me boyo or boychick, a tribute to my mixed parentage, I guess.

We listen to Lester Young wheel and dive on his sax for a minute or two before I ask, "Listen, do you know a guy named Rex Halsey? Thirty, thirty-five maybe. Slick. Real good-looking, from what I understand."

"Don't know him, but I've seen him. Always has a young white chick on his arm."

I reach into my jacket pocket for the vacation snap of Lucy Garrett I cadged from her father and show it to Monk. "Did he ever come in with her?"

Monk takes a look and says, "Oh, yeah. She's one of them."

"What do you mean by one of them?"

"The cat's a pimp, Jack. He deals reefer too. At least that's what the boys tell me."

Bourbon is Monk's drug of choice these days, and he's way too fond of it. There have been plenty of nights when he's been so deep in the bag that he couldn't make it home on his own. I'd bundle him into a cab and tell the driver to collect the fare from Monk's wife, Nellie. Every other player I know smokes reefer, shoots smack, or does both. So did Monk until Nellie straightened him out.

"How old is she supposed to be?" Monk asks, handing me back Lucy's photograph.

"Sixteen," I say.

"Sixteen, huh? That sounds about right."

None of this should shock me, but it does. In my line you see a lot of scandalous, even perverse, behavior, but never involving a kid. That Lucy is off doing things she shouldn't while her father thinks she's playing Mystery Date on the floor of Muffy Palmer's bedroom isn't necessarily a surprise, but turning tricks for the likes of Rex Halsey? I told V I thought Lucy might be in over her head. Now I'm sure she is. I had Rex down as a gold digger, not a pimp hustling underage girls. A pretty little thing like Lucy Garrett must fetch a hefty price. But who's paying it? And how did he get Lucy to go along with it? I can see her being out for a cheap thrill, slumming to give the girls at school something to gossip about, but selling her body to some Park Avenue plutocrat just to please Rex Halsey? That I don't see. And now I'm angry. No matter how much trouble Lucy Garrett makes, she's still just a child. Halsey is not only exploiting her but abusing her—even if she doesn't realize it. It's sick and twisted and I'm going to put a stop to it, but first I have to find the son of a bitch.

I think about spending a few nights hanging around Minton's waiting for Rex to show up, but there's no telling how long that could take. Anyway, I'm not the type to sit on my thumbs. That Halsey deals drugs makes it easier. He's got to have a supplier, and I have a pretty good idea who that might be.

I met Carmine Rizzo in 1944—"met him" sounds like somebody introduced us at a rent party or over drinks at O'Doul's. We actually met crouching in a hole in the ground, trying not to get our heads blown off by a German eighty-eight firing for effect. We were assigned to cross the Moselle at Pont-á-Mousson, but the Krauts were kicking our ass from the high ground on the other side of the river. There's no place like a foxhole to make a friend for life, even if that friend turns out to be not only a soldier in the Eightieth Infantry but one in the Genovese crime family. Actually, our friendship became kind of convenient in my later line of work. And considering most of the drug trade in Manhattan is controlled by Vito Genovese's right-hand man Vincent "The Chin" Gigante, knowing Carmine is a definite plus.

I know I can find Carmine at the Triangle Social Club on Sullivan Street in the West Village. The Chin holds court there. It's not much more than a bar with an espresso machine, but it's across the street from Gigante's mother's apartment, and he and his old lady are close. Now, ordinarily, if a guy like me walks into the Triangle uninvited, he gets his legs broken. The Chin gives me the eye when I come in the door, and I can tell he's thinking he'll have one of his boys do just that, but then Carmine vouches for me, so Gigante doesn't say anything when I take a seat. It's three in the morning and the last thing I ought to be doing is drinking the double espresso Carmine is drawing for me, but I need his help and it pays to be sociable.

"What do you want that pimp for?" he says when I ask about Halsey. Then he leans in close so Gigante can't hear him and says, "The only reason we haven't iced that fucker is The Chin likes 'em young, you know what I'm sayin'?"

Color me shocked.

"Halsey deals for you too, doesn't he?"

"Strictly small time, Jack. Nickels and dimes."

"How does it work with him and the girls?"

"We don't let him come in here, that's for damn sure. The girls do, but not him."

I show Carmine Lucy's photograph. "She ever been in?"

"I don't know, but I don't recognize her," which comes as a relief. The Chin has an apelike quality, and the idea of Lucy turning a trick with him upsets my stomach.

"Do you know how I can get ahold of him?"

"Halsey? No idea. We pay a neighborhood kid to run him dime bags. The kid does a dead drop someplace in the park, but I don't know where exactly. Halsey leaves our cut behind and he's good about it, so we don't take an interest. I wish I could be more help."

"That's okay, buddy," I say. "How's the wife?"

"Fat."

"How's the girlfriend?"

"Also fat, but the best blow job in the business."

"Good to know," I say, and pat Carmine on the shoulder when I get to my feet. But before I take off, I leave a hundred on the table because I know The Chin is watching. There's no such thing as a free lunch or free information as far as Vincent Gigante is concerned.

CHAPTER SIX

My favorite time in the city is just before dawn. The town isn't really asleep, just resting its eyes. It's October, and there's a chill and the smell of burning leaves in the air. I could jump on the subway or try to dig up a cab at this hour, but I don't mind walking back to Perry Street from the Triangle, not on a clear night like this. There's nobody on the street and nothing in the way of traffic. I hear a foghorn, which makes me feel good for some reason, and figure it's a tug in the harbor or the Staten Island Ferry making its first run of the day. Stein's Bakery on the corner of Hudson and Barrow has just opened, and I stop in for schnecken. I haven't eaten in hours, so I gobble the sweet bun down and chase it with another cup of coffee. I pass a couple of kids making out in an alley off West Tenth. They could be up to more than that. The girl has got her leg hooked around her boyfriend, and her shoe is dangling from her toe.

I'm not a block from home now. I know V is there waiting and I'm anxious to see her, so I don't notice the guy lurking on the basement steps of 106 Perry. By the time I hear his footsteps, it's too late.

I must have gone out for a couple of seconds because I hit the sidewalk face-first. By the time I come to, the guy has flipped me onto my back and is about to finish me off with a length of lead pipe. I grab his wrist before he can and throw an elbow that catches him on the side of his head. Somehow I manage to wrench the pipe out of his hand, but before I can squirm free, he's got his mitts around my neck and squeezes for all he's worth. I feel like my windpipe is about to shatter, and I grope around for something, anything, to back him off. I find a rusty eight-penny nail lying on the sidewalk and jam it as hard as I can into his nut sack.

He lets out a yowl and lets go of my neck long enough for me to scramble away.

I don't pack a gun usually—usually, there's no need to—but it seems a wise thing to do whenever I stop by and visit Carmine at the Triangle. I go for my revolver, but the guy's on me just as I get to it.

He slaps it out of my hand and pulls out a .38 of his own.

The thing about the prospect of breathing your last is that it comes with a blast of adrenaline. I ignore the gun, rush the guy, and snatch him off his feet just as he fires.

The bullet grazes my ear, but I'm on an adrenaline high and I heave him up on the wrought iron fence at the foot of my building's stoop. He's hung up on one of the fence spikes and there's plenty of blood, but he's wriggling free. I grab my gun out of the gutter and shoot just as he comes at me again. He topples over backward, crashing into a trash can, and it's only then that I recognize the guy.

It's the slab of cement I ran into in the Beresford's lobby.

It suddenly hits me that the slab might've gotten to V before he got to me.

I tear up the steps and into the apartment, where V is not only unhurt but lounging in the tub, reading *Vogue*.

She takes one look at me, shouts, "For God's sake, Jack, what happened?" and doesn't wait for an answer. She jumps out of the tub, grabs a towel, and tries to stanch the bleeding from my skull, which is profuse.

By the time my cop friend Jimmy Mullen arrives, V has torn a sheet into strips and wrapped them around my head. And though I'm woozy and feel like somebody's banging on my brain with a sledgehammer, I'm pretty sure I'll live.

Mullen, like his father and grandfather before him, became a cop after graduating from high school. He's good at it too, working his way up from a beat in Canarsie to detective. His partner, Bernie Rothstein, is with him. Bernie and I don't get along.

"I didn't have a choice, Jimmy," I say, handing Mullen my revolver before he asks for it. "It was me or him."

"I'd say it was definitely him, Jack," Jimmy says, but Rothstein isn't quick to buy self-defense as an excuse.

"You had him hung up on a wrought iron fence, Coffey. What did you do, put two in his chest as a parting gift?"

"Do you want to see the hole he tried to drill in my head, Bernie?" I start to unwrap the bandages.

"No need for that," Jimmy says, stepping in, "but you'd better tell us what happened."

I run down the night's events, leaving out seeing Carmine at the Triangle because it seems best not to involve him or The Chin. I lie and say that I couldn't sleep and went out for a walk, a lie I know V will back up. The guy came at me from out of nowhere, I tell Jimmy, and I have no idea why he was so anxious to cave in my skull. When I say that I don't know him, but that I've seen him before, Mullen wants to know where. I sketch out a few innocuous details about my meeting with Louis Garrett without saying why he wanted to see me. I give him the name of Garrett's secretary so he can check out my story. I'm not sure Rothstein believes any of this, but Jimmy seems satisfied.

"You're gonna have to fill out paperwork, Jack," he says, "and the ADA will want to go through all of this with you again," which I know and don't really mind. "We'll have somebody come by to collect the stiff," Jimmy says as he makes for the door. Rothstein shoots me a look that tells me he thinks I'm scum before he and Mullen take off.

The minute they're gone, V, who hasn't uttered a word up until now, says, "I don't trust that man."

"Rothstein? He's not so bad. He thinks I'm slime, which offends me as a matter of fact, but he's just the usual idiot cop."

"No, not that one. He just hates you. The other one."

V is savvy when it comes to reading people, particularly men. They usually make the mistake of thinking that she's purely decorative when there's a sharp mind behind that dazzling face.

"I dunno," I say. "I've known Jimmy a long time. He's all right."

"No, he isn't, but I'm not going to argue with you about it," V says, taking my hand and leading me into the bedroom.

This is the happiest I've ever been. That's what I always tell myself when V and I are together in bed. The sex is great, but it's so much more than that. I love V, and when we make love, I feel connected to her in a way I've never felt with anyone before. She draws me into a place that's so intimate and emotionally overwhelming that I swear sometimes I feel like weeping when we're done. And sometimes I do.

Tonight, she's being gentle with me, trying not to rattle my brain any more than it has been. She's straddling me, slowing rocking back and forth. The smile on her face is so warm and inviting that I'm desperate to kiss her. I lift my head to do just that, but she leans forward and whispers in my ear, "Just enjoy it, Jack," and I do.

"Do you know what I don't get?" V is sitting up in bed now, her legs crossed, lighting a Gauloise. She brought home a carton of them from Paris, and the room fills with the sweet scent of Turkish tobacco. "Why did that guy try to kill you? I mean, I know he works the door at the Beresford, but Garrett didn't send him. Garrett's the one who hired you."

My head is still pounding, so I reach for the bottle of aspirin on the nightstand and gobble down a few.

"And do you know what else? I don't buy that Garrett's daughter is just an innocent little thing in over her head."

"Why's that?" I buy it—at least for the moment—but I'm eager to hear V's explanation.

"Maybe, I shouldn't be too hard on her. She's probably got problems I don't know about. And it's not like I was a priss when I was her age. I mean, me and Kyle Gentry used to steal a bottle of Southern Comfort from his daddy's liquor cabinet when I was sixteen, drink it on the beach in Galveston, then go up in the dunes and fuck."

"My, weren't we precocious?"

"My, wasn't I boy crazy? But I think Lucy Garrett is up to a lot more than that. How old did you say this Rex Halsey is?"

"In his thirties, I think."

"Of course, he is. And fun to look at too, I'll bet."

I like doing these postmortems with V. I put up a cynical front because in my job cynicism is generally a safe bet, but the truth is I can be too trusting. Misplaced trust has bitten me on the ass more than once.

A few years back, I did work for a sweet guy, an academic who taught in the English Department up at Columbia. He was convinced that his wife, a PhD candidate in childhood development, was having an affair with her academic adviser. He was more hurt than angry but wanted to be sure it wasn't just his imagination before he confronted her. I followed her around for a week, and though she had long lingering lunches with the adviser, she wasn't sleeping with him. I told the academic that he had nothing to worry about, that at worst it was a harmless flirtation, and his wife probably loved him as much now as she did on the day she married him. The guy was relieved, even laughed about it, and I left him thinking I had done a good deed. Two days later he shot his wife to death on the steps of the Low Library. It wasn't the first or the last time something like that happened to me, which V reminds me of whenever she thinks I'm being naive.

"So, what are you saying, that Lucy Garrett is turning tricks for kicks?"

"I'm saying she's young, pretty, and reckless. You think this Rex character is exploiting her and you might be right, but it's possible you've got it the wrong way around."

"That Lucy's using him? Why?"

"Because she can."

"I don't know, V. Monk says the guy has a whole stable of young girls."

"Then what makes Lucy Garrett so special that he sent somebody to kill you?"

"Maybe it wasn't Rex who sent him."

"Then who was it?"

CHAPTER SEVEN

The next day V talks me into going over to the emergency room at St. Vincent's to make sure my cranium isn't permanently damaged. She tags along so I don't blow it off because she knows I hate going to the doctor more than anything in the world. She says the reason I refuse to get an annual physical is because I'm afraid the freckle on my scrotum isn't a freckle at all but a sign of metastasizing testicular cancer. She says that I'm scared a simple blood test will reveal something catastrophic, leukemia or a nascent but incurable malignancy. I remind her that when I was all of eighteen, I took on the Wehrmacht, fought my way across France, crossed the Rhine under heavy shellfire, and battled into the Ruhr pocket. V says she's impressed but that I'm still frightened to death of having a gloved finger shoved up my behind, and she's not entirely wrong.

The emergency room doc takes a look at me, shines a penlight in my eyes, and tells me that I have a concussion, which doesn't exactly come as news. He stitches up the gash in my scalp—it stings like hell when he does—and tells me I should take it easy for a while, maybe spend a couple of days in bed.

V thinks that's a good idea too, and she buys me *Brilliant Corners*, Monk's newest album, and Sonny Rollins's recording *Way Out West* to keep me entertained at home. But by the next morning, I've worn out the grooves on both records, and I'm too antsy to stay in bed. V has another shoot scheduled at Avedon's studio, and I pester her into taking me along, which she says she'll do only if I promise to sit quietly and not interrupt her while she works. I agree because staring at the apartment's four walls is making me stir-crazy.

Dick Avedon and I have nothing in common other than we're both city boys, but I like him anyway. He comes from money. His old man, who Dick despises, is in the retail *schmate* business with a store on Fifth Avenue unsurprisingly called Avedon's Fifth Avenue. His mother's family is in the *schmate* business too, and they're also well heeled. Dick was in the service—assuming you consider the merchant marine the service, which I do—mostly as a photographer. After the war he parlayed that and some pretty amazing department store work into becoming *Harper's Bazaar*'s in-house photographer. Now he's the hottest fashion photographer in town. V tells me his work is revolutionary, that before Avedon came along, models stood like statues with frozen looks on their faces. Now they're alive, human, and laughing, and that's Dick Avedon's doing. His photographs are so famous that I remember seeing one even before I met V. It was of a woman in a black floor-length evening gown standing between two enormous circus elephants, an image almost impossible to forget.

V tells me the woman in that photograph was Dovima, Avedon's longtime muse. Now V plays that part, and she and Dick are close, gossiping, laughing at private jokes, whispering into each other's ear, and holding hands like lovers. Ordinarily, I would be incandescently jealous, but Dick is married and devoted to his wife. And V told me that he also likes guys, which I didn't understand at first, seeing that he's married, until V explained it to me.

Avedon's studio on East Forty-Ninth Street is like no place I've ever been. Sinatra croons "I've Got the World on a String" from the hi-fi, and there are flowers, balloons, wild headdresses, rolls of colored-paper backdrops, and a Santa's workshop full of oversize toys. The latest fashions are hanging on pipe racks, and today Avedon had an actual living horse brought up in the freight elevator. V sits on it bareback as one of Dick's assistants puts the finishing touches on her makeup while another adjusts her lighting. A camera assistant, a pretty blond girl dressed in a black turtleneck and black leotards, bustles around while Avedon stands behind his Rolleiflex, peering through a handheld viewfinder.

There's a delay of some sort, a lighting glitch or something, and the horse has taken an enormous dump that needs to be cleaned up. I'm doing as I promised, keeping my mouth shut and sitting on a velvet love seat against the back wall of the studio reading the *Daily News*, when Dick comes over and sits down next to me.

"Do you follow football, Jack?" he asks, which surprises me. I figure a guy like Avedon for opening night at the Metropolitan Opera, not freezing his ass off up at the stadium on a November afternoon. "I've got season tickets to the Giants, you know?" he says. "This kid Gifford is really something to see. What do you say we go to a game together sometime?"

I'm really not much of a fan, but Avedon is making an effort and I want to oblige him, so I say, "Sure. Sounds great. I'd love it."

"It'll have to be next month though. I'm scheduled to do a shoot in Milan in a couple of weeks and I'll be away, which is really what I want to talk to you about."

"Why? What's that got to do with me?"

"I'd like to take Victoria along, make her the centerpiece of the layout, but she says that she doesn't want to leave you in New York."

This also surprises me. V enjoys working in Europe. They treat her like royalty there, and she comes home with stories of guys offering her wildly expensive gifts if she'll go with them to their villas in Cap d'Antibes or other such tony places.

I tell Dick that V's life is her own and she does pretty much whatever she pleases. "Anyway, I wouldn't try to stop her," I say. "I don't think I could even if I wanted to."

"She told me somebody tried to kill you the other night."

Now I really wish V would go to Milan with Avedon. This business with Lucy Garrett isn't as advertised, and I'd just as soon she wasn't around to see how it plays out.

"I'll talk to her," I tell Dick.

"Don't get me wrong," he says. "I'll find somebody else if I have to. I don't want her to go if she'd rather be home with you. Listen, you don't think she's in any real danger if she stays, do you?"

"Definitely not," I say, hoping that I'm right, then I vamp, "This isn't really about V worrying, you know? She would never admit it, but the truth is—"

"She likes mothering you."

"I'm not sure what that makes me exactly."

"Lucky," Dick says.

"Mr. Avedon." It's his camera girl. "We're ready for you," she says, but Dick ignores her.

"Why don't you find something else to do with your life, Jack? Something safer. I mean, you're obviously a smart guy. You'd do well at most anything."

"Yeah, but I like what I do."

"Mr. Avedon?" The camera girl is insistent.

"Just a second," Dick barks at her, then turns back to me. "So, did they ever catch the guy or what?"

"Which guy?"

"The guy who tried to bash your head in."

"Oh. Yeah. Sort of."

It's nearly ten by the time V's done, and I hire a limo to take us back downtown to Perry Street. This is not something I usually do, mostly because I can't afford it, but V looks exhausted and I don't mind paying twenty-five bucks for her to ride home in style. But she doesn't want to go home. She wants to go to Toots's joint for a vodka martini and a blood-rare steak, both of which sound pretty good to me.

Crosstown traffic is jammed up on Fifty-Sixth, and the limo is barely moving. V rests her head against my shoulder. I take her hand and say, "Go with Avedon to Milan."

"I will if you drop the Garrett case."

"I can't. I need the money."

"I'll give you money."

"Why don't you have my balls bronzed and mounted on the wall while you're at it?"—which comes out snider than I mean it to sound, and V slugs me in the arm for saying it. "I'm not going to live off you, V," I tell her, but she says that's not what she's asking me to do.

"I've got a real bad feeling about this one, Jack. Something's not right about it. I'd bet the farm Garrett's lying to you about his daughter and somebody still wants you dead."

Of course, V's right. The slab didn't come at me because he felt like it, and whoever sent him isn't going to back off because he ended up in the morgue instead of me.

"I don't have a choice, V. Until I find Lucy Garrett and get her home, I'm still a target. In the meantime, I'd feel a whole lot better if you went with Dick to Milan and I knew you were safe."

"And worry that you're lying in a gutter somewhere? I'm not going to Milan, Jack, or anyplace else and that's final. Now, feed me, get me drunk, then take me home and have your way with me, or I'm really gonna get annoyed."

CHAPTER EIGHT

"Well, would you look at what the cat dragged in?" Toots says as we walk in the door of his saloon. "What're you doin' with this bum?" he asks V. "He's a mutt, he don't got a pot to piss in, and he ain't too much to look at neither."

Toots Shor is gruff, fat, and rude, and if he doesn't insult you the minute he sees you, he doesn't like you. Earl Wilson once said about him, "There's nothing the matter with Toots except he's an egomaniacal jughead and as phony as a three-dollar bill," which I think he meant as a compliment.

"What can I tell you, Toots?" V says. "The guy's grown on me," and she kisses him on the cheek.

"Yeah, I get it. Like a tumor. Now, give me a couple of minutes and I'll find you bums a table."

If I came into Toots Shor's on my own, he would make me cool my heels for an hour or two before getting me a table next to the kitchen, assuming he bothered to get me a table at all. Not that I'd be insulted. He treats everyone the same way, which is to say like they're shit on his shoe. I once saw him give Sinatra a dollar bill and tell him to go across the street and buy him a paper and to be quick about it. But V is V, a guy's girl, and Toots would open a vein for her.

We go over to the bar. V orders a vodka martini from Joe the bartender in her sexiest voice, giving Joe a cheap thrill and making him smile. I order a Maker's Mark neat, and we settle in.

I stuck out like a sore thumb at Avedon's studio. His people were nice enough and treated me like I belonged, but we all knew that I didn't. Toots's place on the other hand is my place. I've been coming here for years. I know most everybody, and most everybody knows me. But as usual V is the center of attention. I don't mind really. The guys here know we're together. They flirt and make a fuss over her, but it's all pretty harmless—harmless, that is, until Frank Gifford shows up with his Pepsodent smile and NFL championship ring.

I didn't tell Avedon that I know Frank, but I do. He's a great-looking California kid and he's been the toast of the town since he was drafted by the Giants out of Southern Cal, but I don't like the guy. He comes on like the all-American boy, but he's really a philandering bastard in disguise. He's got a wife and kids stashed in the suburbs somewhere, and he comes into Toots's whenever he's in the city to drink and get laid. Gifford nudges in between me and V at the bar like I'm supposed to make way. He comes on to her with some phony boyish patter about how he has always wanted to meet her and does she know Eddie Fisher and Elizabeth Taylor, who Gifford claims are friends of his.

V doesn't know Eddie Fisher or Elizabeth Taylor, has nothing against them, but doesn't really care whether they live or die. She doesn't say that though. Instead, she looks over Gifford's shoulder at me and rolls her eyes.

But Gifford keeps at her. V can usually take care of herself without any help from me, but he isn't taking her cold shoulder for an answer and he's getting handsy, so I butt in and tell him to back off.

"Who the fuck are you supposed to be?" he says, expecting me to be not only impressed but intimidated. The kid may be a football hero, but I guarantee you he's never been in a real brawl in his life. I could put him on the floor with a quick punch to the throat, and I'm thinking about doing just that when Toots intervenes.

He smells a fight brewing, which is a major no-no in his joint, and moves in to head it off by telling me our table is ready. I pick up on his cue and spare Gifford the beating he so richly deserves. Instead, me and V get up from our seats at the bar and follow after Toots, but not before V turns back to Gifford.

"Frank, you're cute, I'll give you that," she says, "but your fly's open, your breath stinks, and from the way the girls tell it, your equipment doesn't always work, so thanks, sweetheart, but no thanks."

Then V smiles and saunters off, leaving the half-dozen guys who've overheard her bent over laughing.

Toots seats us and tells me to leave Gifford alone. "Okay, he's a bum," he says, "but he brings in the suckers, so be nice." I get the message. Toots will serve anybody short of Hitler if he thinks it will fill his saloon, which he knows I know, and he swats me across the back of the head before moving off so I don't forget it.

V ordered another martini before Gifford stuck his nose in, and a waiter sets it down in front of her. She winks at me and drains it in one long gulp. Drinking makes the lady amorous, and her hand is on my knee, making its way to my fly, when a guy calls out "Jack Coffey!" loud enough to startle us both.

"I had a feeling I'd find you here," he says, which is weird because I've only met Bob Carson the one time—right after seeing Garrett—and I didn't stick around long enough then for him to have any feelings about me at all.

He introduces his wife, a plain-looking woman in her thirties. She's made an effort tonight. Her dress looks new and so do her shoes, but the sad fox stole she's wearing has seen better days. She has been to the hairdresser's too and keeps fluffing at her curls as if she isn't used to having them.

"You're somebody, aren't you?" Carson says to V.

The wife whispers to him, "Victoria Hemming," but he has no idea who that is.

"Do you mind if we sit down?" Carson asks, and he doesn't wait for an answer. Unlike her husband, the wife doesn't want to intrude and seems pretty desperate to leave.

V takes pity on her, makes room at the table, and when the wife finally does sit, V says, "I love your dress," hoping it will take the edge off her embarrassment.

"You know, Lou Garrett couldn't stop raving about you," Carson tells me. "Whatever you said to him the other day impressed the hell out of him."

That Carson is a colossal boor is obvious, but why is he bothering to suck up to me? Garrett and I have a business arrangement. I don't care whether he likes me or not, and I'm sure he feels the same way.

"You know, Lou is a great judge of character," Carson goes on, like he's trying to sell me something. "There's no telling where this might lead, Jack. He can make you a very rich man."

No doubt Garrett could, but why would he? Obviously, Carson has an angle, and I want to know what it is, so I say, "Is that so?" just to egg him on.

"Louis Garrett is extremely wealthy, but he didn't get that way without making enemies. He's been looking for someone to oversee security for him. We talked about it, and I think he's about to make you a very generous offer."

I don't believe a word of this. If Garrett wanted to offer me a job, he'd do it himself. He wouldn't send Bob Carson to preview it for me.

"There is something else, though," Carson says, and he leans forward like he's going to tell me big a secret, though he doesn't bother lowering his voice. "Don't tell Lou, but I heard from Lucy. We've always been close, you know? I've known her since she was a little kid and I'm kinda like an uncle to her. She doesn't want to be found, Jack. Things between her and Lou are bad. Real bad. She told me she doesn't care what he thinks, and she's not coming home."

"When was this?"

"Just a couple of days ago. She means it, Jack."

"Do you know where she is?"

"She wouldn't say, and to be honest, I'm not sure I'd tell you if she did. She trusts me. I'm probably the only person in the world that the kid does trust."

I'm not sure what to make of this, but Carson doesn't exactly strike me as the trustworthy type. He's also a loudmouth, so I keep at him, hoping he'll tell me more.

"So, what's the real deal with Lucy and her father? They fight a lot, do they?"

"It's worse than that, Jack. Much worse. Do you understand what I'm saying?"

Carson throws me a look and I get it. He's signaling me that Garrett is diddling his daughter. He's not being subtle about it either.

I'm skeptical for a couple of reasons. First, if Garrett really is Carson's partner and a pal, why make these hideous accusations to me? And second, if Garrett is abusing Lucy, why pay me all that money to find her? To shut her up, then shut me up after I do? It's possible, I guess, but abused and emotionally battered doesn't fit with anything else I know about Lucy Garrett—not with what Monk, or Carmine, or even Muffy Palmer told me.

"You'll keep this under your hat though, won't you, Jack? I mean, it's not the kind of thing I want getting around," Carson says, despite having just announced it to half the restaurant.

I let the limo go when we got to Toots's, so I hail a cab out front of the restaurant and V and I climb in, but she goes quiet on the ride home. She's staring out the window, brooding, and I figure it's over what Carson told me.

"I don't think it's true, V," I say, thinking I'm reading her mind. "Okay, I don't know that for sure, but Carson's definitely got some ulterior motive, and when I met Garrett, he seemed to really care about Lucy—"

"You don't know what you're talking about, Jack!" V suddenly shouts. "You don't know what it's like! You can't! Somebody you love, somebody who's supposed to love you back because you're their child, comes into your room at night—" And that's all V can get out of her mouth because the lump in her throat is so big that it's choking her.

I've never seen V cry before, never seen her sob and her shoulders shake like they are now, and it breaks my heart. I reach out to hold her, but she doesn't want that. She doesn't want me to touch her at all. Instead, she tells the cab driver to drop me off at Perry Street, then take her home to Beekman Place.

V hasn't been in her apartment in weeks, but she wants to go there now, and I think I understand why. Her father must have touched her when she was a kid and done it more than once. I'd hop the next flight to Houston and strangle the son of a bitch if he wasn't already dead.

V lets me hold her hand the rest of the way downtown, but she goes back to staring out the cab window, and we don't say a word. When we get to Perry Street, she says, "I don't want to talk about this, Jack. Not now. Not ever." She lets me kiss her on the cheek before I get out of the cab, and as it pulls away, I see her bury her face in her hands before it disappears.

CHAPTER NINE

I ring V in the morning, but she's not answering her phone. It worries me, but I know that she wants room and I'm not going to crowd her. I grab breakfast at a diner on Varick, then walk over to my hole-in-the-wall office in a walk-up on Canal. It's pretty basic: a desk, a couple of chairs, a beat-up leather couch, and a window overlooking the street that hasn't been washed since before the war.

Janie, the secretary I share with Nat Bernstein, the accountant in the office next door, looks up at me when I walk in, then glances at my office door and holds her nose. She doesn't have to tell me who's in there waiting. I can smell Iggy Ivanovich even from a distance.

Iggy's brother, Sergei, and a couple of Hungarians from up in Yorkville were running a protection racket in Chinatown. The game isn't new. The way it usually works is a bunch of hard guys extort cash from local merchants in exchange for not beating the crap out of them. If a local refuses, the guys knock him around until he changes his mind. If he's stubborn and still won't fork over, they might burn him out of his store. It rarely comes to that, though. Usually, the merchant pays, chalking it up to the cost of doing business. But Sergei was a sadistic bastard. He got a kick out of playing rough and wasn't above beating the daylights out of some unsuspecting mark just because the mood struck him.

One day a couple of years back, Tony Chang comes to see me, very upset. He owns the Green Dragon over on Mott, and I stop in there for dim sum a couple of times every week. I like Tony. He's a nice guy, and I want to help him out if I can. He tells me Sergei tried to shake him down, but that he wouldn't bite. Instead of punching Tony in the face, which is pretty standard, Sergei goes over to Tony's apartment, slaps his wife around, and snatches his five-month-old son. He sends word to Tony that if he doesn't come across or goes to the cops, he'll never see the boy again.

Naturally, Tony is beside himself, and I say I'll try my best to find Sergei and the kid and that I'll do it for free.

This does not prove difficult because before too long, Sergei lets Tony know where he can bring the money, five grand in cash—which is a hell of a lot more than his original asking price. Somehow, Tony puts the cash together, and he and I go up to a cold water flat in Spanish Harlem to make the trade, the money for the kid.

But Sergei decides that's too easy and wants to have a little sick fun at our expense. He's got a big pot of boiling water on the stove like he's about to cook goulash. When we walk in, he has Tony's little boy by the ankle and is dangling him over the pot, like he's going to drop him in just for fun. I pull my gun and tell Sergei to put the kid down. Sergei grins at me like the freak he is, and I know he's a heartbeat away from letting go of the boy, so I shoot him in the face. Tony races to his son, who, thank God, is unhurt, but Sergei is lying in a bloody heap on the floor, stone-cold dead.

Despite his brother being a psychopath, Iggy Ivanovich loves and admires Sergei. He hears the shot, rushes into the room, spots Sergei, and lets out a wail so piercing that it chases a flock of pigeons off the windowsill. I still have my gun in my hand, but I don't figure Iggy has one of his own, mostly because he's stark naked, the explanation for which isn't long in coming. A girl appears in the doorway. She might be Iggy's girlfriend or a pro or possibly both, and she doesn't have a stitch on either. Iggy darts across the room to his brother, cradles Sergei's head in his lap, and shouts at me, "I'm going to make you pay for this, you fucking son of a bitch!" before bursting into tears.

I didn't know what he meant by that then. Later I'd find out.

Iggy is sitting behind my desk, eating a pastrami sandwich on rye that he picked up at Katz's Deli. He's chewing with his mouth open, and there's mustard on his chin. It's nine o'clock in the morning, but he has already finished off a pint of J. T. S. Brown. The empty is sitting on my desk. He hasn't bathed in days, but that's not new. Iggy has been living rough on the Bowery, at least he was the last time I saw him, but somehow he can afford that sandwich, so maybe things are looking up.

"What do you want, Iggy?" I ask.

"Money," he says without missing a beat.

I don't like Iggy, but I admire his balls. Somehow he thinks that by virtue of me shooting his brother to death, I ought to pay to keep him alive. It's absurd, but the truth is I float Iggy a few dollars every now and then because I feel sorry for the guy.

But V is on my mind this morning and I'm in no mood to be nice, so I advise Iggy to get lost. He doesn't take this advice, at least not right away.

Instead, he says, "I told you that you were going to pay for killing my brother and you are, you fucking piece of shit."

I don't really mind being cursed at, but I don't appreciate being threatened, especially by a pathetic wretch like Iggy Ivanovich. I fight back the impulse to throw him out the window without bothering to open it first and instead take a seat on my couch.

"Do you know Charlie Thornton, Iggy?" I ask and make a show of examining my cuticles.

"Yeah, what about him?" Iggy answers, like he's a tough guy, but there's an edge of scared-shitless in his voice and I know why. The thing about living on the street is that if you suddenly disappear, nobody really notices or misses you. And everybody on the Bowery knows Charlie Thornton can make that happen for a couple of hundred dollars and a halfway-decent meal.

"I ain't afraid of him," Iggy says, but bravado isn't his strong suit.

"Okay, here's the deal, Iggy," I tell him. "You've got exactly five seconds to clear out of my office, and if I ever see your face around here again, I'm gonna let Charlie know and the two of you can work it out on your own."

This is enough to get Iggy out of my desk chair and onto his feet. He spits, "Fuck you, Coffey," at me as he heads for the door, spraying me with crumbs from his sandwich as he goes. I make a sudden move like I'm going to chase after him, which is enough to speed Iggy on his way. I'm wiping crumbs and bits of pastrami off my lapels when Janie comes in, closes the office door, and sits down.

"I feel like calling the fumigators every time that guy shows up."

"I don't think we'll be seeing much more of him after today," I say.

"Why? What did you do, Jack, threaten to make him take a bath?"

Janie Cantwell is twenty-four, blond, pretty, and from a small town outside Boston. She's smart as a whip, has a degree from Vassar, an MFA from Radcliffe, and could do anything she wanted to, the sky being her only limit. A lot of kids her age come to New York to find a job that pays them enough to live on until they find a husband, but I don't figure Janie for that type. I'm sure she would like to be in love, who wouldn't, but I don't see her playing the pleasant, ever-pliant girl-who-you-can-bring-home-to-mother just to please some guy, mostly because she's so much more than that.

When I tell Janie this, she shoots me a look like I was born yesterday. "What choices do you think I have, Jack? Do you have any idea what it's like for a woman in this town, the kind of crap and creeps we all have to put up with? You know, when I first came to the city with my master's degree and my brand-new wool overcoat from Filene's Basement, I sent out one hundred and thirty-seven resumes, one hundred and thirty-seven, Jack, and do you know how many responses I got back? Two. And they were both rejections." Janie takes off her shoes and begins to rub her feet like the memory is making them ache. "It's cold out there, Jack, real cold, and you can't blame a girl for trying to find somebody warm to cuddle up to, which I wouldn't mind doing at all."

"That's not you, Janie."

"No? You might be surprised."

"Listen, I know she's kind of the exception to the rule, but V does pretty well on her own."

Janie lets out a snort. "Right. Victoria Hemming, one of the most beautiful women in the world, does pretty well. Like that's a fair comparison."

"You're plenty attractive, Janie."

"Thank you, but why should it matter? And what if I looked like J. Fred Muggs? What then, Jack? I'll tell you what. Not only would no one take me seriously, they wouldn't see me at all. I'd be totally invisible. And don't tell me that being smart makes a difference because it doesn't. Sometimes I think it makes it worse. Most of the guys I know are terrified of a woman with a brain in her head."

She's right. All you have to do is spend five minutes at the bar in Toots's joint and you get the idea.

"Do you know, before I came to work here, I was in the steno pool at one of those big publishing houses," Janie says, lighting a cigarette. "Publishing. I thought, there's a business where a woman can get ahead. You hear that, anyway. They hire me and my bosses are all Harvard and tweedy and I think they're probably harmless. Talk about naive. Do you know how many times they grabbed my behind or squeezed my breasts, and in front of other people too? Then do you know what they did? They laughed about it because they thought humiliating me was hilarious."

"Sounds like a real rotten deal, Janie."

"It was, but I shouldn't complain. Every girl I know has to put up with the same thing. Even Victoria, though she doesn't tell you about it."

"She tells you?"

Janie looks at me like I'm an idiot. "You know, I like working for you, Jack," she says, just as my phone rings. "It's kind of thrilling, and in the two years I've been here, you've only looked down my blouse once or twice." She pads over to my desk and answers the phone, "Jack Coffey's office. Oh, hi, Vicky. Fine, thanks. I was just telling your boyfriend here what jerks and idiots men are. Okay, I'll let him know." She hangs up.

"She didn't want to talk to me?" I ask, feeling a little hurt.

"No, but she said that she'll meet you at home later and not to worry, that you may be a jerk and an idiot, but she still loves you."

"That's a relief."

"I'll bet it is. You're a lucky man, Jack Coffey, a very lucky man."

CHAPTER TEN

When I get home, V is bustling around the kitchen. She stopped off at the market for gruyère and thinly sliced prosciutto, whipped up a half-dozen eggs, seasoned them with basil and chives, and now serves me a perfectly crafted omelet. V's a surprisingly good cook—surprising because she eats in restaurants most of the time and doesn't seem to have a domestic bone in her body.

I open a '54 Château Margaux I've been saving for no particular reason, and we finish it off along with a half bottle of port that's been gathering dust in my pantry. We talk and laugh like last night never happened and listen to Dizzy on WNEW with dessert. V moves her chair closer to mine, and we smooch a bit before going into the bedroom.

Sitting on my bed naked, I watch V undress. She's silhouetted against the bedroom window backlit by street light. V has a beautiful body, but she's not so much proud of it as she is at home in it. She drops her clothes on the floor, climbs onto the bed with a grin on her face, and I'm thinking Janie Cantwell is absolutely right. Definitely lucky.

When we finish making love, we hold each other for a couple of minutes before finally spilling apart. While I'm trying to catch my breath, V jumps out of bed and makes for the bathroom. She turns on the tap and I assume she's peeing, but the truth is I'm not entirely sure what she's doing in there. When she comes out, she scampers back onto the bed, switches on the bedside lamp, and apropos of nothing at all says, "You know, when we first met, I didn't think we were going to amount to anything. I mean, you were handsome enough, but not really my type. Don't get me wrong, I liked you and everything, but you were sort of frayed around the edges and I figured probably broke so I didn't think we were going anywhere."

"What made you change your mind?"

"I liked that you were nervous. You played the tough guy, but I could tell it was an act and thought it was kind of cute."

"Why aren't I flattered?"

"You should be, Jack. Most of the men I met before you all came on to me like they were God's gift, flashing their money around, buying me things I didn't want, offering to fly me to Paris for the weekend like the idea was so romantic I couldn't wait to jump into bed with them. Well, I've been to Paris. I've lived in Paris. I didn't need some man to take me there just so he could sleep with me in a suite at the Georges Cinque."

"No. You'd much rather spend your time in my little shithole on Perry Street."

"I would, actually, but as fabulous as this place is, it's definitely not the reason I'm with you. It's that I feel safe with you, Jack. I've never felt that way about a man before, and I love you for it. I always will, you know?"

This really gets to me. V is solid, and honest, and brave, and so much more than a pretty face. I take her by the shoulders, fold her into my arms, and we tumble back onto the pillows about to make love again when the phone rings. I'm ready to ignore it, but V can't abide an unanswered telephone. She rolls over and picks it up.

"You bet you're interrupting something," she says with a laugh and hands me the phone. "It's Monk."

"He's here," Monk tells me, but I don't know who he's talking about, which might be because V has her tongue in my ear and her hand on my erection. "That white boy you were asking me about," Monk says. "He walked in ten minutes ago."

V keeps teasing me even after I hang up with Monk. The last thing I want to do is get dressed and go uptown to Minton's, but if I'm ever going to put this Lucy Garrett business to bed, I have to talk to Rex Halsey. I say this to V, who pretends to pout before she cracks a smile and tells me to wake her when I get home, that if I'm lucky, we'll pick up where we left off.

The house band is doing a set when I walk into Minton's. Monk's riffing at the piano, but he catches sight of me out of the corner of his eye and nods toward Halsey, who's sitting in a booth with a pretty brunette. It's after midnight, but the place is packed. I make my way through the crowd and slide into the booth opposite Rex without waiting to be invited.

"Who are you supposed to be?" Halsey wants to know.

Instead of answering him, I say, "Where's Lucy Garrett, Rex?"

I can tell Halsey's the kind of a guy who prides himself on being able to keep his cool no matter the situation, but he gives me the shifty eyes just long enough for me to know that I've gotten to him.

"Are you working for her father?"

"Where is she, Rex?"

"I'm not sure," Halsey says. "Honestly, I don't know where Lucy is and I'm not real anxious to find out either."

The brunette with him has laid on pancake, a slash of ruby-red lipstick, and dressed herself like a sophisticate, but when I get a good look at her, I see that she's just a kid—not more than about fifteen.

"Does your mother know you're out this late?" I ask her, and she shoots me a look like she's going to slap me.

"Leave her alone," Halsey tells me, but I ignore him.

"How old are you, sweetheart?"

"Old enough," Halsey says like I'm about to accuse him of something.

"No, she isn't, Rex. Not by a long shot. And just out of curiosity, what do you tell them? I mean, how do you convince a girl like this one to turn a trick for some old guy in exchange for a fistful of cash she doesn't need?"

"I don't know what you're talking about."

"He hasn't told you about that yet, has he?" I say to the girl. She's chewing on a strand of her hair now, not because she's trying to be seductive, but because she's scared and wants to go home. "Why do you think he's taken you out to a jazz joint in the middle of the night? I'll give you a hint. It's not because he wants to go steady."

"I want to leave, Rex," the girl says, but Halsey isn't going anywhere.

"Why don't you wait for me outside, Kimberly?"

"I'm not going to stand out there all by myself."

"Just do what I tell you to do!" Rex barks at her, but Kimberly is used to getting her own way, and she doesn't back down.

"If you don't come with me right now, I'm taking a cab home," she says, and glares, expecting Rex to get to his feet. When he doesn't, she snaps, "I hate you!" and storms off.

"Somehow I don't think she's coming back, Rex," I say, but he seems unconcerned.

"There are other girls," he says.

"Right. I heard that about you."

"People hear a lot of things about me, buddy, but doesn't mean they're true." Rex drains the scotch on the rocks he's been nursing, then says, "And since you're so interested, I'll tell you something you probably don't know. Lucy Garrett isn't who her daddy thinks she is."

"Not sweet little Miss Sunshine," I say. "Yeah, I got that already."

"Look, I run a business. You may not like it, but that's what it is. I arrange favors for guys with particular tastes, but I don't force my girls to do anything they don't want to. And nobody gets hurt. I make sure of that."

"How does Lucy fit in?"

"She doesn't. That's just the point. The girl's a psycho."

"Somebody told me you were sleeping with her."

"That somebody got it wrong."

"What about her and her father?"

Halsey looks at me nonplussed. "I don't get it. What's that supposed to mean?"

I try a different tack. "Why did Garrett pay you all that money to get lost?"

Halsey grins at me like he's gotten away with something, then says, "We were shaking him down."

"You and Lucy?"

"Crazy, right? I mean, her old man will give her anything she wants, but she gets some weird charge out of fucking with him, so she tells him that we're in love, that we're going to run away together, and there's nothing he can do about it. Garrett gets one look at me and just about shits his pants. He figures the easy way to make me disappear is to buy me off, and he tries to lay a load of cash on me. I make noise like I'm too in love to be bought, so he ups the price and I finally take his money like I'm making some big sacrifice."

"And Lucy's in for half?"

"You'd think, but she tells me she did the whole thing for kicks and that I should keep the money for myself. Who in their right mind turns up their nose at fifty grand? Like I said, the girl's a psycho."

"Okay, just so I'm clear: you're saying you haven't seen Lucy, have no idea where she is, and you don't know what if anything is really going on between her and her father."

"I already told you. I don't know and I don't want to know."

Back at Perry Street, V is sound asleep, and I don't want to disturb her despite what she promised earlier. I strip down and climb into bed next to her, but Lucy Garrett's on my mind and keeps me awake. She isn't who her father said she was, that's for sure, but if it's so obvious to me, why isn't it to him? Maybe it is. You don't get to be a heavy hitter in this town with a duplex on Central Park West by being somebody's fool, not even if that somebody is your own daughter. And if he's having sex with Lucy—and I still don't know if that's true—is that what made Garrett ripe for a shakedown? And where is she? Halsey may be a scumbag, but I believed him when he said that he didn't know. Finding Lucy and dragging her home is turning out not only to be more complicated than I imagined; it also might be a lousy thing to do to the kid—which is the last conscious thought I have before drifting off to sleep.

CHAPTER ELEVEN

What I should do is march over to the Beresford, bulldoze my way past whoever they hired to replace the slab of cement, and make Garrett tell me what's really going on between him and his daughter. I should say that if he doesn't level with me, he can take that ten-thousand-dollar bonus and shove it right up his ass. I'm sure telling him off like that would make me feel no end of good, but there are two reasons why I won't. The first one is obvious: I want his money. I don't think of myself as being particularly mercenary, no more than the next guy in my line of work, but Garrett's payday is big, making it harder to walk away. The second reason is pretty obvious too: self-preservation.

I saw him last night when I jumped on the subway to go uptown to talk to Halsey. He was trying to make himself inconspicuous, but I made him the minute he stepped onto the train.

A little guy, no more than five foot four, wearing a brown suit, a brown snap-brim hat, brown brogans, and white socks. There's no accounting for taste, I guess, but his—or more specifically his lack of it—made him stick out.

I spotted him again when I left Minton's. He stood in the shadows with his hat pulled down, but it's close to impossible for a white guy to blend in on 118th Street in Harlem after midnight. I hopped into a cab, leaving him behind on the sidewalk, but there he was again when I left the apartment this morning.

What this means is pretty clear. Whoever sent the slab to cave in my skull hasn't lost interest in me. Also, walking away from Garrett, his kid, and his money doesn't mean I'll be left alone.

It's usually best in these situations to establish ground rules, so instead of trying to duck the guy when I leave the apartment on Perry, I walk right up to him.

"Something I can do for you?" he says in a nasal accent that screams Philly—meaning he's muscle from out of town. I see that he's got a gun under his suit jacket, but it's eleven o'clock in the morning, the sun is shining, and there are plenty of people in the street, so I don't think he's going to make a move.

"Well, you could fuck off," I tell him with a smile. He just stares at me like his beady little eyes are intimidating. Normally, I try not to look for trouble, but I don't mind going toe-to-toe if it's to make a point. I suppose the guy could go for his gun, but I've got a foot and at least twenty pounds on him and figure I can drop him before he gets to it.

What I don't count on is his knife.

To call it a knife isn't really doing the thing justice. It's long and sharp, more like an assegai than something you'd pick up at the Army Navy Store. He slashes at me and opens a gash across my chest, turning my shirtfront red.

I don't know how badly I'm hurt, but I don't care because adrenaline sends me into a blind rage. I kick the guy as hard as I can in the nuts, always a good opening move.

When he doubles over, I bring his head down hard against my knee and hear his nose shatter. He falls to the sidewalk, and I roll him over, pull his gun out of his shoulder holster, press the barrel against his forehead, and cock it.

Despite having his .45 shoved in his face, he shouts, "You're a dead man, Coffey!"—the irony in the remark apparently lost on him.

A bunch of people are staring, and it's not going to be long before one of them calls the cops. I figure the little guy has gotten the message, and there are too many witnesses to do anything more drastic, so I let him go.

I'm bleeding pretty badly, badly enough to hoof it over to St. Vincent's to have somebody take a look. It's the second time I've been there in less than a week. The same ER doc who stitched up my scalp tells me that I ought to start being more careful, and I have to agree with him. The gash isn't too bad though. I'm going to have to explain the stitches to V, but at the moment she's the least of my worries. The guy from Philly can't be through with me, which not only means I'll have to watch my back but that walking away from Garrett now is pointless. Anyway, if I'm going to risk my life, I might as well get paid handsomely for it.

I decide to go see Bob Carson. I don't like him, but Carson did tell me the reason Garrett is so anxious to find Lucy wasn't a father's love, not the kind of father's love a daughter wants anyway. I still don't know whether that's true or part of some elaborate con he's trying to pull, but I'm determined to find out.

It turns out Carson isn't the sniveling sycophant that I first thought. He has offices on Broad Street, and they're bigger than I expect. They come complete with plush carpeting, lots of mahogany, a spectacular view of the harbor, and hot- and cold-running secretaries.

One of them intercepts me at the door and tells me that Mr. Carson won't see anybody without an appointment. I tell her who I am, but she's not impressed. She says she'll check with her boss if I want her to, but that it won't do any good. But when she comes back, she's all sweetness and light, leading me into Carson's private office as if I've magically turned into somebody important.

Carson gets up from behind his desk and greets me like I'm a long-lost friend. "I was hoping you'd stop by, Jack," he says, pumping my hand. "Can I get you something? Something to drink maybe? I'm having one." I wave him off, but he goes to a liquor cart and pours himself a stiff one. I get the feeling it isn't his first of the day and I'm right. "Hair of the dog," he says and sits back down behind his desk. He makes a show of lighting a Macanudo. It's the usual big-shot routine: a sterling silver cigar cutter produced from his jacket pocket, a wooden match struck against the base of a humidor, a deep drag making the cigar end glow, and a thick cloud of gray smoke. It's a tell. Guys who go through the ritual of lighting an expensive cigar within a minute of meeting you are not only trying to impress but have something to hide.

"Listen, I know Lucy contacted you," I say, "and seeing as the two of you are close, you must be worried about her. I need to know more if I'm going to find her and keep her safe—more about Garrett too. I was hoping you could help me with that, you know, fill in some of the details." I figure giving Carson the impression that I'm not just going to deliver Lucy up to her father—which I very well may not—is a good opening gambit.

"I told you, Jack. She doesn't want to be found."

He could be helping her hide. If he's really as close to Lucy as he says, it would make sense. "Look, I get why you have her under wraps, but you do know where she is, don't you, Bob?" I say and watch his face for a reaction, but there isn't one.

"I wish I did, Jack. I really do."

"Okay, let me make sure I've got this straight. Lucy Garrett called you out of the blue a couple of days ago to say she was all right and doesn't want to be found. But she didn't tell you why she ran off, where she is, or what she's doing now that she's on her own."

Carson exhales a stream of cigar smoke but doesn't say anything.

"Look, if Garrett has been messing with her, hiding from him isn't going to help. She's underage, and somebody is going to take her to go back to the Beresford sooner or later. What she really needs to do if she wants her father to leave her alone is go to the police. Hell, I'll take her there myself. I don't care how much he promised to pay me, there's no excuse for fooling around with your own kid."

"I told her that myself, Jack, but she won't go. She's just too scared." Carson is shaping the ash of his cigar on the edge of a cut-crystal ashtray when he says this and won't look me in the eye. I'm not sure how much of his story is a lie—most of it probably—but if Garrett isn't abusing his daughter, why is Carson making it up? Maybe he knows where Lucy is and won't tell me because he really does care about her, but he doesn't exactly strike me as the noble type. He said he worked with Garrett when we first met, making it sound like he's Garrett's business partner, but I got hold of Murray Bloom over at *Esquire*, who covers such things, and he told me Garrett doesn't have a partner. So why that lie?

"Let me ask you something," I say, trying one last time to draw him out. "If you were looking for Lucy, where would you start?"

Carson leans back in his chair and puffs on his cigar with a wistful look on his face, like he's conjuring a memory. "I used to take her to the Automat when she was a kid," he says. "Something about putting a dime in a slot and walking away with a wedge of apple pie fascinated her. I took her to the zoo in Central Park too, and to the carousel. She loved riding on that carousel."

This is such obvious horseshit that I have to suppress the impulse to laugh. The Lucy Garrett who hangs around with a pimp like Rex Halsey and shakes down her own father just for the fun of it is not whiling away her afternoons on a merry-go-round or in the reptile house at the Central Park Zoo. I don't say this, though. There's no point. Carson knows more than he's saying, but he's not about to tell me what that is, no matter how nicely I ask.

I make my excuses and get to my feet. He comes out from behind his desk, grips my hand like he's trying to prove something, slaps me on the back, and ushers me out the door.

That night I hit the jazz clubs on Fifty-Second Street. Seeing that Halsey took Lucy uptown to Minton's, it's a good bet he's taken her to these joints too. Mo Levy owns Birdland, and I show him Lucy's photograph. He glances at it and says, "Wait a minute. I thought you were with what's-her-name, you know, that big-time model. Or did she dump you already?"

"I'm just looking for the girl, Mo. Have you seen her?"

Mo takes a second look before handing the photograph back to me. "Sorry, Jack. I can't help you. All those little blondies look alike to me. How about I buy you a drink on the house?"

Dizzy's combo is on the bandstand and they're wailing so I'm tempted, but I've got work to do so I beg off. "Thanks, another time, Mo," I say and head for the door.

I ask around at the Three Deuces, Leon and Eddie's, the 21 Club, and Jimmy Ryan's, but nobody has seen Lucy in those joints. I go downtown to the Vanguard and the Gate, but still no luck. The girl's a rich kid and jazz might be Halsey's passion, not hers, so I stop in at some of the swankier places uptown—the Rainbow Room, the Stork, El Morocco, even the Copa—but it's no dice in those high-end boîtes either.

It's late by the time I'm done, but I stop in at O'Doul's in the old neighborhood on my way home. I've been coming here since I was sixteen, and I know all the rummies and the regulars. Kevin O'Doul runs the place now. His dad did when we were kids, but when Frankie O'Doul passed, Kevin took over.

"Jesus, I thought you were dead, Jack," he says when I sit down at the bar. I don't come in as often as I used to, and Kevin always gives me a hard time whenever I do.

"They keep trying, Kev, but they haven't gotten me yet," I tell him and order a Maker's Mark on the rocks.

"You know, Jerry Moran got out," Kevin says, pouring my drink. "He came in last night. That time he did in Elmira really took it out of him. The poor guy just isn't the same."

Jerry, Kev, and I all went to high school together. I dropped out in '43 to join the army. Kevin went to work in his old man's bar when he graduated, and Jerry became a bank robber, a poor career choice. Jerry's younger sister Bridget hung around with us too. She was a sunny freckled-face redhead who tagged after us like a puppy. I haven't seen Bridget in years.

The bell over the bar door rings. A girl ambles in and slides onto the barstool next to me. She doesn't say anything, just waits for me to notice her. After a couple of minutes, Kevin comes over, nods at the girl, and asks me, "Who's your friend?"

"Lucy Garrett," I tell him.

CHAPTER TWELVE

Lucy flashes a phony ID at Kevin and orders a shot of tequila. Kev knows it's a phony but serves her anyway because he thinks she's with me. I can't figure out how Lucy knew where to find me, but I don't feel like giving her the satisfaction of asking. She throws back the shot like it's nothing new and motions to Kevin to pour another one.

He looks over at me, and I shake my head. Lucy shifts her weight in my direction, props her elbow on the edge of the bar, rests her cheek against her palm, and studies me for a couple of seconds before asking, "Do you live around here, Jack?"

"No. In the Village."

"In the Village, huh?" She sighs. "Oh, well." And the next thing I know, she squats between my legs and reaches for my belt buckle.

"C'mon, cut it out," I say and pull her back to her feet. It's only now that I realize just how glassy her eyes are. That shot of tequila probably wasn't her first of the night, but I don't think it's drink that's made a pretty young girl like Lucy Garrett look this gray and drawn. Muffy Palmer told me she smokes reefer with some of the guys up at Minton's, but it looks to me like Lucy's been chasing something harder. I don't know for sure, and I can't check her arms for tracks because she's wearing long sleeves. I guess I could just grab her, push back those sleeves, and see for myself, but I'm not sure I want to get any more involved with the Garretts than I already am, so instead I ask her, "What do you say I take you home?"

I expect her to say no. I expect her to kick and scream, stomp her foot, and say that she isn't going to let me take her back to her old man or anyplace else. I figure she might even panic and make a break for the door, but instead Lucy grins and says, "Not yet. Daddy hasn't suffered enough."

This might be payback for his abuse, which I get and her old man might deserve, but I can't just let her wander the streets in the middle of the night looking for her next fix. I could bring her over to the Eighteenth Precinct and let Jimmy Mullen take it from there. That seems like a pretty good idea, so I say, "Listen to me, Lucy, I heard about what's going on, and if your father is—"

"Is what, Jack? If my daddy is what?"

I can't bring myself to say it out loud, so Lucy says it for me.

"Fucking me? Is that what you think?" She starts to giggle.

This is so blunt and raw that it throws me. I'm hardly an innocent, but to hear a sixteen-year-old girl ask something like that with a grin on her face would throw anybody.

"I'll bet Bob Carson told you that. He did, didn't he?" Lucy starts to laugh.

"Then it's not true?" Instead of answering me, Lucy shoots me a salacious look like she really is sleeping with her father and doing it just for kicks.

I have choices, none of them particularly appealing, but any one of them might get me out of this mess. I could snatch Lucy by her Peter Pan collar, haul her over to the Beresford, deposit her in her father's duplex, and wait for him to write me a check. But if Garrett is abusing her, that seems a callous and generally lousy thing to do. I could drag her over to the precinct and see if Mullen can squeeze the truth out of her, but arresting a guy as rich and powerful as Louis Garrett for screwing his underage daughter is probably a bridge too far for Jimmy. He wants to become a police commander one day, and a vengeful Garrett would put a quick end to that, which means he'll punt Lucy right back at me.

Or I could wash my hands of the whole sordid business.

I'm thinking that's my best move when Lucy suddenly says, "Okay, it's true. Daddy and I sleep together sometimes, but it's no big deal. Anyway, it was my idea, not his."

Where can this possibly come from? Is it supposed to shock me or is bravado how she copes? There's no way I can find out now because Lucy is beginning to jones. She's drumming her fingers on the bar like she's waiting for somebody, then starts scratching at her arms. Her nose is running, her eyes are bloodshot, and because I'm a nice guy—or more likely, because I'm just another mark—I take Lucy outside, flag down a cab, and tell the driver to take us to Perry Street.

V is not thrilled. She likes her creature comforts, and the idea of giving up her bed to a sixteen-year-old rubs her the wrong way. She's also skeptical. I thought she would be sympathetic, but she suspects it might all be a rich kid act, and it gets her hackles up.

"She's playing you, Jack," V says to me when we're alone in the kitchen. She thinks she's whispering, but she's pretty furious and isn't exactly keeping her voice down.

"What was I supposed to do, V, leave her alone in that bar?"

"Yes! Look, I know you think you're a tough guy, but you have a soft heart, Jack. I love that about you, but it makes you a sucker for a sob story. And like most men, you understand almost nothing about women."

"She's not a woman, V, she's a kid."

"That's just the point. She's a kid. She doesn't get that all the crazy things she's saying and doing have consequences. I mean, sleeping with her father was her idea? Do you actually believe that?"

"I don't know what I believe, but I can't just take her home. I couldn't live with myself if I did and he's really—"

"Don't you see? She's counting on that," V says, cutting me off. "She's counting on you believing her so she can use you against her father."

"Then what do you want me to do?"

"You're Victoria Hemming, aren't you?" Lucy says this from our bedroom doorway. She's stark naked and smoking a Gauloise she's cadged from the carton V keeps in my bureau.

Rather than answer her, V grabs Lucy by the wrist, drags her back into the bedroom, and slams the door behind her.

I don't know if it's what V said to her or if she took off in search of a score, but Lucy's gone in the morning. We spent the night on my living room couch, and neither of us heard her leave. She rifled V's purse before she left and pocketed the couple of hundred in emergency cash that I keep rolled up in a sock on the top shelf of my closet. It was a shitty, spoiled thing to do, but totally in character. I should have expected as much.

I set a pot of coffee on the stove and watch it percolate while V's in the shower. After a few minutes, she comes out of the bathroom in a terry-cloth robe with her hair wrapped in a towel. I fill a cup for her, pour another for myself, and we sit down at the kitchen table to assess the damage.

"She filched my diamond earrings and my Cartier Tank watch," V says, more in resignation than in anger. "I don't mind the earrings so much, but Dick bought me that watch and I really liked it."

"You were right, V. I should have left her at O'Doul's."

"You're going to walk away from all this now, aren't you, Jack? I mean, that girl's dangerous. Can't you find a nice little divorce case to work? I know it won't pay as much, but at least I'll know you're safe."

"Yeah, I'm done. I'll let Garrett know."

"Good," V says, then she leans across the table and gives me a kiss before disappearing into the bedroom to get dressed.

When I get to my office, Nat Bernstein is waiting for me. Nat's a buddy and does my books gratis, which I appreciate, but I frustrate him. "How many times do I have to tell you to keep your receipts, Jack?" he says when I walk in. "If you don't, I can't itemize your deductions and you're gonna owe Uncle Sam a fortune come tax time."

"Receipts for what?"

"Business expenses, entertainment."

"Who do I entertain?"

"Will you please stop being such a schmuck and just keep your receipts!"

I like Nat a lot. He invites me out to his beach club in the Rockaways a couple of times every summer, and I always look forward to going. I like his wife, Bernice, too. She's a prosecutor in the Brooklyn DA's office, the only woman prosecutor out of a couple hundred guys, which tells you what you need to know about her. She's sweet as pie to me, but underneath that nice Jewish girl exterior, Bernice is as tough as nails. I wouldn't want to be in the dock with her trying to put me away.

"You'll figure it out, Nat," I say to him. "You always do." Nat's sitting in my desk chair. I walk behind him and start massaging his shoulders. "You'll sharpen your pencil, put on your green eyeshades, and Uncle Sam will owe me by the time you get through."

"And here I thought we agreed you were going to stop being a *shvantz*," Nat says, taking off his glasses and rubbing his eyes. "By the way, Bernice wants you to come to Shabbos dinner Friday night. She's making pot roast. And she says to bring Victoria."

"Love to, Nat. I can't guarantee V will come, but you know how much she likes Bernice's pot roast." My phone begins to ring. I hear Janie pick it up in the outer office.

"Jack?" she calls out.

"Who is it?"

"Jimmy Mullen."

CHAPTER THIRTEEN

I hate the morgue for the obvious reasons. It's cold, antiseptic, and despite the medical examiner's best efforts, it still stinks of rotting flesh. Jimmy and Bernie Rothstein are waiting for me next to one of the morgue's stainless-steel slabs. A body is lying on it, covered by a pea-green sheet.

"Friend of yours?" I say to Jimmy, nodding at the stiff.

He peels back the sheet and asks, "Do you know this guy?"

It's Rex Halsey. At least, I think it's Rex. Somebody has pounded his face into hamburger so it's hard to tell. His corpse is bloated too, and one of Rex's legs is missing. "Rex Halsey," I tell Jimmy. "What'd you do, fish him out of the river?"

"Yeah, but it ain't the river that killed him." Jimmy nods to one of the morgue assistants, who turns Rex's body over. There's a bullet hole in the back of his head.

"He was executed."

"Looks like it. Powder burns. Stippling. Whoever plugged him held the barrel right up against the guy's skull."

"What made you get hold of me?"

"Your name and telephone number were scribbled inside a matchbook in his jacket pocket. We also found this shoved halfway down his throat."

Jimmy shows me a small Plasticine bag of what looks like heroin. I'm thinking maybe Rex got out of line and The Chin had him iced.

"What happened to his leg?"

"Not sure. A boat propeller sheared it off maybe."

"There's a pleasant thought."

"So, is this guy a friend of yours or what?" Bernie Rothstein growls at me. I get the feeling he isn't inclined to believe anything I say, so I decide to keep it simple.

"He was involved in a case I'm working."

"What do you mean? What case?"

"That would be confidential, Bernie."

"Don't give me that, Coffey. Nothing's confidential when it comes to murder and you know it." Rothstein's got a point, but I don't think I could explain Lucy Garrett and her father to him even if I tried.

"Maybe so," I tell him, "but the last time I looked, keeping my mouth shut wasn't against the law."

"Yeah?" he says. "How do I know you're not the shooter?" This threat isn't exactly subtle, but it's pretty empty.

"First off, Bernie, you don't have a lick of evidence, not a print, not a fiber, and not a witness because I wasn't there, wherever 'there' turns out to be. I also don't have anything close to a motive. And seeing that I'm not in the habit of gunning down guys for no good reason, there isn't a chance in hell you can make a case. Now, if you gents will excuse me, I have a lunch date with a corned beef sandwich over at Katz's and I don't want to be late."

Rothstein is fuming. I can see his wheels turning. He'd love nothing better than to come up with some bogus excuse to arrest me, but he can't think of one. I don't think Jimmy is too pleased with me either, but there's nothing he or his partner can do to stop me from taking off, so I do.

But I don't go to Katz's. I told V that I'd drop the Garrett case, but it's still giving me indigestion. I don't know what the *emes* is with either Lucy or her father, and all of a sudden Rex Halsey turns up dead with a bullet in his head? No way that's a coincidence, so instead of enjoying a corned beef on rye and a bottle of Milwaukee's finest at Katz's Deli, I walk over to the Fulton Fish Market.

Carmine's there—he is almost every weekday afternoon—playing dominoes and keeping an eye on things for Socks Lanza. Socks has been running the fish market for the Genovese family for decades. He's getting on a bit though and doesn't pack the punch he used to, so Vito's tapped Carmine to back up the old guy.

"Pull up a crate, Jack," Carmine says when he sees me coming. He and a few of Genovese's foot soldiers are sitting around a card table slapping down dominoes. "What can I do you for?"

"Somebody hit Rex Halsey," I tell Carmine.

"Yeah, I heard that. Not that I give a shit, but I heard."

The other guys at the table haven't given me a second look, but because I'm after information, I say to Carmine, "Maybe we ought to talk someplace private."

"Say what you gotta say, Jack. These mooks don't hear nothin' unless I tell them they hear it, and before you ask, no, we didn't ice Halsey. We're not real happy about it either. It was our call to make, if you take my meaning."

Rex might have been a minor player in his operation, but The Chin felt like he owned Halsey. Beyond being a small-time dealer and supplying Gigante with a steady supply of young girls, Rex was probably kicking back a percentage of his take, not only as a dealer but as a pimp. If somebody was going to put a bullet in him, it should have been one of The Chin's crew, not some stranger. But if Gigante didn't order the hit, who did?

"Not a clue," Carmine says when I ask.

"Whoever did worked Rex over pretty good before they put him down. You could barely tell it was him."

"Yeah, I heard that too. Not our style unless you're a rat."

"Which Halsey wasn't, mostly because he didn't know enough to be one," I say.

And Carmine winks at me before slapping another domino down on the table.

When I get back to the office, there's a message from Louis Garrett waiting for me. He wants me to meet him at Bemelmans Bar in the Carlyle Hotel. I'm not an uptown guy, but I like Bemelmans. It's sophisticated without being stuffy. There's always something new to discover in the murals of winter scenes Ludwig Bemelman painted on its walls, and they serve hot chocolate to kids whose cheeks are still rosy from playing in the park.

It's four in the afternoon when I get there, so the place is nearly empty. Garrett sits at a table by the window, nursing a scotch on the rocks and staring out at people walking by on Madison Avenue.

He's cleaned up since the last time I saw him. The three-piece pinstriped suit he's wearing is elegant and looks like it was hand-stitched. He shaved, had his hair cut, and the Rolex Submariner on his wrist goes for more than I make in a year. But despite the dapper appearance, Garrett might be an incestuous sexual abuser, maybe even a pedophile depending on when he started sleeping with Lucy, assuming that he actually has, so I'm not sure how I want to play this. I could confront him, get up in his face with the accusation, and see how he reacts, but moral indignation isn't really my style. Still, the idea of pretending I believe he's a doting and concerned parent makes me nauseous. I guess I'll listen to whatever it is he has to say, then decide how to handle him.

Garrett barely looks up when I sit down, and he doesn't offer me his hand. "Your services are no longer required," he says without bothering with a preamble. "Lucy is in hand and you're no longer needed." This dismissal is delivered with a bloodless dispassion, and I might have been insulted if Garrett didn't reach into his jacket pocket and hand me a check for ten thousand dollars, a bonus I didn't earn. It's meant to buy me off, meant to buy my silence anyway, and for a moment I think about handing the check right back to him.

Instead I say, "Lucy must be home then."

Garrett just repeats, "She's in hand," and he gets to his feet.

Now I'm annoyed. He's fobbing me off with plutocratic noblesse oblige, which is one of the reasons rich people get under my skin.

"You know, she's got a lot to say about you," I tell Garrett, "and she's not the only one with a story to tell."

Something flashes behind his eyes, but all Garrett says is, "I'm sure they do," and he walks away.

CHAPTER FOURTEEN

That night I take V out to dinner at a French place we like on Christopher Street. I order a '53 cab, a bottle I usually can't afford, but I've decided to deposit Garrett's check rather than rip it up. The son of a bitch lied to me and tried to use me in a sick roundelay with his daughter, so my conscience is clear.

"Now that the Garrett thing is over," I say to V, "you can go to Milan with Avedon."

"Too late," she says, "he's taking Suzy Parker." Parker is V's big-time rival, and I figure she must be disappointed, but I'm wrong, "To tell you the truth, I really didn't want to go, and not just because I was worried about you. I'm not sure I want to do it anymore, Jack. The modeling, I mean."

This is new. I know V is sometimes bored standing around for hours with people fussing over her. She sometimes feels like the whole business is too superficial and frivolous to put up with, but that feeling usually passes. Anyway, I've always assumed she enjoys what she does, enjoys the money and the attention at any rate, but I've never actually asked her so I don't know for sure.

"I know most girls have it much tougher than me. They don't have a lot of choices and I do, so I shouldn't complain, but is this all that I am, Jack? Is this all that I'll ever be, somebody staring back at you from the pages of a glossy magazine? Isn't that all everybody thinks I am?"

"I don't," I say and expect V to tell me that I'm in love with her so my opinion doesn't count, but instead she retrieves a Gauloise from her purse and says nothing. A passing waiter can't light it fast enough and V thanks him, but after he moves off, she nods toward an older woman with a blue tint in her hair and says, "Do you think that waiter would have been as quick to light her cigarette?" and we both know the answer.

"One day my looks are going to fade," V tells me, "and when they do, who will I be exactly? What will I do? What do I know how to do other than stand around looking pretty? I've never told you this before because I was too embarrassed, but I didn't finish high school. I could have. I made good grades. I could have gone to college too, to UT or SMU, but one day a man showed up at the door with a bucket full of cash and offered to take me to New York. I had to go, Jack. I had to get away."

"Away from your father."

"That's right. Away from my daddy. I don't want you to think that he broke me because he didn't. I wouldn't let him. And I had this face and it got me places. I relied on it, Jack. Now, I rely on it too much and I'm scared that when the time comes, I won't be smart enough or educated enough to do anything other than become some man's wife. Don't get me wrong, it's not that I don't want a husband someday, it's just that I want so much more."

I've been happily holed up with V on Perry Street, V with her career and me with mine. I'm ashamed to say it, but I've never really thought much past that. I'm not one for long revealing talks that go on half the night, not even with V. That kind of intense intimacy makes me nervous. But would I marry V if that's what she wanted? I haven't thought much about that either, but the truth is I would in a heartbeat.

"Where is this coming from?"

"I've been thinking about it ever since that horrid man and his wife sat down with us in Toots's place. I wanted to slap the snide look off his face when he was telling you about Lucy Garrett and her father. I know I said that I don't want to talk about what happened to me and I don't, but it changes you, Jack. It changes you forever."

I take V's hand walking home after dinner. We don't say very much, just sort of stroll along. Two young guys come out of a bar on West Tenth Street. They're holding hands too. They smile at us as they pass, and we smile back.

Two tough-looking teenage kids making like they're James Dean in leather jackets and pompadours come out of an alley. They start hassling the guys, pushing them around, spitting at them, and shouting, "Fucking faggots!" like they're spoiling for a fight, which they are.

Normally I wouldn't get involved, but one of the kids hauls off and smacks one of those perfectly nice guys in the mouth, drawing blood while the other dances around him cackling. It's ugly and I don't like it.

I shout at them to cut it out, but they tell me to fuck off like I'm some nobody, so I walk over, grab one of the kids by the collar and smash his face up against a wall, knocking out a couple of his teeth.

I figure that should make things even, but his buddy doesn't agree. He pulls a stiletto out of his jacket pocket and waves it in my face. This kid has seen the movie *The Asphalt Jungle* too many times, and when he lunges at me, I grab his wrist, twist, and break it. When he doubles over in pain, I kick him in the ass for good measure, and he and his friend stumble off.

I take a look at the guy's split lip. There's a lot of blood and it might need a stitch or two, but it's not too bad. I take out one of the handkerchiefs V gave me for Christmas and tell him to hold it against his mouth to stanch the bleeding until he gets home.

He thanks me and says that I'm his avenging angel, which in a way I guess I am. We shake hands like we're old friends, then the guys head off. When I get back to V, she smiles at me, gives me a big kiss, slips her arm through mine, and we walk back to the apartment.

Over the next couple of weeks, a few cases come in over my office transom, none of them too challenging. Bobby Rafferty has gone missing, and his wife, Hilda, is afraid Bobby took his paycheck and went on a bender. She's worried there isn't going to be enough left in their bank account to buy groceries for her and their six kids, and she asks me to find Bobby before he pisses all their money away. It isn't the first time

Rafferty has taken off without telling his missus. I ask around and discover that it isn't booze but a waitress that's besotted him. She lives in a three-room railroad in Washington Heights. I take the train up there and knock on her door. Rafferty is lounging around in the girl's kimono, and I say he'd better get home before I let Hilda know what he's been up to. He puts up a stink like the waitress is the love of his life, but I know he's just showing off, and an hour later Bobby is back in his Brooklyn apartment, begging Hilda to forgive him.

There's also a Hasid in the jewelry district who thinks his nephew is stealing from him, but he's wrong. There's a housewife in Peter Cooper Village who's afraid her husband has gambled away the family nest egg at the track, and she's right. And there's an Upper East Side matron who's sure her Pomeranian has been kidnapped and won't I find out who snatched him and bring him back home? I hardly have the heart to tell her that her little darling was hit by a Dellwood milk truck on Lexington Avenue and his carcass was found lying in the gutter. Like I said, none of these cases are exactly compelling. I take them because they provide a distraction, but Garrett and his daughter are still stuck in my mind.

I promised V I'd let the case go but I can't, not even after Garrett so officiously told me to get lost that afternoon in Bemelmans Bar.

I decide to get hold of Red Smith over at the *Herald Tribune*. Red is the preeminent sportswriter in the city, and I've known him for years. I give Red a call and ask if he can get me into the paper's archives. I figure the *Trib*'s financial reporters must have covered Louis Garrett over the years.

I spend the better part of the next week in the newspaper's basement poring over their files on the guy.

Initially, I'm disappointed with what I find. It's the usual self-made man stuff. Garrett comes from nothing, gets a job in the mailroom at the House of Morgan right after World War One, and through skill, acumen, and cunning makes his first fortune, at least that's what the paper says. He sees the '29 crash coming, sells all his equities before it hits, then times the market perfectly when he gets back in. He's on the board of a dozen big companies and gives money to the opera, the Metropolitan

Museum, and the Henry Street Settlement House. I study photographs that the paper has published of Garrett with Cardinal Spellman, J. P. Morgan, Mayor LaGuardia, and even Franklin Roosevelt.

I'm about to give up when I run across a snapshot of Garrett taken when he was a kid. It's grainy and faded. In it he looks to be about thirteen, wears a blouse, baggy trousers, and a cap, and he's standing on the sidewalk with a bunch of his friends. Two things about this picture get my attention. The first is that Garrett is standing in front of a kosher butcher shop on what looks to be the Lower East Side. The other is that I think the good-looking kid standing next to him is Benjamin Siegel, better known to most of the world as "Bugsy." I pocket the photograph.

The next day I take it over to Katz's and show the picture to Mort Steinberg. Mort works the counter there, but he grew up on Delancey Street and knows Siegel from the old days.

"Yeah, that's Benny," Mort says after slipping on his glasses to take a look. "And that's Meyer."

"Lansky?" I ask him.

"Yeah. And the kid in the middle," Mort says, pointing at Garrett, "the one you think you know. That's not Louis Garrett, that's Abie Gotbaum."

CHAPTER FIFTEEN

V has flown to Miami Beach for a shoot. It's been cold and rainy in New York for the last week and a half, and she's put her doubts about her career on hold so she can spend time in the sun. Meyer Lansky lives in Miami Beach, and I want to talk to him about Garrett without letting V know I'm still nosing around, so I say I want to join her there, which makes for a good excuse.

Arranging a meeting with Lansky isn't easy. Carmine sends word down to Meyer through a Genovese family intermediary, asking if I can talk to him about Louis Garrett. Naturally, Lansky is reluctant, but Carmine vouches for me, guarantees that I won't stick my nose in where it doesn't belong, and after a few days, Lansky sends word back that he'll give me a half hour.

I like Florida. It's not just the weather. I like the smell of the place. It's hot and tropical and dotted with great weird attractions, monkey farms, flamingo sanctuaries, and billboards advertising guys who wrestle alligators. I don't even mind the humidity.

I meet Lansky at Wolfie's on Collins Avenue. The aroma of brisket and whitefish hits me the second I walk in the door, making my mouth water, a sort of Jew-boy Pavlovian response. Meyer is sitting in a booth by the window and barely looks up when I slide in opposite him. A waiter takes his order: *motzoh brei* and a glass of iced tea. He doesn't ask if I want anything, and the waiter doesn't hang around long enough to see if I'm hungry.

Meyer's an unprepossessing sort of guy, short with a bulbous nose and a weak chin. He carries none of the physical menace of, say, Lucky Luciano or Joe Adonis, much less that of the late and little-lamented Bugsy Siegel, but if Meyer wants you dead, you'd better have your affairs in order.

"That little *shvantz* has come up in the world, hasn't he?" Lansky says, reaching for one of the pickles in a wooden bowl on the table.

"You mean Garrett."

"No, I mean Abie Gotbaum. That Garrett business doesn't fool anybody."

"He thinks it fools a lot of people."

"You know why Abie lives on Central Park West? I mean, the real reason? It's because no Jews or dogs are allowed on Fifth Avenue. No, I take that back. They'll let you have a dog."

"So, the society types know that he isn't who he pretends to be."

"They know he isn't in the Social Register, that's for sure. Let me tell you something about those Jew-hating WASP shits. They're happy to take Gotbaum's money for their charities, but even if Abie gave them all the money in the world, it still wouldn't get him into the Union Club. How did you find out about him anyway?"

I pull the snapshot of Garrett, Meyer, and Ben Siegel out of my jacket pocket and hand it to Lansky. He looks at it and does something almost no one has ever seen Meyer Lansky do. He smiles.

"I remember that day," he says. "The *Herald* sent a photographer down to the old neighborhood, you know, to do one of those how-the-other-half-lives stories. We had just beaten the piss out of another kid, I don't remember why anymore, and the guy thought he had found himself a real slice of street life, so he lined us all up on the sidewalk and took our picture." Lansky hands the snapshot back to me and takes a big bite out of his pickle.

"Mr. Lansky," I say, calling him that because it pays to be extra polite when talking to a mob boss, "did Abie come by his money legitimately?"

"Nobody's money comes legit," he says, "but that's not the story you're looking for."

"What is?"

"You're the private dick, figure it out," Lansky says, then he picks up a copy of the *Racing Form*, which has been lying on the banquette beside him, and buries his nose in it. I've been dismissed, so I slide out of the booth and take off.

V is staying at the Fontainebleau. The place is plenty cush and a hit with celebrities. I spot Judy Garland in the lobby with a drink in her hand, laughing at a joke Buddy Hackett just told her. Ordinarily, those two would attract a crowd, but the hotel has hired armed guards to keep the gawkers away.

V is posing for Irving Penn on the "Stairway to Nowhere," which is exactly what it sounds like, a staircase that leads only to the lobby's ceiling. She's wearing the latest from Cristóbal Balenciaga. It's an odd-looking black billowy number cinched at the waist. It looks to me like V's modeling a hot-air balloon, but I'm sure it costs a pretty penny, so what do I know? I don't want to disturb her, so I just wave as I pass by and V gives me a wink.

I've got the rest of the afternoon to kill, and I'm debating whether to grab a drink in the Poodle Bar or drive out to Hialeah to watch the ponies run. I decide it's too hot to go to the track, so I wander into the Poodle and see him sitting at the end of the bar.

He's left his brown suit and brogans at home. Instead, he's wearing a loud plaid sports jacket over a Ban-Lon shirt, but I still make him for the guy from Philly. I assume he's packing under that jacket, but the Poodle is pretty crowded so I don't think he'll make a ruckus. I decide to have a little fun with him, so I take a seat on the barstool next to him and wait for him to say something. I don't have to wait long.

"You're a dead man, Coffey," he sneers, apparently the only threat he knows by heart.

I grin at him and say, "You'd be surprised at how often I hear that."

"And I'm gonna enjoy shutting that smart mouth of yours," he says, and I'm surprised that he doesn't growl at me like a rabid dog.

It's a lame attempt to bait me, but I don't rise to it. Instead, I motion to the bartender and order a shot of Maker's. He pours it for me, and after he moves off, I say, "Out of curiosity, who sent you down here? I mean, you're a nobody, but somebody must be paying your freight."

"None of your fucking business."

I reach across the guy, grab a handful of pretzels from a bowl on the bar, gobble down a couple, and toss back my drink. But before I get to my feet, I say, "Just so you know, I don't really mind you coming after me, but if you go for my girl, I'll rip your heart out of your chest with my bare hands," and smile.

They've booked V into the honeymoon suite, which is as ritzy as you'd think. I go up there to retrieve my piece because, despite my threat, the guy from Philly is as likely to take a crack at V as he is at me. I don't want to scare her, but with Penn's shoot wrapping at the end of the day, the safest thing to do is get V out of town as quickly as I can.

Eastern's last flight out of Miami International is at nine, but I hate to fly, so I book us a sleeping compartment on the Pullman to New York and start to pack her things. It's amazing how light the woman travels, given that her life has been fashion since she was seventeen. Other than her makeup kit and lingerie, V's only brought along a couple of silk blouses, a pair of high-waisted linen slacks, a bathing suit, ballet shoes, and a simple black scoop-necked cocktail dress that she wore on the one night we went out on the town. I throw my stuff together, snap our suitcases shut, and line them both up by the door. After a while, V comes in and asks me where we're going.

"Home," I say.

When she asks, "What's the rush?" I tell her that she doesn't want to know.

By midnight, our train is somewhere north of Jacksonville and we're in the bar car. We're on a couch, and V is resting her head on my lap. I'm nursing a nightcap and thinking I really have to do something about the guy from Philly and do it before he does something about me.

"He talked to me, you know?" V says all of a sudden. "At least he tried to."

I thought she was asleep. "Who did?"

"The man we're running away from." V delivers this tidbit of information casually, like it's no big deal, but my heart thumps.

"What did he say?"

"Only that I should watch myself. He wanted to say more, but one of the hotel's guards chased him off."

"When was this exactly?" I ask, but what I'm really thinking is that when the train gets into Penn Station tomorrow, I'll put V in a cab and have the driver take her to Beekman Place and out of harm's way.

"While you were off talking to that mobster."

Then I'll take down the guy from Philly, who's probably hopped on the nine o'clock flight and is already in Manhattan.

"Don't worry," I tell V. "I'll make sure he doesn't bother you again."

"I've got a surprise for him if he does," V says, and she reaches into her purse and pulls out a nickel-plated Smith and Wesson snub-nose .38. We're alone in the bar car but for a Black waiter who pretends not to see the gun.

"Do you even know how to use that thing?" I ask.

"I'm from Texas, Jack. Of course I do."

CHAPTER SIXTEEN

I figure it won't be long before the guy from Philly makes his move, but I'm wrong. I wait a week and then another, but there's no sign of him.

I've been bunking in with Dolores Ryan, who lives across the street from me on Perry. I've helped her out a couple of times with her Neanderthal ex-husband, so she's happy to let me stay. I set up a cot in Dolores's front room and keep watch on my apartment from there. I figure when the guy finally turns up, he'll be armed to the teeth, so I'm packing too.

And two or three times each day I creep around the neighborhood to make sure I haven't missed him. I check out my building's basement and the basements of the buildings next door. I even peek in the alleys off Greenwich and Washington Streets, but he's not there either.

This isn't the way it usually works, but I keep watch for another week just to be on the safe side before thanking Dolores and moving back into my apartment.

I've called V every day since we got back from Miami to make sure she's all right. We shoot the breeze for a few minutes about nothing in particular, but we're both happy to touch base and talk. I don't go uptown to see her though. I have a fairly good sense of when I'm being followed, but it's not infallible, so I don't take the chance. V's been a trooper through all of this, turning down jobs and sticking close to home, but after three weeks of wandering around her apartment with nothing to do, she's bored to death, and frankly so am I.

We decide to risk meeting up at Minton's. Actually, we're not taking too much of a risk. If the guy from Philly was going to move on me, he would have by now. Still, I decide to take one last prowl around the neighborhood before I jump on the subway and head up to Harlem, but there's still no sign of the guy.

Art Blakey's group is playing when I walk into Minton's. I look around for V and spot her sitting at a table in the back with Monk. They're with a balding white guy with a scraggly beard and an elegant woman in a mink stole. When I sit down, Monk introduces me, saying the guy's name is Ginsberg and he's a famous poet. I've never heard of him, but that doesn't mean anything.

Apparently, Ginsberg published a poem last year that was a big sensation. V tells me that everybody is talking about it, and I pretend to know what "Howl" is just to be polite. Ginsberg says he's just back from Morocco after visiting a writer named Bowles. I don't know who that is either, but V does. So does Monk and the woman in the mink stole, and I'm beginning to feel like an unsophisticated rube. Ginsberg cuts me some slack though. He probably knows I'm lost, but he's a jovial sort and doesn't hold my being an ignoramus against me.

He's brought along a hunk of hashish that he bought at a souk in Marrakesh and asks me if I want to go out in the back alley and smoke it with him and the "Baroness." I don't particularly—drugs aren't really my deal—but V does, and I tag along despite having no idea who the Baroness is either.

She turns out to be Pannonica de Koenigswarter. The name is a mouthful, but Ginsberg calls her Nika and so do I. She's attractive and looks to be around forty. She's also a Rothschild and an heiress to a piece of that vast fortune. Around the jazz clubs in Manhattan though, she's known as the Bebop Baroness, not only because she's a big fan but because she's a patron, helping out musicians who are strung out or just down on their luck. I like her. I didn't expect to. I have a natural suspicion of anybody who has more money than God, but Nika's all right.

It's freezing outside in the alley, and we all huddle together. Ginsberg takes a hand-carved pipe out of his pocket, drops a shard of hashish in the bowl, and lights it with a kitchen match. He passes the pipe around, and everybody hits it but me. The smell of burning hash is sweet and enticing, but I'm not a fan of that high, and given what's been happening lately, it seems best to keep my wits about me.

It's after three in the morning by the time we wander back inside, and Minton's closes at four. Blakey and his combo have packed up and gone home. Monk and Ginsberg decide to do the same, but V says she's not tired and neither is the Baroness. Nika invites us to a predawn breakfast up at her apartment in the Pierre Hotel, and the three of us pile into her limousine and are driven over there. Naturally, the place is spectacular with views of the skyline and Central Park.

A room service waiter delivers scrambled eggs in a chafing dish and serves them along with a rasher of bacon, freshly squeezed orange juice, and coffee in a heavy silver pot. He opens a '51 Roederer Cristal brut, pours each of us a flute, and I begin to think I might have been a little hasty to sneer at the lap of luxury. When we finish breakfast, Nika puts an old Bix Beiderbecke recording of "Clarinet Marmalade" on her hi-fi, and we all relax in her living room.

Now, I don't think that all the rich people in the city know each other, but they do tend to run in the same circles. They go to the same charity galas and Broadway opening nights. They belong to the same country clubs in Westchester or on the North Shore and reserve the same boxes at Forest Hills and the Metropolitan Opera. Nika might be something of an exception, but I get the feeling she knows everybody who's anybody, so I ask her if she knows Louis Garrett.

"I thought you were all through with that," V says, and I can tell she's annoyed. We've just spent our first night out together in weeks, and I don't want it to end on a sour note.

I'm ready to drop the subject when Nika says, "He's an awful little man, isn't he?" When she asks how I know him, I give her the basics, that Garrett hired me to find his daughter and that when she made her way home on her own, he let me go. Nika reaches for a sterling silver cigarette box, fits a Pall Mall into a lacquered holder, and tells me, "Garrett is an absolute fraud, you know?"

"Meaning he's a Jew," I say and instantly regret it. The Baroness is a Rothschild and, of course, Jewish herself, though the boys down at Ezrath Israel on West Forty-Seventh Street might have a hard time recognizing her as one of their *landsman*.

"He's what they call in Paris *un pervers*," she says, but I don't know what that means.

"It's French for 'pervert,'" V tells me, then turns to Nika and says, "Jack thinks he's sleeping with his own daughter. That's what she told him anyway, but I'm not so sure."

"I wouldn't put it past him," Nika says, "but I don't think that's Garrett's perversion of choice." Nika is as sophisticated as anyone I've ever met, and the fact that she's reluctant to explain what she means by his "perversion of choice" when I ask her speaks volumes. But having smoked Ginsberg's hash earlier in the evening and having just finished off a bottle of champagne with our help, the Baroness lets her guard down long enough to say, "He likes to beat them up. That's what I've been told anyway."

"Beat who up?" V wants to know, and so do I.

"Girls. They're terribly young apparently. That might not be all that he does, but I'm told it's what he enjoys best. I've heard other horror stories too. That he has someone film him while he's doing it. One can only imagine what he does while he watches those films."

"Jesus," V gasps, and I know how she feels. Incest is horrifying enough, but add to it rape and the fact that it's all on film almost beggars belief.

Nothing in this setup has ever been what it seems, not Garrett, not his daughter, not her disappearance, not Rex Halsey's blackmail, none of it. Meyer Lansky told me that Garrett's past wasn't the story I was after, and now I think I know what he meant.

"Of course, I'm not entirely sure that it's all true," Nika says, reading the shock on our faces, "but I suspect most of it is. I don't suppose there's anything one can do about it, not unless one has proof." Nika stubs out her cigarette, clears her throat, and says, "But let's talk about something else, shall we? Something more pleasant."

A week later a woman named Hillary Cady is sitting in my office, fingering a diamond pendant that's worth a small fortune. Her husband Ronald "Skip" Cady made his fortune, which is considerable, shipping ore from the Minnesota Iron Range across Lake Superior to various points south. Hillary, who affects an English accent for no particular reason, tells me Skip has been up to no good, that he has several "tootsies," as she describes them, stashed around town, and she wants me to catch him in flagrante delicto so she can sue for divorce and take Skip for all he's worth. She says that I come highly recommended and that she's willing to pay "quite nicely" for my services.

It's a straightforward proposition and I probably should take to it, but I don't. I can't get Lucy Garrett out of my head. This won't be the first job that I've turned down since Lucy's father hired me to find her. He also fired me, but paid me off before he did, so it's not like I'll starve if I don't take on Hillary's case. I tell her that I'm sorry, but she'll have to find someone else, a rejection the woman does not take with grace. In fact, she snorts at me as if I'm beneath contempt and storms out, leaving a cloud of Chanel Number Five behind. When she's gone, Janie pops her head into my office.

"What's the matter with you?"

"What do you mean?"

"Did you just tell another potential client to get lost?"

"Well, yeah. Why?"

"Then how do you propose to pay me? With magic beans?"

"Who says I don't have the money to pay you?"

"Right. Blood money," Janie says, and she's not too far from wrong.

I decide to talk to Lillian Crouse. Garrett's secretary isn't hard to find. She's in the book. Lillian lives in Queens, on Thirtieth Avenue in Jackson Heights. I'm working a hunch. If she knows what her boss is up to and I lean on her a bit, maybe she'll tell me where he has those movies stashed. Gal Friday types like her usually know their bosses' secrets and are usually paid well to keep them to themselves, but Lillian lives with her mother in the modest apartment she grew up in. She doesn't own a car, and it looks to me like she buys her clothes at J. C. Penney's or Montgomery Ward, hardly the headquarters of high fashion. She could have money stashed away somewhere, but when I follow her into the A&P, she hands the checker a sheet of S&H Green Stamps to save herself a few dollars.

I'm tailing Lillian on a Saturday afternoon, and after shopping for groceries and then for shoes at Stride Rite, she stops in at a coffee shop on Northern Boulevard. She takes a seat at the counter and orders a tuna salad sandwich on rye and a bottle of Cel-Ray.

I take the seat next to her and say, "Remember me?"

Lillian instantly jumps to her feet and makes for the door.

I don't try to stop her, not physically anyway, but I do say, "I'm good at this, you know, Lillian. You're going to talk to me sooner or later, so why not sit back down and let me buy you lunch?" I figure she's going to ignore me and leave, but she hesitates, so I play what I think is my trump card. "You know, I spoke to Father Grogan over at Blessed Sacrament about you. He said that he can't remember the last time you or your mother missed a Sunday mass. Father Grogan celebrated your first holy communion, didn't he? He told me you've always been a good girl and a favorite of his."

Reluctantly, Lillian returns to her seat at the counter. She doesn't say anything. Instead, she carefully spreads a paper napkin across her lap, picks up her tuna salad sandwich, and begins nibbling at it.

"I've heard ugly rumors about your boss. Do you know if any of them are true?"

Lillian dabs at the corners of her mouth with her napkin and says, "I open his mail, answer his phone, schedule his appointments, and that's all that I do."

"But you know about those rumors, don't you? About the girls?" I watch Lillian's face for a reaction.

"That has nothing to do with me."

"Have you seen Garrett with them? Somebody told me he makes movies starring those girls. What do you know about that?"

She's barely touched her sandwich but reaches into her purse for her wallet. "Nothing, and I'm through talking to you."

"Lillian, if you haven't actually seen him with the girls, how do you know if the rumors are true?"

"Because I've seen the poor things after he's through filming them," she says and snaps her purse shut. It's an inadvertent admission, but just the one I'm looking for.

Lillian gets to her feet and heads for the door. I call after her, "What can you tell me about the daughter, Lillian—about Lucy?"

"Lucy Garrett?" Lillian closes her eyes for a moment, then says, "Lucy Garrett is the devil incarnate," and walks out.

CHAPTER SEVENTEEN

I'm sitting in Washington Square Park, watching a beagle sniff at a basset hound's behind. Their owners, two young women with Beat affects—one is actually wearing a beret and black leotards—are holding their dogs' leashes, smoking cigarettes, and chattering about an exhibition they saw at the Cooper Union. V is out in Montauk working for a few days, and I've been sleeping in. This morning I got up around ten, stopped in at Sal's on Bleecker for a cruller and a white coffee to go, and walked over to the park to read the paper before going into my office on Canal. It's a beautiful November morning, the sun is out and the air cool and crisp, but all I can think about is where Louis Garrett has those movies stashed and how I can get hold of them. Assuming I can somehow, I could hand them over to Jimmy Mullen, but the problem with that is the films alone don't really prove anything. I'm sure the girls in them look plenty young, but unless I can find one who's willing to come forward and tell the DA exactly how old she was when the films were shot, they aren't enough. Still, it's a place to start.

I'll need to get inside, but the question is how? I could try to talk Lillian Crouse into helping me out, but that would take a lot of convincing, and I can't really blame her if she doesn't want to get involved. Lillian might think Lucy Garrett is the devil, but she's the sole support of her mother and probably wants to hang on to her job. I couldn't get a good read on Burton, Garrett's butler, but he didn't strike me as the type to turn on his boss either. Actually, he seemed more the type to be working the camera while Garrett got his jollies slapping those girls around. There's Bob Carson, but I'm still not sure how he fits in. He claims he's like an uncle to Lucy, but that might mean almost anything. If I'm going to have any chance of getting at those films, I'll have to get into Garrett's duplex when nobody's around, and that's a tall order. I'll have to stake out the Beresford and watch not only for Garrett's comings and goings but Lillian's and Burton's as well. I'll have to get past the doorman too, and I'm trying to figure out just how to do that when the first shot whizzes past my cheek and ricochets off a tree behind me.

The guy from Philly is on the other side of the park, firing his automatic as he comes running toward me. The young women walking their dogs scream and duck for cover.

I hop over the back of the bench, dash through a thicket of bushes, scramble over a wrought iron fence, and tumble out onto MacDougal Street. The guy keeps firing away, but he keeps missing. It's not necessarily that he's a bad shot, but firing a handgun from a distance and hitting a moving target is a lot harder than it looks. I race down MacDougal just as he clears the fence. There's a narrow alley between two of the old town houses lining the street, and I dart down it. It runs perpendicular to another alley, but one end of it is closed off by a fence topped with razor wire and the other is blocked by a lumbering garbage truck. I'm trapped.

I hear the guy coming. I'm not carrying a piece of my own, and when I look around, the only thing resembling a weapon is a No Parking sign set in a heavy cement stand. The guy barrels around the corner ready to smoke me, but adrenaline being what it is, I pick the sign up over my head and brain him with it.

I hadn't really meant to kill him. Fracturing his skull would have been enough to do the trick, but blood and bits of his brain are matting his hair and spreading across the pavement. Now, I could call Jimmy Mullen and try to explain myself. Obviously, it was self-defense, but I already told Mullen and Rothstein that when I put away the slab of cement. I'm not sure they'll buy that excuse a second time.

I do have an alternative though: friends in low places, friends I've helped out of more than one jam, and I'm fairly sure they'll return the favor. I wedge the body under a dumpster and hustle over to a phone booth on West Fourth. I ring O'Doul's from there, and when Kevin answers, I ask him if the Dugan brothers are around.

Joe and Eddie Dugan work as muscle for a few of the local shakedown artists, and I've known them since they were kids picking pockets in Times Square. Eddie gets on the phone, and I say that if he and Joe don't have anything better to do, there's a stiff under a dumpster in an alley behind MacDougal Street that needs collecting. I tell him there's a couple of hundred in it for each of them, but Eddie says he won't take my money. I give him the address, and he tells me I shouldn't hang around, that he and Joe will take care of it. I thank him, hang up, and walk away.

That night I meet Carmine out in Sheepshead Bay. He's fishing off Pier Two on Emmons Avenue. Seeing that Carmine spends most of his days at the Fulton Fish Market, you'd think trying to catch fluke and flounder in the middle of the night is the last thing he'd want to do, but he says fishing relaxes him. He also says that his wife Estelle's snoring is prodigious and that the sea air beats staring at his television set's test pattern.

"Some mook tried to kill me this morning," I tell Carmine, but if he's surprised, he doesn't show it.

"Which mook is that?" he asks, and I tell him that I'm not sure.

"He was out of Philly, I know that, but that's all I know."

"Was?"

"Yeah. Let's just say the guy won't be going back home anytime soon, not upright anyway."

I know that Vito Genovese has a lot of clout with Joe Ida, the head of the Philly mob. In fact, a lot of people think that Ida's crew is just a franchise of the Genovese crime family. I have no problem with Ida and I'm pretty sure Joe has nothing against me, so the guy who tried to tap me must have been working freelance. Still, I figure he had to be connected—meaning Carmine might know who he is and who sent him.

"What did he look like?" Carmine wants to know. I tell him short, dark, a lousy dresser, good with a knife, not so good with a gun.

"Big schnoz?" he asks.

"Yeah, I guess you could say that."

"Dante Cerone. Dante's one of Ida's guys, but he hires himself out when things get slow."

"Who do you think sent him?"

Carmine bites into the salami-provolone-and-peppers panini he's brought along, then says to me, "You didn't leave that business with Garrett alone, did you?" and when I tell him that I didn't, Carmine says, "There's your answer."

"But Garrett has no reason to gun for me—didn't until recently, anyway. Besides, who'd hook him up with Cerone?"

"He doesn't need to be hooked up, Jack. Garrett knows guys. None of those Wall Street types have clean hands."

"That's what Lansky told me."

"Yeah? Well, Meyer would know, wouldn't he?" Carmine tosses the rest of his sandwich to a passing seagull.

CHAPTER EIGHTEEN

I own a car, a 1949 forest-green Nash Rambler with four on the column. I keep it in the garage Lynn Murphy owns near the Lincoln Tunnel. Lynn changes the points and plugs a couple of times a year and charges me twelve bucks a month to garage it. I don't drive it around town, that's more trouble than it's worth, but V bought a cottage in the Berkshires a couple of years ago and she likes to drive up there on weekends when we can both get away.

The Rambler also comes in handy when I'm on a stakeout. There's nothing worse than standing on a street corner in the middle of the winter freezing my ass off waiting for a cheating husband and his paramour to appear so I can take their picture.

I find parking on West Eighty-First Street outside the Beresford where I can keep an eye on both the building's front and side entrances. I've been here for the better part of a week now, clocking Garrett's household. Lillian is easy to track. She comes into work at eight every morning, puts in a nine-hour day, and takes the subway back to Queens in the evening around five. Burton doesn't show up until ten. He ducks into the side entrance and doesn't reappear until one or two in the morning. A limousine picks up Garrett just before the stock market opens, and I assume his driver takes him to an office on Wall Street because he's always home an hour after the market closes. I haven't seen Lucy. There could be any number of reasons for this, but my bet is either her father has locked her in her room and thrown away the key or she's taken off again.

I spot Lillian leaving the building and hailing a cab. She's too conscientious to take off in the middle of the morning, and it's too early for lunch. She must have an appointment of some sort, which I take as my cue to make a move. The building's loading bay and freight elevator are around the back. The Beresford's management hired a guard to keep watch there, but the guy's a rummy and drinks on the job. I'm not exactly a master of disguise, but I'm good enough to get past him. I put on a work shirt and a pair of overalls with "Al" stitched in red thread on the front pocket, which I have stowed in the trunk of my car, grab the toolbox and bathroom plunger I borrowed from Lynn, and tell the rummy I'm the plumber.

He buys this because he's in the bag and has no reason not to. I get on the freight elevator, close the cage, ride it up to Garrett's floor, and step into a narrow utility alcove off the duplex's kitchen. There's a locked door here, but the lock doesn't take long to pick. Nobody's in the kitchen, so I slip into the duplex as quietly as I can. I might get lucky and somehow run across Garrett's dirty movies, making this little caper especially worthwhile, but the apartment is so enormous that doesn't seem likely. Still, it's worth a shot.

Lillian's desk sits outside Garrett's library. I pad over to it and take a look in her diary. I'm right. "Dr. Anderson" has been penciled in at eleven thirty, and I'm guessing that she won't be back for at least another hour.

Burton is around here somewhere so I have to be careful, but I'm in luck: there's music coming from the library, something classical I don't recognize, and the library door is ajar. I peek through the crack in it and see Burton sitting with his feet up on Garrett's antique desk, smoking one of his boss's cigars and reading the newspaper. He doesn't see me, but when I turn around and start to creep away, I nearly collide with Gertie, Garrett's housekeeper.

"That upstairs toilet is clogged again, ain't it?" she asks.

"Yeah. I'm kinda lost though. Maybe you could show me the way."

Gertie Hess, dressed in a gray maid's outfit complete with a lace cap, leads me up a staircase to the duplex's second floor and into Garrett's bedroom. It's bigger than my apartment, and I let out an involuntary whistle. She smiles and says, "How the other half lives, huh?" and points me toward Garrett's bathroom. I rattle around in there for a while, banging on the pipes and the porcelain in case Gertie's suspicious and still in the bedroom.

After a few minutes, I pop my head out, see that she's gone, and begin looking around. The bedroom's decor is understated and masculine. There's art on the walls, signed Lautrec and Matisse lithographs. The books on Garrett's bookshelf are bound in leather but look like they've never been cracked and read. I open an inlaid teak jewelry box that he keeps on his bureau. In it are sterling silver cuff links, gold shirt studs, and three expensive-looking watches. Garrett's bedroom window overlooks the Hayden Planetarium, and there are kids playing in the park that surrounds it. It's all very impressive, but there's no way he's stashed those films in here, not with Gertie coming in to clean, and the duplex is so massive that it could take me days to find out where he does keep them. I don't have that kind of time, so instead of craft, I'm going to have to charm Gertie into telling me where they are—that's if she knows.

Gertie lives out in Canarsie. She's forty-five and plump but wears a wedding ring, so sweet-talking her into showing me around isn't going to be easy. I head back downstairs to look for her. I hear her in the kitchen, wander in there, and ask her for a glass of water.

It's a working stiff's kind of request, and Gertie says sure, but tells me there are beers in the fridge and maybe I'd like one of those instead. It's just the icebreaker I'm looking for. She retrieves a couple of bottles of something imported, grabs a church key from out of a utility drawer, and we both sit at the kitchen's Formica table. I crack open the beers and hand her one. Gertie pulls a pack of Camels out of her apron pocket, offers me one, and we both light up.

"How long have you been working here?" I ask, and she tells me that it's only been a couple of months.

"Nobody lasts too long," she says, "but the pay's good so I'll stick it out for as long as I can."

"Did all the others quit?"

"That or they got fired. Mr. Garrett isn't easy to work for. He's very particular. Like if I don't make his bed so tight that you can bounce a dime off it, he gets annoyed."

"Is he married?"

Gertie hesitates, then says, "You know what? I don't think I should say. I mean the man deserves his privacy and I work for him, so—"

"Aw, c'mon Gertie. The housekeeper always knows the gossip. What's this guy's real story?"

Gertie takes a long pull on her beer, swallows hard, sizes me up for a moment, then cracks a smile. "Who are you, Mr. Nosy? Why do you want to know anyway?"

"I'm just curious is all. I mean, a guy with all that dough. It's not like he found it in a paper bag in the gutter. How'd he come by it anyway?"

"How should I know? Rich guys don't talk to the help."

"But you hear things, right?"

Gertie takes another sip of beer, then says, "I think he was once. Married, I mean."

"What happened to her?"

"The wife? No idea. Look, if I tell you something, do you promise to keep it to yourself? I'm serious now, don't repeat it to anyone." After I nod and say that I won't, Gertie stubs out her cigarette and says, "He's got girls coming in and out of here all the time."

"Why's that a big secret?"

"They're young. I mean, really young. And they don't look too happy when he's done with them."

I don't want to jump on this too hard. If I do, Gertie's liable to get suspicious and clam up. My best move is to let her run with it without too much prompting.

"They're all really upset when they leave," she says. "You know, crying like he did something terrible to them. I don't know what that something is, and to tell you the truth, I'd just as soon keep it that way."

"How young is young?"

"They look like school kids to me. The thing that I don't get is that he's got a daughter the same age."

"And she's here while all this is going on?"

"She was. A couple of guys showed up the other day and took her away. I don't know what that was all about either, but she was screaming her head off when they did."

This isn't necessarily surprising. When the wives or kids of the well-heeled are too hard to handle or just plain nuts, sometimes they get sent off to a sanatorium to cool down, but I'm pretty sure the explanation for dragging away Lucy is a lot more complicated than that.

"Did her father say anything when they took her?"

"He said she'd brought it on herself. I don't know what that means, but he said it."

It means Rex Halsey's story wasn't entirely horseshit. He and Lucy must have thought they could leverage Rex's pimping for Garrett against him. Not only was that a mistake, but it's why Lucy was carted off and why Halsey ended up floating face down in the East River.

"You'll keep all this to yourself, right?" Gertie reminds me. "Because I'm not supposed to know about any of it. Mr. Garrett would kill me if he thought I did." She doesn't mean this literally, but it may not be too far from the truth. "Not that I worry about it too much though. He doesn't really notice me. I mean, I'm the maid. I doubt the guy even knows my name." Gertie slips her pack of Camels back into her apron pocket and gets to her feet. "Listen, it's been really nice talking to you, but I got a lot of work to do."

"Me too," I say and collect the empty beer bottles off the table while Gertie rinses out our ashtray in the kitchen sink. I dump the bottles in the trash and head for the door, but before I go, I can't resist asking, "Where does all this happen? I mean, where does he take those girls?"

"There's a suite of rooms upstairs that I'm not supposed to go near, but I saw him come out of there once. I think he films them. I didn't get a real good look, but I thought I saw a camera on a tripod and there's padding all over the walls like they're soundproof or something."

The Baroness was right. Garrett gets off filming the girls, then later—later I don't want to think about. And that suite must be where he has the movies stashed. "Do you think you could take me up there? I don't want to get you in trouble or anything, but I'd love to get a look for myself."

"I couldn't even if I wanted to. It's all locked up tight as a drum, and Mr. Garrett's got the only key."

CHAPTER NINETEEN

When I get home, V is sitting on the couch in the living room. She has her feet tucked up underneath her, and she's reading. V reads a lot. She regrets dropping out of high school and is determined to do something about it. She takes classes at the New School whenever she has the time and stops in at the Eighth Street Bookshop for a paperback a couple of times a week. Her tastes are eclectic: the Russians, the English Romantics, Agatha Christie, Hemingway and Fitzgerald of course, and that kid Mailer everybody keeps shouting about. Tonight she's reading John O'Hara.

"What did you find out?" she asks when I flop down on the couch next to her.

"He does his dirty work in rooms on the second floor, rooms that are soundproofed so nobody can hear the girls scream."

"Jesus."

"I think Rex Halsey was procuring for him, then tried to turn the tables, and it cost him."

"Wasn't that the man you met up at Minton's?"

"Yeah, that's the one. He was grooming the girls, probably grooming the kid I saw him with that night. Rex seduces them, and once he gets his hooks into them, he traffics them to Garrett for a fee, but he must've gotten greedy."

V puts her book down. "You think Garrett murdered Halsey."

"More like had him murdered, but yeah."

"You are being careful, aren't you, Jack?

"Always," I say, trying to sound reassuring, then I haul myself to my feet and go to the front window to retrieve the bottle of scotch I left on the sill. It might be paranoia, but when I glance out the window, there's a guy lurking in front of the building across the street, dressed against the cold. The headlights of a passing car reveal him. He could be cooling his heels, waiting for somebody, somebody who isn't me, but I don't think so.

"Garrett got rid of Lucy too," I tell V when I sit back down. "Had her put away. I just wish I knew where."

"Payne Whitney probably," V says, stretching out on the couch and resting her head in my lap. "You know, like me."

Payne Whitney is a high-end psychiatric clinic in Upper Manhattan. V had herself committed there for a time. Starving yourself so you can fit into a size two can make any girl crazy, but it was love that did it. Before we met, V was involved with an older man. She won't tell me who. I assume he was somebody famous, but whoever he was, he didn't treat her very well. She was barely twenty-one then and in love in that all-consuming way you can be at twenty-one. Anyway, it ended badly, and when it did, V fell apart. She holed up in her apartment on Beekman Place and wouldn't see anybody. She couldn't bring herself to eat, didn't shower or get dressed, and refused to answer the phone. Dick Avedon finally went up there to find out what was what, and when V wouldn't open her door, he got the super to let him in. He convinced her to check herself into a clinic. She didn't make much of a fuss about it. I guess she knew she had lost the plot and needed help. V seems rock solid to me, maybe the sanest person I know, but now that she's told me what her father did to her, those months she spent in Payne Whitney make more sense.

"My guess is that Garrett wants Lucy isolated," I tell her. "Isn't she liable to run into somebody she knows at Payne Whitney?"

"The Hayden Institute then."

"What's that?"

"A sanatorium upstate. It's in the middle of nowhere and they don't allow visitors. Rumor has it that if you don't behave yourself, they can keep you for years."

I want to make sure V's right, so over the next few days, I nose around various other high-end psychiatric hospitals in the city, slipping a few dollars to secretaries and orderlies, bribing them to get a look at their patient lists. Lucy isn't on any of them. I even go over to Bellevue, but she isn't there either. It's just as I suspected—Garrett has stashed her someplace where she won't be recognized.

It takes me nearly four hours to drive upstate to the Hayden Institute, and after I'm out of the range of WNEW, I snap off the Rambler's radio and wonder about the guy I saw in the shadows last night. I'm pretty sure he's not a civilian, which brings me back to the same question I had after I was attacked by the slab of cement and the guy from Philly. Who is so intent on seeing me dead? Garrett is the obvious answer. He must have ordered the hit on Halsey, and he wouldn't think twice about taking out a contract on me. Still, both the slab and Philly came at me before I knew about Garrett and his girls. But there is no one else, no one who grew up with Meyer Lansky and Ben Siegel at any rate, and no one who knows where to hire somebody connected to carry out a hit.

The Hayden Institute sits on fifty-seven acres outside Wheelerville, New York. The architecture is Gothic and gloomy, and the place looks like it should be in the Carpathian Mountains, not in the rolling hills of Fulton County. It's surrounded by a stone wall that has to be at least ten feet high, and the entrance to its long sloping driveway is blocked by an enormous iron gate.

As I pull up to the gate, a guard carrying a clipboard waves me over to the side of the road. He's not going to let me pass, not without an explanation, so I make up a story. I tell him that Louis Garrett sent me, that there's been a family emergency, and I have to see his daughter Lucy posthaste.

The guard doesn't buy it. He says nobody gets in unless Dr. Hayden himself puts their name on a list, and not only is my name not on any list he's seen, but there isn't a Lucy Garrett in the place, so I should get lost. The guard looks to me like the kind of guy who moves his lips when he reads, and I don't believe for a second that he knows the name of every patient in the place by heart. Hayden must have given strict instructions to keep anybody asking for Lucy out. Good to know, but I'm not going to be able to bulldoze my way past him or scale those ten-foot walls without a rappelling hook. I'll have to find another way in.

There's a diner out on Route 29, the kind of place locals drop into for a cup of coffee and a slice of pie. Truckers stop in there too. They wolf down greasy burgers on their way down to the city and other points south. I pull the Rambler into the diner's dirt parking lot and get out. I walk into the place and take a seat at the counter. A high school kid takes my order. Tuna on rye and a Coke seem a safe bet. While she hands the chit to a short-order cook, I amble over to the jukebox to see what kind of music the customers favor. It's the usual crap. Elvis. Pat Boone. Perry Como crooning "Round and Round." It's enough to make anyone with a lick of musical taste sick, but the Diamonds' "Little Darlin" has a bluesy up-tempo backbeat, so I drop a dime into the slot and let it play.

A guy wearing a toggle coat has parked himself on the stool next to mine. He's clean-cut and looks to be about twenty-five. I nod at him when I sit back down, and after the high school kid puts my sandwich down on the counter in front of me, I turn to him and ask, "Are you from around here?"

When he says that he is, I say, "You know that big stone building down the road? What is that place?"

"You mean the looney bin?"

"Is that what it is?"

"Yeah. It's spooky, isn't it? When I was a kid, I used to think Dracula lived there. I've never been inside though. I don't know anybody who has except for my buddy Pete's dad. He works for the laundry service they use."

The Hudson Valley Cleaning and Supply Company is run out of a warehouse in Saratoga Springs. It's pretty much what you would expect: a dozen or so industrial-size washing machines and dryers and local women doing the sorting and folding at long wooden tables. It services most of the hospitals in the area, including the Hayden Institute.

Pete's dad, John Carpenzano, drives a delivery truck for Hudson Valley. He's fifty, needs a shave, and his arms are thick with prison tattoos, meaning he's done time in Coxsackie, which isn't too far away. The guy in the toggle coat handles the introductions, but Carpenzano is suspicious. I'm sure doing time made him that way, and convincing him to give me a hand getting into the Hayden Institute isn't going to be easy. I manage to talk him into going with me over to a local tavern, where I buy him a boilermaker and make him a proposition.

I say I'll pay him a couple hundred bucks if he'll look the other way while I take his truck and make his next delivery to the institute. "No way," Carpenzano says. "If I get caught, I'll lose my job, and my parole officer will have me back inside in no time." Then he lights a cigarette and changes his tune—sort of. "I'll tell you what I'll do. Make it five hundred and I'll think about it. Make it seven fifty, and I'll throw in my Hudson Valley windbreaker; in fact, make it seven fifty or it's no deal." Seven fifty is a little rich for my blood, but I don't see another way, so I tell Carpenzano okay and we shake on it.

CHAPTER TWENTY

If the guard recognizes me, it'll blow my con out of the water, so I buy a cheap pair of sunglasses, borrow Carpenzano's John Deere cap, and pull it down over my eyes. When I ease to a stop at the Hayden Institute's gate, the guard peers into the cab of the delivery truck and wants to know where Carpenzano is.

"Stomach bug," I tell him. "He called in and said he was puking his guts out all last night, so I took his shift."

The guard seems pretty dubious, but he doesn't make me, at least I don't think he does.

"It's going around," he says after a brief stare-down. "The wife had it last week and couldn't keep anything down." Then he opens the gate and waves me through.

I pull the truck around to the delivery entrance and open the tailgate. Freshly washed and pressed white lab coats, sheets, towels, and bedding are stacked in a large canvas hamper. I roll the hamper out of the truck and wheel it through double doors into the institute.

I'm trying to make myself inconspicuous, but it isn't easy. Maybe I've seen *The Snake Pit* too many times, but I counted on the inmates careening around screeching and blithering to distract anyone from noticing me. But the arched, high-ceiling hallways are empty, and my footsteps are echoing off the marble floors.

A couple of orderlies are loitering outside one of the wards smoking and gossiping. I wheel the hamper past them like I know where I'm going, but when one of them spots me, he barks, "You're not supposed to be here."

I play dumb. "Why? What's the big deal? I'm just making a delivery."

"The big deal, buddy, is that the linen supply closet is at the other end of the building. These are locked wards, and nobody's supposed to get anywhere near them."

I don't want to be reported, so I say, "Sorry. I'm kinda new and somebody told me it was this way."

"Down the corridor and to the left," the orderly tells me, but before I trundle off, I stop and take a look through the locked ward's glass observation window. I'm looking for Lucy, but all I see is a bunch of sad-looking women weaving lanyards and sewing wallets or just staring blankly off into space.

"So, these are the nutjobs, huh?" I say to give my act a little credibility, but the orderlies ignore me and I move off.

When I round a corner into another corridor and out of sight of the orderlies, I strip out of Carpenzano's windbreaker and doff his John Deere cap. I toss them in the hamper and slip into one of the white lab coats. A nurse smiles at me when she walks by and a doctor does the same, so my ruse must be convincing.

As far as I can tell, the institute is divided into two wings. In the one I've just left, patients spend their nights in small cell-like cubicles and their days in a common room with little more to do than contemplate the four walls. In the other wing, the one I'm wandering around in now, better-heeled patients occupy suites complete with a bedroom, a sitting room, and wide picture windows overlooking the institute's grounds. I figure they've probably put Lucy in one of them, but when I go to investigate, I find all their doors are locked, all except for one.

When I ease it open, I see an attractive woman in her late thirties sitting in a straight-back chair, sipping a cup of tea and listening to Charlie Mingus. There's something familiar about her. I know I've seen her before, but I don't know where.

"That's Mingus's new one, isn't it?" I ask when the woman looks up at me. But before she has a chance to say anything, there's a tap on my shoulder.

"A little outside your usual bailiwick, aren't you, Mr. Coffey?"

When I turn, I'm confronted by Dr. Wallace Hayden, a tall, thin, desiccated-looking guy with a hook nose and cheeks so sunken that you can almost see his skull. The guard from the gate and the two orderlies I saw earlier stand behind him, ready to manhandle me.

"Listen, I'm not looking for trouble," I tell Hayden, "but there's somebody here that I really need to see."

"Lucy Garrett?"

"That's right."

"It might be best if you and I talk in my office." Glancing over my shoulder, he says to the woman, "Sorry to disturb you, Susan. It won't happen again." She smiles, and Hayden closes her door when we leave.

"Who is that?" I ask him.

"Privacy is essential to the work we do here, Mr. Coffey."

"Meaning you won't tell me."

"Exactly. Now, if you'll just come this way."

I follow Hayden down a long hallway to his office. It's large and formal. Framed diplomas, awards, and citations are hung on the wall behind his desk. His bookshelves are crammed with academic-looking volumes, knickknacks, and keepsakes. A knitted afghan is draped over a leather divan in a corner of the room. Hayden's patients must lie down on it when they confess their sins or whatever else is on their minds.

He indicates a chair, and I take a seat. Hayden perches on the end of his desk and leans forward as if he's about to share a confidence.

"I'm surprised that you haven't asked me how I know who you are," he says.

"Do you want me to guess?"

"I spoke to Louis Garrett a few minutes ago, if that's any help."

"Oh yeah? What did he have to say?"

"That as long as I don't violate the sanctity of the doctor-patient relationship, I should tell you whatever it is you want to know."

You have to give the guy credit for being inventive. Hayden could have just said that he didn't know Lucy, wouldn't tell me even if he did, and then had his goons throw me out. That's not going to be his play.

"Okay," I say, like I'm buying what he's selling. "So where is Lucy?"

"Right now? I don't really know."

"You're not keeping her here?"

"We don't keep anyone, Mr. Coffey, but to answer your question, no, Lucy Garrett is not here at present."

At present. Hayden uses this phrase deliberately. He wants me to think Lucy was here, and then what happened? She got better?

"As I said, I don't know where she is right now, but I have been treating her in my office in the city. I'm afraid Lucy is not at all well and really does need my help."

The good doctor is being intentionally vague, which irritates me, so I say, "Define 'not at all well.'"

"Mind you, I'm ethically bound not to reveal too much," he says, "but I will tell you that Lucy is a borderline personality given to flights of fancy and delusions of grandeur and perversity."

Ethically bound? If ethics were Hayden's strong suit, he wouldn't have told me anything about Lucy at all. The cat and mouse of this conversation is not only beginning to bore me, it's also not telling me anything that I don't already know. Despite the diplomas on his wall, I'm not afraid to match wits with Hayden, but it's time we get to the point.

"So, you're telling me Lucy isn't sleeping with her father. Do I have that right?"

"My God. Where did you get such an idea?"

Hayden's affronted act is anything but convincing, and I've had enough. "It came to me in a dream, which I'm sure you'll appreciate," I tell him, then I get to my feet and offer him my hand. "I'd like to say it's been a pleasure, Doctor, but we both know that's not true."

"I'm sorry to disappoint you, Mr. Coffey, but if there's nothing else I can do . . . ?"

"Oh, there's plenty you can do, but I'm sure you'll keep on gaslighting me, so I'm going leave before I lose my temper."

Psychoanalysis is all the rage these days. V swears by it, and I'm sure it has helped her, but I can't imagine spending time pouring my heart out to a supercilious prick like Wallace Hayden. Anyway, I'm not much for self-reflection. I suppose if I did "the work," as V calls it, I might discover things about myself that I didn't know. I might even be able to understand why I went into this line of work, which is plenty frustrating just at the moment. But I don't want to think about that now.

What I want to do is find that woman Hayden stopped me from talking to.

I'm positive I've seen her before, so instead of leaving, I sneak back and knock on her door.

"I hope I'm not disturbing you," I say when she opens it.

"Not at all," she says. "I've been expecting you."

CHAPTER TWENTY-ONE

"Is tea all right? I'm sorry I can't offer you anything more than tea and one of the butter cookies I took from the cafeteria. They let me have this little fridge, but they won't let me go to the market, so I never have very much."

"Tea is fine. Thanks."

She sets a kettle on a hot plate to boil, then walks over to her hi-fi. She thumbs through a pretty decent-size album collection, picks out one, lays it down on a turntable, and Miles's "'Round about Midnight" begins to play. I'm sitting at a small table by one of her picture windows.

When she comes over and sits down opposite me, I ask, "Do you know who I am?"

"No, but I've seen you before." She lights a cigarette, then delicately plucks a flake of tobacco off the tip of her tongue.

"Where was that?"

"The Onyx Club, I think. Or Leon and Eddie's. It might even have been the Royal Roost. The truth is, I don't remember very much from those days."

I'm trying to imagine her younger. The Roost closed seven or eight years ago, so it had to be before then. And there's something a little off about her, like the light behind her eyes has gone dim.

"I do remember how handsome you looked in your uniform though."

It must have been right after I enlisted. After basic, they gave us a week's furlough before we shipped out. I hit every club in town that week. It was a long time ago, so I'm a little hazy on the details. Could I have spent the night with her? No, that's not possible. I would have remembered. I wasn't much for one-night stands, even back then.

"I was sleeping with Coleman, you know," she says suddenly, "which horrified everybody, especially my parents."

She must mean Coleman Hawkins. Coleman is Black, and she couldn't be more lily white. That alone was enough to cause a scandal back during the war. It still is.

"To get me away from him, they sent me to finishing school in Switzerland. That's where I met him. I don't know what he was doing there. Something not very nice, I'm sure."

Who is she talking about?

"I knew he could be mean. I liked to think he was a spy. At least that would explain all the time we spent with those terrible men. Do you think he really was a spy?"

I'm not sure how far down this rabbit hole I want to go. The woman doesn't strike me as completely off her rocker, but we are in a mental institution and the story she's telling me doesn't make a lot of sense.

"I don't know how he got us back to New York. There was a war on and we shouldn't have been able to go anywhere, but he managed it somehow. And then I got pregnant. He didn't like that one bit."

I don't know who "he" is, and she might be making all of this up, so I'm watching her closely for some sort of tell, but there isn't one. Hayden must have her on drugs—sedatives and antipsychotics probably. That would explain her flat affect. Or maybe she's just delusional. Maybe when I knocked on her door, she let me into a private world where she goes places she's never been and meets people who don't exist.

"Of course, he wanted me to get rid of it, but I wouldn't. That wasn't the first time he hit me, but it was the first time he meant something by it. He never forgave me, you know? Not even after she was born. I was afraid he might take it out on her too, but I couldn't have been more wrong. He doted on her."

In my job you meet a lot of troubled people, people whose husbands or wives are betraying them, whose business partners are cheating them, people who are in danger of losing their livelihoods or even their lives. As sad as some of those cases are, and some of them are downright tragic, I try not to get emotionally involved. There isn't any point. I do what I can for them, admittedly for a price, but when the job is done, I walk away. I'm not sure what makes Lucy Garrett different. I don't know why I keep chasing after whatever the truth of her is, especially considering I'm not getting paid for it anymore. And I don't know why I keep listening to this woman spin castles in the sky when she's probably out of her mind.

"He arranged for everything, wet nurses and nannies. He filled her bedroom with stuffed animals and had luminous stars painted on the ceiling so they glowed at night. I wanted to nurse her myself, but he wouldn't allow it. The only thing he would let me do was kiss her goodnight. But after he went to bed, I'd creep into her room just to watch her sleep. I wanted to hold her, but I was afraid if she woke up and started to cry he'd come running and find me there."

She isn't making this up. Her pain is too real. "Would you like to see her picture?"

When I say that I would, she disappears into her bedroom, comes out a moment later clutching a snapshot, and hands it to me. In it, a pretty little blond girl smiles for the camera, and the woman holding her on her lap is Lucy Garrett's mother.

"She's beautiful, isn't she? Her name is Lucy. After my grandmother."

"When was the last time you saw Lucy?"

"Oh, I don't know. Days here crawl by so monotonously that it's hard to keep track of time. But I don't think it could have been more than a week ago. She didn't recognize me, but I recognized her the moment I saw her."

What could that moment have been like? How long had it been since Susan last saw her daughter? Her child was forcibly taken from her and then Garrett put her away to make sure she would never see the kid again. I wonder if Lucy knew her mother was being held here. Or did Garrett tell her the same thing he told me—that she was dead?

"Louis wanted to lock her up and throw away the key just like he did with me. I told her that too, but she didn't believe me. And when I went to hug her, to hug my own little girl, she was so stiff. It was like she didn't want me to touch her."

This is the way it must have gone. Like Lucy, her mother was a wild child. Lying about her age, she hit the jazz joints. She drank too much, smoked reefer with the boys, and probably slept with more than one of them. When Susan's parents found out she was with Coleman, they wanted her to break it off, but she refused. So they shipped her off to one of those fancy finishing schools in Switzerland, and that's where she met Garrett. She was young then, and he likes them that way. But when he knocked her up, she wasn't young anymore. After Lucy was born, Garrett was through with her, but he had to do something to get rid of her, and the Hayden Institute was the perfect place to stash her.

"She's expecting, you know?"

"Who is?"

"Lucy. You can hardly tell. She hasn't really begun to show."

Is Garrett the father? Maybe that's why he had Lucy taken here. Warehousing somebody as inconvenient as his wife and later his pregnant daughter probably isn't the only service the Hayden Institute provides. I'll bet that if you're willing to pay the freight, they'll arrange for an abortion. Dr. Hayden might even do it himself.

"I really need to speak to Lucy," I tell her mother. "Do you know where she is?"

"Oh, she's not here anymore."

"Did your husband come and get her?"

"No, she left with another man. Wait, I remember who you are now. Your name is Jack, isn't it? That's right. You're Jack Coffey."

CHAPTER TWENTY-TWO

It was far from the first beating I've ever taken, but it might have been the most professional. It feels like they cracked a couple of my ribs, and my nose is broken. I didn't hear Hayden's goons come into Susan's room, but one of them must have hit me with a sap because all of a sudden, I was seeing stars. It's a good thing they threw me into the cab of Carpenzano's delivery truck after they were done working me over. I'm not sure I could have made it there on my own. It was all kind of unnecessary though. All they had to do to get me to leave was ask.

I pull into a gas station on my way home and get the key to the restroom. The guy looking back at me from the smudged restroom mirror is a mess. His right eye is swollen and a sort of nauseating purple, and both his nostrils are caked with blood. They split my lip too, and it's still oozing. I'd hate to have V see me like this not only because it's liable to scare her but because I'm afraid that one day she's going to say that she's had enough of the mayhem and that I'd better find another line of work or she's leaving. Given the way I look now, I could hardly blame her.

The restroom sink is thick with soap scum, but I run the tap anyway and clean myself up as best as I can. When I crack my nose bone back into place, the pain is so intense that it shoots right up through the top of my skull, but it had to be done. I'm not going home to V with my face on crooked. I stagger back to the Rambler and get in behind the wheel as gingerly as I can. I'm probably going to be laid up for a couple of days. I make a mental note to get hold of Carmine and have him send one of his boys over with a bucketful of Dilaudid.

Driving back down to the city, I manage to get WNEW on the car radio again, and Monk's "I Mean You" helps clear my head. Ordinarily, I'm pretty good at judging the angles my cases take, but just when I'm beginning to make sense of Garrett and his daughter, I stumble across something that makes their story even more complicated and bizarre. Garrett's wife was a disturbing surprise. I ought to try to do something about getting Susan Garrett away from Hayden and off the stew of psychotropic drugs he must have her on, but that will have to wait. Right now I'm trying to figure out who sprung Lucy, but nothing is coming to me. There aren't a lot of possibilities. It wasn't her father, that's for sure. It might have been Bob Carson, but I don't think he'd cross Garrett. They're in business together in some opaque way, so I don't think he'd break Lucy out no matter how "fond" of her he is.

Maybe Lucy has another boyfriend that I don't know about, some poor schmuck she can manipulate into doing whatever she wants. That seems likely, but the only guy I've ever known her to be with is Rex Halsey, and what's left of Rex is lying in an unmarked grave in Potter's Field. There must be other men, older men probably. Like the saying goes, there's no fool like an old fool, something I'm sure Lucy learned at her father's knee, or more likely on it.

I go with the idea of an older man, a man not only Garrett's age but one as connected as he is. And if I'm right, she's probably convinced him to order up the slab of cement and the guy from Philly to try and hit me. Lucy knows that her father hired me to find her, but she didn't want to be found, and she probably knows that I'm still looking for her. What better way to put an end to all of that than putting an end to me?

I try this theory out on V while we're driving up to the cottage in the Berkshires. V's at the wheel. She's wrapped my ribs with an Ace bandage, and she's having me hold an ice pack against my swollen nose.

"You might be right, but I don't want to talk about that right now," she says. "I'm pretty furious with you, Jack, in case you haven't noticed, and the last thing I want to discuss is Lucy Garrett or whoever it is that's trying to kill you."

V was horrified when I came home with my face rearranged, so I say, "Sorry, V. What can I tell you? It comes with the job," which I know won't mollify her, but I've got to say something.

"That's just it, Jack. It doesn't come with the job, not the part of the job you get paid to do. And why do you care what happens to these people? Why don't you just leave them to their own sick devices so we can get on with our lives? Anyway, what do you think you're going to find out that you don't already know? I mean, I feel sorry for Lucy. She's a deeply disturbed girl with a psychotic father, but nothing you do is going to change that. I know you like to play the white knight, which I love you for most of the time, but just who do you think you're rescuing here? And don't say Lucy Garrett because I'm not sure she wants to be rescued."

V's right. Sometimes I do see myself riding to the rescue, saving poor souls who need saving, sometimes even saving them from themselves.

"What if I promise you not to talk about the two of them while we're up at the cottage?" I say. "What if we spend the week in bed listening to music and doing whatever else comes into our heads? What do you say to that?"

V sits on this idea for a couple of seconds, scowls like she isn't about to let me off the hook that easy, then says, "Okay, here's the deal. You cook and do all the grocery shopping. When I say I want to take a long walk in the country, you don't make up some phony-baloney excuse about being a city boy and how the fresh air makes you nauseous. You just come with me. And you're going to take me out to the movies, Jack. I know you hate to get dressed and leave the house when we're up there, but you're going to put on your pants and take me over to the Pickwick because Bud's in something new, and I really want to see it." I tell her that I'll happily do all of that, and V snorts like she doesn't believe me. "I just wish I didn't love you so much," she says, "but for some completely insane reason, I do." I can't stop grinning.

I acted like one of the Bowery Boys when we first started going up to the cottage. My New York accent got thicker, and I began to talk out of the side of my mouth. It was the quiet. I'm used to hearing the city making a racket, the subway rumbling, cab drivers leaning on their horns, drunks shouting and cursing as they stumble home in the dark. But lying in bed next to V those first few nights in the country, I was so spooked by the silence that I couldn't sleep a wink. And when I heard something—the house creak, the wind in the trees, mice skittering under the floorboards—I wanted to make a run for it: grab my bag, jump in the car, and drive back to the city as fast as I possibly could.

When I confessed this to V, she thought it was hilarious. Growing up in East Texas, she loved the country, thrived in it, and had bought the cottage in West Stockbridge the minute she saw it. And when I groused that I couldn't see how anybody wanted to live in a place that didn't stink of car exhaust and garbage, V gave me a kiss and said that I'd get used to it eventually, which I didn't buy for a second.

But I did get used to it, more than used to it. Now, I stumble after V when she takes me for hikes in the woods, swim naked in the pond out behind the house, and barbecue on a potbelly grill. And in the winter, I chop wood. I don't want to particularly, but the cottage is heated by a wood-burning stove, and V says we'll freeze to death if I don't. This seems unnecessarily primitive to me, doesn't come naturally, and I nearly buried the axe blade in my shins a couple of times before I got the hang of it.

I do take V over to the Pickwick to see Bud's latest just as I promised her. It's after ten by the time the movie gets out, and it's starting to snow. They pretty much roll up the sidewalks here after dark, but neither of us feels like going home. There's a bar that's open until eleven, but it's a depressing dive. Amelia's Café is a sort of twee coffeehouse that stays open late catering to the movie crowd, and after taking a stroll around town, we stop in.

We sit at a table by the window, and Amelia's daughter Trudy takes our order: a hot cider for V and a cup of coffee for me. V starts telling me about a yard sale over in Lenox that she wants to go to. She says that she needs to find a new quilt for the bed, and pretty soon she's deep into a recitation of the relative merits of block quilts versus scrap and crazy quilts. I'm only saved when Trudy comes back with our order. After she sets the cups down, V tells her to take a seat, and the two of them fall into a conversation about the movie. I glance out the window.

That's when I see him standing across the street, smoking a cigarette. He's wearing the same greatcoat, scarf, and woolen cap that he wore lurking in the shadows on Perry Street, and that's how I recognize him. V and Trudy are both startled when I push my chair away from the table and get to my feet, but I don't have time to explain.

Outside, the guy sees me coming, tosses his cigarette, and is walking away like I'm supposed to think he's a local.

I grab him before he gets very far and spin him around, but instead of trying to fight me off, the guy pleads, "Don't hurt me, okay? Just don't hurt me."

"Who are you?"

"Nobody," he says, and I'm inclined to believe him. The guy's fifty if he's a day, and there's something soft about him, like if I slap him, he might start to cry.

"Who sent you up here? And don't tell me nobody again or I'm liable to get annoyed."

"I don't know who he is, I swear it. This guy gives me five hundred in cash and says I should tail you no matter where you go and call him twice a day to tell him where you are. He says he'll give me another five hundred when I'm done, but he doesn't tell me his name and I wasn't about to ask."

"Why you?"

"We both know people, you know what I'm saying?"

This guy is strictly small-time, a bookie maybe or a numbers runner. I crowd him like I still might smack him and say, "What did this guy look like?"

"Slick. Thirty-five maybe. Snappy dresser. Like I said, I don't know his name, but don't rat me out, okay? He'll get steamed if you do, and I think he likes to hurt people."

CHAPTER TWENTY-THREE

V is irritated with me. I've only been gone for five or ten minutes, but she shoots me a nasty look as soon as I walk back into Amelia's. She's too polite to let me have it in front of Trudy, but V is holding on to that look when she asks, "Who was that supposed to be?"

"Nobody," I say, "at least that's what he told me," which I think is clever, but V doesn't. "I thought I recognized him from the city, but he turned out to be somebody else." This seems a serviceable lie, one that Trudy believes, but not one that I can get past V.

"Trudy," V says, "what do you do when your boyfriend makes up a story that you know is a complete lie, but tries to sell you on it anyway?"

"I don't have a boyfriend," Trudy says.

"Lucky you."

"Honestly, V. He really wasn't anybody. I'm just a little jumpy these days, you know, for the obvious reasons."

Now Trudy's interested. "I don't understand. For what obvious reasons?"

"Jack's in the damsel-in-distress business," V tells her. "It doesn't pay very well, but somebody's got to do it. Right, Jack?"

V and I have been together long enough for me to know when to let a dig like that pass, but Trudy doesn't.

"I still don't get it," she says.

V pats her on the arm and tells her that I'm a private investigator, which seems to thrill Trudy no end. She starts pumping me for details, probably expecting sordid stories of gun molls and psychopathic gangsters, but I disappoint her. I tell her that I do divorce work mostly or occasionally find a lost puppy or a demented geezer who has wandered away from home.

V doesn't like it when I hide my light under a bushel, so she tells Trudy about Ernie Norwood.

Nine-year-old Ernie Norwood lives with his mother, Florence, and his father, Ralph, in Pelham Bay. Ralph sells cars at a Chevy dealership in Yonkers—that is, he sells them when he isn't too busy gambling away his paycheck on the ponies. He rarely goes out to the track though. Instead, he makes his bets through a bookie named Petey O'Brien. Petey's from the old neighborhood, but he's at least a decade older than me, so I don't know him all that well. His reputation is good though: he gives track odds, pays off on time, and usually doesn't go in for the rough stuff when somebody can't come across right away. But Ralph is in deep with Petey, so deep that Petey can't let it slide, so to encourage him to pay what he owes, he grabs little Ernie and lets Ralph know that if he doesn't come up with the money, he won't get the kid back. He doesn't mean it, but Ralph doesn't know that and panics.

I arrange a sit-down with Petey at his place out on Staten Island. A gunsel opens the door when I knock and pats me down before leading me into Petey's living room. I don't know what I expected to find there, little Ernie trussed up in a corner maybe, but instead the boy is sitting on the living room floor, eating Cheerios straight from the box, and watching cartoons on TV.

"Just so you know, I don't like this one bit," Petey says, "but the guy keeps stiffing me. What else am I supposed to do?"

"You could just have his legs broken, Petey. Isn't that standard procedure when it comes to this kind of thing?"

The good news is that Petey O'Brien isn't a sadistic extortionist like Sergei Ivanovich. He isn't going to hurt Ernie because he enjoys it or just for sport. In fact, he isn't going to hurt Ernie at all. Petey got fed up with Ralph, snatched his kid without thinking it through, and now he's backed himself into a corner and is looking for a way out.

"How much is he into you for?" I ask, and Petey tells me ten grand, which we both know Ralph doesn't have. "Okay, let's say we do this. Let's say he gives you five hundred now and pays you a hundred a week until he clears the debt."

"What's the vig?"

"Five percent," I say, and Petey pretends to think it over, but before too long he throws up his hands and says, "Go ahead and take the kid home, but tell that shitbird father of his that if I don't see the five hundred first thing in the morning, I really am gonna break his legs." Ralph pays Petey the five hundred and a C-note every week like clockwork, and that's the end of it.

But the way V tells this story, I might as well have had an *S* sewn on my chest. In her version Petey isn't a perfectly respectable bookmaker, but a drooling child molester who spends his time hanging around the playground outside PS 111. And his gunsel, who was sitting on the floor sharing Cheerios with Ernie the last time I saw him, isn't a harmless mug but a killer who, if I hadn't been quick-thinking enough, would have murdered me and Ernie in cold blood. She tells Trudy that I busted into a rat-infested warehouse in the Bronx rather than ambled into a split-level ranch house in Arden Heights. She says I found Ernie there, picked him up, threw him over my shoulder, and narrowly escaped in a hail of gunfire. None of it is true, but V is convincing, and by the time she's through, Trudy's mouth is hanging open.

I have no idea what possessed her to concoct a story like that. When I ask her in the car on the way back to the cottage, V says that she just felt like it, and where's the harm in Trudy thinking that I'm a hero? Then she slides across the front seat and rests her head against my shoulder. I wrap my arm around her, and we stay that way until I pull up in front of the cottage to find every light in the place burning,

This is not good. V always turns off the lights before we go out. Somebody's been in the house and might still be there. I tell V to wait in the car, reach into the Rambler's glove box to retrieve my .38, and shove it in my waistband.

I'm trying to be as quiet as I can as I approach the cottage, but my footsteps are crunching against the snow loud enough to give me away. I peek in the front window to see if I can spot anybody. I can't, but the front door is wide open. I creep across the threshold and slip inside. There's a fire burning in the fireplace. I smell cigarette smoke and hear somebody talking. It turns out to be the radio, but I don't know that yet.

I pull out my .38, ease back the hammer, and I'm moving toward the sound of the voice, when Jimmy Mullen says to me, "I poured myself a drink while I was waiting, Jack. You don't mind, do you?"

Mullen is sitting in a rocker by the fire with his feet up. He has a tumbler full of Irish in his hand and a cigarette stuck in the corner of his mouth. "You wanna put the piece away?" he says to me.

"As soon as you tell me what you're doing here, Jimmy."

"The girl. Is she with you?"

"Are we talking about Lucy Garrett?"

"Yeah. That's the one."

I admit that I'm surprised. I always figured Mullen was clean. I guess I was wrong. "You're on her old man's payroll, aren't you, Jimmy?"

"Let's just say I help Mr. Garrett out when I can."

I ease myself down into a chair, the .38 in my lap. "Is that what you're doing here? Helping Mr. Garrett out?"

"Don't make this difficult, Jack. Is the girl with you or not?"

"Not," V snaps, suddenly at my side. "Now get out of my house."

Jimmy looks up at her and smiles. "Give it a rest, sweetheart. Go powder your nose or something. I mean, isn't that what you do for a living?"

V doesn't hesitate. She grabs the .38 out of my lap and pulls the trigger. A bullet whizzes past Mullen's ear and blows a hole in the wall behind him.

Jimmy nearly faints.

V missed on purpose, at least I think she did, but she isn't going to again. "Get out of here," she shouts at Jimmy, "or the next one is between your eyes."

I'm grinning. I can't help it. The woman never ceases to amaze me.

"Self-defense, Jimmy, open and shut," I say, getting to my feet. "You broke in here. You were armed. You were lying in wait. Justifiable homicide all day long, my friend." I yank Mullen's service revolver out of his shoulder holster and grab the snub-nose that I know he's got strapped to his ankle. "Now, you'd better do what the lady says and take a walk."

CHAPTER TWENTY-FOUR

Stillman's Gym is filthy. The toilets are backed up, the locker room reeks, the windows are sealed shut, and a pall of cigar and cigarette smoke hangs over the place like a radioactive cloud. Rotting food and old newspapers are strewn everywhere, and the floor hasn't been mopped in years. Lou Stillman, the owner, likes it that way. Stillman is seventy, has a face that looks like a patch of bad road, and is so moody that he's liable to take a swing at you for no good reason. He keeps the place as unsanitary as possible for the fighters' own good. "If I clean up, they'll catch cold from the cleanliness," he says. But all the greats have worked out at Stillman's: Dempsey, Carpentier, Billy Conn, and Joe Louis, to name just a few. When I walk in the door, Rocky Marciano is hitting the heavy bag.

I come into the gym every once in a while to break a sweat, but Bud is here most every afternoon when he's in town. He goes about one-eighty-five these days, making him a light heavyweight, and he's surprisingly agile for a guy that size. I've seen him mix it up with Archie Moore and Ezzard Charles, and Bud just about holds his own. Of course, ever since he became a famous actor, he attracts a crowd, which is just fine with Lou. Stillman charges Bud's fans a buck apiece to sit on folding chairs and gawk at him while he works out. The Dugan brothers are regulars here too. Eddie was a ranked heavyweight until he had his bell rung once too often and gave it up. Joe worked his corner as a cut man.

When I approach the ring, Bud is sparring with a Black kid, who's carrying him not so much because he's Marlon Brando but because he doesn't want Bud to get hurt. But Bud clips him with a pretty good right cross, so then the kid counters with a left that puts Bud down on the canvas.

"Serves you right for dropping your shoulder," I say, and Bud smiles up at me through his mouthpiece.

"You want to go a few?" he says, and I say sure. Bud has about five pounds on me and he's quick, but there isn't much power behind even his best punch, and I'm pretty positive that I can take him.

I've got my gym gear in a canvas bag, so I duck into the locker room, strip down, and inside of a few minutes, me and Bud are squaring off. Stillman himself decides to work the bout as the ref. The bell rings, and Bud and I are dancing. We jab at each other to no great effect. I throw a right hand that he ducks under. Bud counters with a right of his own, but it misses. We go at it like this for a while until I connect with an upper cut that has Bud backpedaling. I'm moving in to work his body when somebody yells out, "Coffey! Telephone!"

I make the mistake of turning my head, and Bud throws a left hook that knocks me on my ass.

"Gotta protect yourself at all times, pal," he says, standing over me with a grin on his face before helping me to my feet.

There's a pay phone in the gym, but Lou doesn't like anybody to use it. The coin slots are taped over to make sure we all get the message. No one knows I'm here, so I'm suspicious when I pick up the receiver.

"Who's this?" I say in my best tough-guy voice, but it's Janie, my receptionist, calling.

"You'd better get over here as soon as you can, Jack," she says. "Some kid is here to see you and she's so nervous that it's all I can do to keep her from jumping out of her skin."

"Some kid like in Lucy Garrett?"

"No. Some other kid, but she's pretty desperate, so step on it, okay?"

"Yeah, okay, but just out of curiosity—how did you know where to find me?"

"Who do you think you are, Jack, the Shadow? You're not home. You're not with Vicky. You're not in O'Doul's. Where else are you gonna be on a weekday afternoon when you should be in the office?"

Bud is standing next to me when I get off the phone, and he wants to know what's up. I tell him that I've got to get back to my office pronto, and he asks if he can tag along. This strikes me as odd.

"You're a big movie star now. Don't you have anything better to do?"

Apparently he doesn't, so I tell him okay and we take off.

Muffy Palmer is about the last person I expect to see. She's sitting in the office reception area, gnawing on a cuticle, her stringy dishwater-blond hair falling in her face. She pays no attention to Bud, but Janie recognizes Mr. Brando. Her mouth drops open the second we walk in the door, and I'm pretty sure I just heard her whimper.

Muffy can't bring herself to look me in the eye. "I shouldn't be here," she says, staring at her lap. Not only is the kid terrified, but she's speaking so softly that I can barely hear her. "I wasn't supposed to, but I had to tell somebody."

"Listen to me, Muffy, everything is going to be all right," which is probably a lie, but I have to say something. "Now, why don't we go into my office and you can tell me all about it." I help the kid to her feet. It's freezing outside. Muffy has been in the office for a while, but she's nervous as a cat and her hands are still cold as ice, so I tell Janie to run down to the candy store on the corner and buy her a hot chocolate.

But my secretary's too busy gawking at Bud to hear a word I say.

"Janie!" I bark loud enough to break the spell. "Go! Now!"

I usher Muffy into my office and into a chair. I sit on the edge of my desk. Bud leans up against the office doorframe, his arms folded across his chest.

"He was waiting for me after school," Muffy tells me.

"Who was?"

"I don't know who he was. A man."

"What'd he look like?" Bud asks, and it's only then that Muffy recognizes him.

"Aren't you in the movies? He is, isn't he?" she says to me.

"The man, Muffy," I say. "Was he tall or short? How was he dressed? Was he wearing a suit and tie or casual clothes?"

Instead of answering me, Muffy snaps open the white patent-leather pocketbook she's been clutching and hands me a scrap of paper with an address near Times Square scrawled on it. "He gave me this," she says.

"Did he say anything to you when he did?"

"Only that she's real sick and somebody needs to get over there right away."

"Did he mean Lucy?"

"I think so. I'm not in trouble, am I? I mean, if my mom finds out. Don't tell her I was here, okay? Please, or she'll get real mad."

To call the Washington Arms a dump is to be generous. They rent rooms by the hour to hookers and their johns, who stream in and out night and day. The guy behind the desk is obese, bald, and glistening with sweat. He's protected by a thick sheet of plexiglass in case a stray bullet happens along or some irate customer tries to get in at him. An ashtray piled high with butts is on the desk in front of him, and the guy's body odor is so pungent that it seeps out into what passes for the hotel lobby.

"There's a girl here," I say to him. "A kid. Which room is she in?" The guy ignores me. He's reading the late edition of the *Daily News*, licking his fingers each time he turns the page.

"Don't make us call the cops," Bud chimes in, and frankly I'm a little embarrassed. It's a cheesy threat like something out of a B movie, which I'm thinking is beneath an actor of Bud's caliber, but it's enough to make the guy look up.

"You're Marlon Brando," he says, like Bud is an apparition turned suddenly real. "Wow. I'm a big fan, Mr. Brando. I mean, *On the Waterfront*, I must've seen it a dozen times."

This I hadn't counted on. If I had pulled my gun and threatened to blow the guy's head off, I wouldn't have gotten as quick a response as Bud does when he says, "Listen, pal, help us out here. Which room is that girl in?"

"One-twelve," the guy says. He can't get the words out of his mouth fast enough. "Meanwhile, do you think I can get an autograph?" He slides a pencil and a piece of paper to Bud through a slot in the plexiglass along with the key to room 112. "And could you make it out to 'my friend Myron,' you know, so the wife doesn't think I'm making it up when I say we met?"

I grab the key, and before Bud finishes scribbling his signature for Myron, I'm bounding up the hotel stairs. I unlock the door to room 112 and burst in.

Lucy Garrett is sprawled half-on and half-off the bed. She's unconscious, and there's a bloody needle lying on the carpet next to her. If she really is pregnant, she still isn't showing.

I check for a pulse. Bud appears in the doorway. "Is she dead?"

"Alive," I say, "but not by much."

I haul Lucy onto the bed and give her mouth-to-mouth. Bud is about to run downstairs to call an ambulance when she comes around.

"What are you doing here?" she says, grinning at me like she's not only surprised but happy to see me.

"Can you stand up?" I say.

"Why?" she wants to know. "Where are we going?"

CHAPTER TWENTY-FIVE

Al Murphy is the doorman in V's building on Beekman Place. He's seen more than a few tenants stumble home in various stages of inebriation so nothing much shocks him. He is a bit surprised though when he sees me and Bud help Lucy out of a cab and carry her into the lobby. He offers to give us a hand taking her upstairs, but I figure the less he knows about all this, the better. I tell Al no thanks and slip him a ten-spot so he'll keep his mouth shut if anybody asks after us. He lays a finger against the side of his nose to let me know he gets the message.

I've taken Lucy over to V's mostly because I can't think of another place to stash her. I have a spare key, so getting in is no problem. Lucy is still on the nod but bound to jones for another fix before the night is out, and I want to make sure she's someplace safe when she starts to get sick.

I've got a ton of questions for her, but I don't really want to spend the next eight hours mopping Lucy Garrett's fevered brow and waiting for answers. Bud doesn't either, so I call over to Stillman's Gym to see if Joe and Eddie Dugan are still around.

It takes forever for anybody to answer the phone, but when somebody finally does, it's Joe. I fill him in on the situation and ask if he and Eddie wouldn't mind coming over to Beekman Place to babysit Lucy until she gets straight. I tell him there's a bottle of bourbon in V's liquor cabinet with the Dugans' name on it and that the Chinese restaurant around the corner delivers. Apparently, this is enough of an enticement.

Joe tells me they'll be here inside of an hour, and I call downstairs to let Al know they're coming.

Bud and I tuck Lucy into V's bed. She dozes off with her thumb in her mouth, looking the picture of innocence.

"Poor kid," Bud mutters. "She's what, sixteen? And she's got a shit for a father, right? I mean, the worst mine did when I was her age was knock me around a little and tell me that I'd never amount to anything. I won the goddamn Academy Award last year and I can still hear the bastard's voice telling me I'm no good."

"Listen, it's not like I don't feel for her, but I don't trust her," I tell Bud. "Her old man is abusing her, which is probably the reason she's acting out, but she's capable of almost anything. As a matter of fact, I think she might have convinced some mook to gun for me, so I'm just gonna sit on her until I find out what's really what."

"But it's Garrett you're really after, right?"

"Yeah. Why not?"

"I'll tell you why not. I know guys like him out in Hollywood. Two-bit chiselers and cheap hoods who bully and bullshit their way into money and power. They don't mind screwing underage girls either. They play for keeps, Jack, and if you don't watch it, you're liable to end up in a plain pine box. I know this kid's had a tough time, but it's not worth risking your life trying to save her. Anyway, how do you know she wants to be saved?"

I grin, and Bud wants to know what's so funny. "V told me exactly the same thing," I say just as the house phone rings. It's Al from downstairs. The Dugans are in the lobby.

Al is with the brothers when they knock on V's door just to make sure they really are who they say they are. The Dugans don't know it, but he's carrying a knuckle-duster in his coat pocket. He's used it on more than one miscreant who mistook his paunch, his snow-white hair, and his smiling Irish face for an easy mark and thought they could take him. I reassure Al that these are the right guys, and he takes off. The Dugans know Bud from Stillman's Gym, and handshakes go around before Joe breaks out the bottle of bourbon I promised him and takes a healthy swig.

V's TV set is a major attraction. The Dugans don't own one, and they turn it on and settle onto her couch to watch *Have Gun—Will Travel* while passing the bottle back and forth. I figured them for fans of the *Friday Night Fights* or wrestling, but they relate to the show's gunslinging hero mostly because the actor playing him is as pockmarked as they are.

Before Bud and I leave, I tell the boys to keep an eye on Lucy. "I put a bucket beside her bed so it's there when she starts to puke. Just make sure to keep her warm when she gets the shakes. She's gonna try to bolt the minute she feels better and might even offer to blow both of you, but don't fall for it, at least not until I get back."

The Dugans grin at me in a way that's a little disturbing. I know they're not above collecting sexual favors, particularly from a girl who looks like Lucy Garrett, so I promise them a night at Kitty Malone's brothel over on Tenth Avenue but only if they behave themselves.

A cold wind is howling when Bud and I hit the street, and we aren't dressed for it. We're hoping to hail a cab, but it's late and there isn't one in sight. We're about to hop on the subway at Fifty-First Street when somebody calls out my name.

"Jack? It is you, isn't it, Jack?" A woman emerges from the shadows of a storefront on Third Avenue, but I don't recognize her. "Sure it is. Jack Coffey. You're still the best-looking boy on the block, aren't you Jack?"

The last time I saw Bridget Moran, she was fifteen. She sparkled then, her curly red hair falling to her waist and her green eyes bright, but that sparkle is gone. Her skin is sallow now. There are deep bags under her eyes, and I'd be surprised if she weighs a hundred pounds. She's wearing a fake-rabbit-fur jacket, a skirt that leaves nothing to the imagination, fishnets, and ridiculously high heels. What Bridget is doing with herself these days is hardly a mystery. Third Avenue is thick with ladies like her selling themselves, even in the cold and at this time of night.

"You got a light, Jack?" she asks, fishing a cigarette out of her purse. I don't, but Bud does. When he lights her cigarette with a Zippo, the flame illuminates his face, but Bridget either doesn't recognize him or just doesn't care who Bud is. Her hands are shaking so badly that she can barely bring the cigarette to her lips.

"Bridget, why don't you get out of the cold and go on home?" I tell her. "You look like you're about to freeze to death."

"I can't," she says, "not until my man tells me it's time." I assume her man is a pimp.

"Would that man be somebody I know?"

"Probably not. He's Spanish, but he treats me good. I just gotta earn for him is all. Speaking of which, you and your friend aren't interested in some fun, are you? I could show you both a real good time, you know?"

This just breaks my heart. Sweet little Bridget Moran trying to sell herself to me. I feel like taking her home to her mother, but her mother was a bad drunk and died a long time ago. "Not my style, Bridge, but if you could use some cash, I got about fifty on me and I'm sure Bud won't mind chipping in."

Any money I give Bridget is likely to go for booze, or in her arm, or into her pimp's pocket, but I can't leave her standing out here in the freezing cold. I empty my wallet and Bud ponies up another hundred. Bridget takes our money and, without even a thank-you, clatters off down the street, teetering on those high heels.

Bud looks at me, expecting an explanation, but I don't feel like giving him one, and he lets it go. It's then that he spots an empty cab coming our way and whistles it to the curb.

"C'mon, we'll split it," he says. "I'll take it crosstown and then you can take it down to the Village."

But I beg off. I can't stop thinking about Bridget, a young girl who used to follow me around the neighborhood, now desiccated and down on her luck. The truth is, after seeing her like that, I'd just as soon be on my own.

"You go on ahead, Bud," I tell him. "I'm gonna walk."

I was lucky. I don't appreciate that enough. I survived combat, and a lot of guys I knew didn't. I went to Fordham on the GI Bill when most of my friends from the old neighborhood dropped out of high school. The Jesuits were a tight-assed Stalinist bunch, but no one else could have gotten me to read Aquinas and Thomas More.

I wasn't the only one to escape. Some guys got grandfathered into the unions or became cops or firefighters. There was even a doctor or two. And I once ran into a judge in the courthouse downtown who used to run numbers for Owney Madden when we were kids. Not everyone ended up like Bridget, but she wasn't the exception either.

I'm thinking about her and guys I used to know like her. I'm not watching where I'm going, so I don't pay much attention to the footsteps coming up behind me. In fact, I don't pay any attention to them at all until I feel the business end of an automatic in the small of my back.

"When you killed Sergei, I told you I was gonna make you pay, Jack. Today is the day."

I should have smelled him coming. "Oh, for Christ's sake, Iggy, give it a rest, will you please?"

"Just keep walking, hotshot."

I'm about to tell Iggy his act is getting old when I hear him jack a round into the chamber of his gun.

I have a split second to take stock. If I don't move fast enough, there's going to be a bullet hole where my left kidney used to be. And it strikes me that Iggy is broke, living on the street, and so fundamentally deep in the shitter that he has nothing to lose by killing me. My only possible saving grace is the street sweeper lumbering toward us. I have to make my move now or I'm a dead man, so I throw back an elbow that catches Iggy square on the jaw. It's enough to jar his automatic, and he misses when he pulls the trigger. I spin around, grab him by his coat lapels, and heave him in front of the street sweeper. There's an ominous thump, the sweeper's brakes squeal, and the driver grinds the thing to a halt. He gets out of the cab and joins me on the sidewalk to assess the damage.

"Never saw him," the driver says. His hands are in his jacket pockets, and he's stamping his feet on the cement against the cold. There's plenty of blood, and Iggy isn't moving. "Think he's dead?"

He isn't dead. Iggy isn't really underneath the street sweeper's wheels but under one of its big circular brushes.

"No, he's still with us," I tell him. "He must've cracked his head on the curb, but he'll come around after a while."

"You wanna call the cops?"

"Not really. You?"

"None of my business," the driver says before he climbs back into the cab of his street sweeper, backs it away from Iggy, and drives off.

CHAPTER TWENTY-SIX

I do Iggy the courtesy of calling an ambulance from a pay phone before taking the subway down to the Village. I was going to walk, but the temperature must be in the single digits and my teeth are chattering. I let myself into the apartment as quietly as I can. I figure V is asleep in the bedroom, and I don't want to disturb her.

I'm wrong. She isn't there. This isn't necessarily a reason to panic. I know V is working a shoot for *Town and Country* in Connecticut. If the shoot ran late, she might have decided to spend the night in a hotel up there. It is a shame though. I was looking forward to climbing into bed with her and snuggling up close—not only because I love her but because I'm still shivering and want to get the chill off my bones.

I also wanted to tell her that Lucy is passed out in her apartment where the Dugan brothers are looking after her. V isn't going to be very happy about that, and I probably would have waited until the morning before letting her know, but that doesn't matter now. By the time V gets home, I'll have figured out what to do with Lucy, gone back to Beekman Place, and cleaned up whatever mess she and the brothers leave behind.

And my gut is rumbling. It has been for the past couple of hours, and I have to eat something before I pass out. I root around in the fridge but can't find very much. There's some sliced roast beef V bought at a deli on Seventh Avenue last week that still looks edible and a couple of slices of swiss. I know there's a half loaf of rye in the bread box, and I'm praying that it hasn't gone completely stale and moldy. It has mostly, but I fix myself a sandwich anyway, pop open a bottle of beer, and settle down at the kitchen table.

I'm about to take a bite out of my sandwich when there's a knock at the door. This not only makes me suspicious, it pisses me off. I'm hungry and don't feel like seeing anybody, so I ignore whoever it is, but they keep at it.

I grab my snub-nose in case Iggy has decided to put in a return appearance and go to see who's there.

I open the door and am surprised to see Burton, Garrett's butler, standing in the hallway outside the apartment. He's wearing a long cashmere coat, a thick woolen scarf, and a black knit longshoreman's cap pulled down over his ears.

"I'm guessing you don't want to come in," I say.

"Mr. Garrett would like to see you."

"I bet he would. Here's an idea. Why don't you tell him to go fuck himself and see how he reacts?" Burton doesn't have much of a sense of humor; he doesn't so much as crack a smile. In fact, he says nothing at all.

"What does he want?" I ask him.

"There's a car downstairs," is all that Burton is willing to say, and he walks off down the hall as if I'm sure to follow.

I grab my coat and do just that. However, I am not an idiot. When I get downstairs, Garrett's limo is double-parked with its engine running, and Burton is holding the back door open, expecting me to climb in. I'm packing, but I'm not about to get into a car with a guy I know doesn't like me very much. Instead, I amble past the limo with my hands in my coat pockets. It takes a couple of seconds, but Burton gets the idea and he slides into the front seat next to Garrett's driver. The driver slips the limo into gear, and it creeps slowly behind me as I walk down the street.

It's after two in the morning, and the only place open is a bar over on Christopher Street. The place is frequented by homosexuals mostly, which I figure is bound to make Garrett uncomfortable and plays to my advantage. I know Larry Siegel, the owner, who's a good egg and a big-time movie buff. I stop into his bar once in a while to shoot the breeze because he's a smart guy and usually has something interesting to say. I came in with Bud one time, and Siegel nearly fainted at the sight of him. I've been drinking for free there ever since.

Despite the hour, the bar is crowded. This isn't surprising. The cops and local hoodlums give Siegel's clientele an incredibly hard time and aren't above beating the piss out of them for no good reason. Larry pays off a police captain over at the Sixth Precinct to keep his minions and the neighborhood toughs away after midnight so that his customers can relax and drink in peace.

When I come in, I have a word with Larry, who's tending the bar. I nod toward the limo, which we can see through the front window, and tell him what it's doing there. He comes out from behind the bar, shoos a couple of guys away from a table in the back, and I take a seat.

After a few minutes, Louis Garrett walks in with Burton and a beefy guy I take to be his bodyguard. The bar goes silent. Everybody is staring at them, which is exactly what I hoped they would do.

"You have interesting friends, Jack," Garrett says as he pulls up a chair. "I didn't know you hit from both sides of the plate."

"I'm just full of surprises, aren't I? Now, what can I do for you?"

"Where's my daughter?"

"No idea," I say, but for some reason Garrett doesn't believe me.

"You know, Jack, it's a mistake to go up against me, a mistake you don't want to make." He says this with a supercilious menace that makes me want to smack him. "Now, why don't you tell me where she is so we can all go home without anybody getting hurt?"

"Here's the deal, Garrett," I tell him. "First off, she's your kid, not mine, and where she goes and what she does makes absolutely no difference to me. And second, I'm not the one who gets his rocks off diddling her friends—you are. Why don't you ask one of them if they know where Lucy is?"

This is not actually the way I feel about Lucy, and I don't expect the remark to go over well. It doesn't. Garrett's bodyguard reaches inside his coat like he's going to pull his gun if I don't watch what I say. Larry, who has been watching and eavesdropping, grabs a Louisville Slugger out from under the bar and makes a show of slapping it against the palm of his hand.

Garrett isn't impressed. "How's your girlfriend?" he asks.

This gets my attention, but I decide to brazen it out. "She's in my bed waiting for me. Why do you want to know?"

"Funny. I thought she was in Connecticut modeling for *Town and Country*," he says, and it takes every ounce of my self-control not to reach across the table and rip out Garrett's throat. "Let me make myself plain, Jack. You'll deliver Lucy to me in the next twelve hours or Victoria Hemming has graced her last magazine cover."

The threat might be a bluff, but I can't afford to ignore it. I'm not going to put V in danger under any set of circumstances, especially not to protect Lucy Garrett from her father. Bud's right: guys like Garrett will stop at nothing to get what they want.

"I'll bring her by the Beresford by noon tomorrow," I tell him, "but only if your goon here isn't tailing me."

Garrett's bodyguard takes offense at this and really does go for his gun, but Garrett stops him. "Is she in one piece?" he asks.

"Barely," I tell him. "She was breathing the last time I saw her anyway."

"Just bring me the kid, Jack," Garrett says and pushes away from the table.

I wait for him to clear off, then sprint back to Perry Street, hoping against hope that V has come home while I've been out. But she hasn't. I'd call her agent to find out exactly where she's shooting, but it's just after three in the morning and he's not going to be in his office. I'd try him at home, but I barely know the guy's name, much less his telephone number.

Instead, I call V's apartment to check on Lucy. I let the phone ring at least a dozen times, but no one answers. This is not good. The Dugan brothers could have finished off the bottle of bourbon I left them and passed out. Or maybe they're too busy watching the late late show on V's TV to pick up the phone. They aren't exactly two of the most responsible people in the world, so they might have blown me off and gone home.

Whatever's happened, I've got to get over to Beekman Place and make sure Lucy is still there and still alive. She's probably deep in withdrawal by now, and I might have to hold her hand until she gets straight, but I've got to get her home. V's life might depend on it.

I call a cab service, and there's a Checker waiting for me when I get downstairs. The sun isn't up yet and there's no traffic, so it doesn't take but fifteen minutes to get uptown. Al, the doorman, isn't on duty when I jump out of the cab, which is a little strange. I suppose his shift might have ended and his replacement off taking a piss, but the management of an address as ritzy as Beekman Place expects their people to be on duty around the clock. They're strict about it too, and abandoning your post even to take a leak is a fireable offense.

I pass by the counter in the lobby where Al sorts the mail, but he isn't there either. I don't think too much of it though. Instead, I ring for the elevator and watch the dial above the door count down the floors.

The elevator door slides open. I'm about to step aboard when I see Al sprawled on the floor in a pool of his own blood. His chin is resting on his chest and there's a quarter-size bullet hole in his forehead. I check his carotid for a pulse, but I know he's dead. Whoever did this must have been going for Lucy and clipped Al on his way. I pull out my gun and hit the button for V's floor. I spin the snub-nose's cylinder to make sure it's fully loaded, and when the elevator door opens, I peek out to see if anyone is there laying for me. No one is, at least no one that I can see, but V's apartment door is wide open.

I'm not sure of my play here. I could back off and call the cops, but after my run-in with Jimmy Mullen, I'm not inclined to make that my first move. And if Lucy's dead, I'll want to know it before trying to explain to the police what she was doing in V's apartment.

I creep toward the apartment door, hesitate at the threshold, but I don't hear anyone moving around, so I step inside. The television is on in the living room with the volume blasting. Eddie Dugan is sitting on V's couch with his pants down, staring blankly at the screen, shot through his head. A trail of blood leads from the living room across the hall and into the kitchen. I follow it and find Joe Dugan face down on the linoleum. He's taken two in the spine and a third execution-style in the back of the neck. I move to V's bedroom and ease open the door expecting the worst, expecting to find Lucy Garrett lying there dead too, but she isn't dead.

She isn't there at all.

CHAPTER TWENTY-SEVEN

Bernie Rothstein isn't happy. Dead bodies keep piling up around me, and that not only makes him suspicious, it offends him. Bernie likes things to be neat and tidy, and he became a cop hoping to bring order to the chaos of the city. Now, he and I are sitting at V's kitchen table while a forensic team scours the grisly scene. I hand over my snub-nose, and he takes a whiff of the barrel. Satisfied that it hasn't been fired, he unloads it, pockets the bullets, and hands the gun back to me.

"Jimmy taking the night off?" I ask. I can't help being a wise guy around Bernie mostly because it's fun to get a rise out of him, but my heart isn't really in it. Lucy Garrett might be anywhere, and unless she decides to go back to the Beresford on her own, which is wildly unlikely, Garrett is liable to hurt V.

The thought scares the hell out of me, and I guess it must show because Bernie asks, "Something eating you?"

"Yeah. Sort of. It's too complicated to explain."

"Everything always gets complicated around you, doesn't it, Coffey?" I'm sure Bernie expects a smart-ass remark in return for the crack, but I don't have it in me.

"I take it you know these guys," he says, meaning the Dugans.

"Yeah," I say, "I had the Dugans come over here as a favor. The truth is, Bernie, they were looking after Louis Garrett's daughter for me, but now they're dead and she's gone, and I don't know how any of it happened."

Rothstein doesn't like me very much and the feeling's mutual, but he's an honest cop and I trust him. Unlike Jimmy, he wouldn't take a dime from Garrett or anybody else. He takes a moment to consider what I've just told him, then says, "I don't get it. What does Garrett's daughter have to do with you?"

Maybe it's because of the mood I'm in, but I decide to be straight with Bernie, mostly straight anyway. With the Dugans dead, Lucy missing, and V in real danger, this is no time to play it cute, so I tell him about being hired by Garrett. I tell him about Lucy and Garrett and his girls. I tell him that Garrett has been sleeping with his own daughter and now she's pregnant with his kid—at least, I think the kid is his. The irony, I tell Bernie, is that Garrett couldn't have been behind killing the Dugans because I was with him not much more than an hour ago and Garrett didn't know where I had Lucy stashed. And because I'm interested in his reaction, I also let Bernie know that Jimmy Mullen is on Garrett's payroll and that despite being Rothstein's partner, he's crooked. But being told that Mullen is bent doesn't surprise Rothstein in the slightest.

"Assuming you didn't do this, Jack, and neither did Garrett, who do you think did?" It's a good question, one I wish I could answer.

"You're not going to like this, Bernie, but I have no idea. What about the neighbors? Didn't they see or hear anything?" When Bernie shakes his head, I say, "Listen, I don't want to tell you how to do your job, but this looks very professional to me." Joe and Eddie Dugan knew how to handle themselves. Whoever took them out had to have skills.

"Your friend in the living room takes a single shot clean through the skull, and his brother takes one in the back of the neck to make sure he's dead. Yeah, I'd say it looks professional, but I've only been on the job for nineteen years, so what do I know?"

I don't mind the dig. I probably deserve it.

"What about the guy who put a contract out on you?" Bernie wants to know. "Maybe he sent the shooter. Did you ever find out who that was?"

I haven't, but it's an angle I should consider. Whoever sent the slab of cement and the gunman from Philly to kill me didn't decide to drop the contract just because I beat those guys to the punch. Maybe this shooter was gunning for me too—but then he snatched Lucy while he was at it? I don't see how that fits, unless she was in it with him.

"I'm going home, Bernie," I say, pushing away from the table. "I haven't slept in twenty-four hours and I'm dead on my feet."

"You know how this works, Jack. Don't leave town."

"Not a problem. Where am I going to go?"

"The Hemming girl's place in the Berkshires for starters."

"How do you know about that?"

"The same way I know Mullen is on the take." Bernie's grinning now, and I'm not entirely sure what that means, other than he knows more than he's willing to tell me, but I'm too tired to ferret out whatever it is.

"You know where to find me," I say, then I get up and leave.

I haul myself back to Perry Street, hoping V will be there waiting, but she isn't. I collapse on my bed without taking off my clothes, pull my pillow over my head, and the next thing I know, it's nine o'clock at night and V still isn't home.

Now I really am scared. Even if she spent last night in Connecticut, she should have been back by now. It may mean Garrett has her.

I go into the bathroom to splash cold water on my face, hoping it will clear my head. I'll never forgive myself if anything happens to V. I figured Garrett was using the threat against her as a bargaining chip, a way to make sure I delivered Lucy, but now I'm not at all sure. I'll tell you one thing though. If he lays a hand on V, I'll kill him. I'll put a bullet in his head even if it means one of his goons takes me down when I do.

I'm not thinking straight. I'm letting my emotions get the best of me, which means I'm liable to do something stupid. I need to talk to somebody I can trust, somebody who will stop me from bursting into the Beresford with guns blazing, so I call over to the Triangle and ask for Carmine.

"V hasn't been home in more than twenty-four hours, Carmine, and I'm pretty worked up about it," I tell him. "It's not like her to disappear like this, not without getting word to me somehow, and I have this really bad feeling that Garrett's got her. I know this isn't the way you usually work, but can I count on you if I take him on?"

"Garrett ain't got her, Jack," Carmine says like I'm panicking for no reason, and when I ask him how he could possibly know that, he says, "Because I'm sitting here looking at her."

I introduced V to Carmine in a restaurant on Mulberry Street. We had spent a couple nights together by then, and I guess we were being lovey-dovey at the table because Carmine comes over with a smirk on his face, sits down, and asks, "*Minchia, chi è sto pezzu di fimmina?*" without saying so much as hello. I don't speak Italian and have no idea what he's talking about, but V does. She learned the lingo working in Milan, so she says, "*Chi lo vuole sapere, stronzo?*" to Carmine, and he bursts out laughing. Like I say, I don't understand a word, but all of a sudden, they're nattering away like a couple of old women until Carmine slams the flat of his hand down on the table and says, "This one, Jack! I like this one," which coming from Carmine is high praise.

Tonight, when I walk into the Triangle, V is sitting at a table with Carmine and The Chin. They're on their second bottle of grappa, and Gigante is regaling V with stories of hijacking trucks as a kid. He's leaving out the part about murdering guys in the process, but I think V knows that. She's listening to him with her chin in the palm of her hand like she's fascinated, which maybe she is. She glances up at me when I approach the table, smiles, and pats the seat next to hers. I don't know whether to kiss her or strangle her, and I'm standing there like a schmuck with a dumb look on my face when Carmine says, "Cop a squat already, will ya please, Jack? I mean, what are you waiting for, a written invitation?"

I'm still furious, so I say, "You know, V, maybe you ought to think about letting me know before you decide to pay a visit to a couple of made guys instead of coming home"—a remark that goes over well with nobody.

Carmine rolls his eyes like I've just put my foot in my mouth. Gigante shoots me a look that tells me another crack like that and I'll find myself lying in a shallow grave in Jersey. And V glares at me like I've just humiliated her.

"Okay, so maybe that didn't come out the way I meant it," I say, trying not only to save face but my life, "but I was worried about you."

"What was I supposed to do, Jack, sit around the apartment and watch you sleep?" V drains her glass, refills it, and to make sure I get the message, she won't look at me.

I realize I ought to be grateful that she's alive and well, so I shut up and sit down. Later, V tells me that when she came home from Connecticut, she heard me snoring and didn't want to wake me. She stashed her bag and went out to meet Irving Penn, who was hanging a show at the Cooper Union. Apparently, they had a drink together, and then on a whim, V decided to walk over to the Triangle for an espresso and cannoli with Carmine, and The Chin sat down with them.

A word here about The Chin. He's dressed in flannel pajamas and a ratty old terry-cloth bathrobe, which is the way he always dresses when he's out in public. To people walking by him on the street, this might seem odd, nuts even, which is precisely what The Chin wants them to think. He wanders around the West Village in his pj's, mumbling to himself like he's lost his mind. It's an act, one that's not only convincing but savvy. If the local DA or the Feds try to prosecute him for murder, racketeering, obstruction of justice, or any other of the myriad crimes The Chin has committed, he'll plead insanity. This is a novel and neat trick, and so far, it's worked. When he beat Tony Murillo, a foot soldier in the Lucchese family, to death, The Chin was sloppy and left behind enough evidence to make the case against him open and shut. Frank Hogan, the New York DA, had him indicted, and Gigante was looking at a minimum of twenty to life, assuming the jury didn't give him the chair. But when he went to trial, he showed up in his bedroom slippers and Dr. Dentons, sucked his thumb, and talked to himself constantly. Instead of prison, he was committed to a state mental institution. Six months later, his lawyer got him sprung, and he was back at the Triangle doing business.

The Chin keeps staring at me, which is disconcerting, then he leans over and has a word in Carmine's ear. The expression on his face doesn't change, but the one on Carmine's does.

He goes a little white, and now he's looking at me like he's just been told that he has to put his dog down. "Okay, but let me take care of it," he says to The Chin.

"Just make sure you do," Gigante says before getting to his feet and heading to the john.

It strikes me that this little exchange doesn't augur well, and I'm right. "You'd better hit the bricks, Jack," Carmine tells me, and I know better than to ask him why.

When I get up from the table, so does V. Gigante sees this and shouts, "Not her."

But before he can make too much of a stink, V says to him as sweetly as she can, "It's getting late, Vincent, and I have a shoot in the morning so I have to get up early. But thanks for the coffee and cannoli, and I'll come back to see you real soon, I promise." It takes a slightly terrifying moment, but this seems to mollify The Chin. He nods and grunts, then disappears into the bathroom.

We walk outside with Carmine. He lights a cigarette, tosses the match, and says, "He'll get over it, but you'd better stay away from here for a while." I tell him that's not a problem. We shake hands, and V kisses Carmine on the cheek before we walk away.

We're not far from Perry Street. V slips her arm through mine and rests her head against my shoulder as we amble along. We don't say very much, just listen to our footsteps echoing off the sidewalk.

Then V apologizes, "I didn't mean to scare you, Jack, if that's what I did. You have to know I'll always come home to you. What did you think happened to me?"

I could tell her about Garrett's threat to snatch her, about the Dugans and Lucy. I probably should, but instead I say, "Listen, can you take some time off?"

Surprised by the question, she says, "Not really. I'm booked all the way into next year. Why?"

The thought isn't a very practical one and it came to me from out of the blue, but suddenly it seems important. "Cancel your bookings, and let's go somewhere."

Ordinarily, when neither of us is working, I like nothing more than hanging around the apartment, listening to Monk or Trane, and I don't want to go anywhere.

V says, "We could go up to the country for a week, I guess. The pipes are probably frozen and we won't have running water, but I don't mind, if you don't."

But the Berkshires aren't what I have in mind, so I tell her to forget it.

"No, I won't forget it. What's bothering you, Jack?"

With Lucy missing, snatched by God-knows-who, I should stay in town until I find out what happened to her, but I've had enough. There are moments in this job when you get too close, when a case starts chasing you instead of the other way around, and I'm beginning to feel that happening to me.

"I just need to get out of the city," I tell V. "Not up to West Stockbridge, but someplace else, someplace far away."

"Far away? Like where?"

"I don't know."

We walk about another half block when V suddenly grins and says, "I do."

CHAPTER TWENTY-EIGHT

A couple of days after our encounter with The Chin, V comes home with a tin of caviar, a '53 Cheval Blanc, and two first-class cabin tickets on the *Liberté*. I can barely afford the Cheval Blanc, much less a luxury cruise to Europe, but V says she wants to spoil me. She says that I look worn out. She says that I told her I wanted to go someplace far away and that Paris seems just about far away enough. She says that she knows I don't like taking expensive gifts from her, but that she's canceled all her bookings and that I should cut out the He-Man crap and just say thank you.

I am reluctant to let her buy me things. It's not just a question of my male ego, though to be honest that's a part of it; it's that V makes a lot more money than I do, and I don't want people to think I'm taking advantage of her. No one does, according to V, but where I come from, living off a woman makes you the worst kind of deadbeat. Still, I can see how happy and excited she is at the prospect of running off to Paris together, so I swallow my pride and pretty soon I'm in the middle of the Atlantic Ocean, sitting in a deck chair and freezing my nuts off despite being wrapped in three layers of wool blankets.

Bernie Rothstein called me before we left New York. He told me that forensics didn't find any trace of the Dugans' killer in V's apartment—not a print, not a hair, not a fiber.

"The guy's a pro, just like you thought, Jack," Bernie says, making me glad that I'm leaving town. I've spent the last few days looking over my shoulder. I usually have a pretty good sense of when somebody's following me, but every time I hear a floorboard creak, a neighbor moving around their apartment, or footsteps in the hall, I go for my gun. Just because you're paranoid, doesn't mean somebody isn't after you, or so the saying goes, and to tell you the truth I'm plenty nervous. Whoever hit the Dugans was brutal and efficient, and the more I think about it, the more I think whoever did it was really after me. And where in God's name is Lucy? I promised Garrett I'd deliver her posthaste, but she's on the loose again—that or holed up with the guy who killed Joe and Eddy. Both possibilities are liable to end in disaster. I hoped to save her from disaster—still mean to, but I can't, not right now anyway. I'm perfectly capable of taking care of myself, but not exactly the fearless tough guy V sometimes thinks I am, and if there's somebody out there really determined to finish me off, there isn't a hell of a lot that I can do about it. And as much as I hate to abandon Lucy and an attempt to get something like justice for the Dugans, there are times when self-preservation wins out over nobility, and this is one of them. I don't tell Bernie I'm leaving the city though. He'll only give me a hard time if I do, and I don't want Rothstein or anybody else to know where we're going.

This isn't the first time I've been abroad. This time is different though. This time a bunch of Krauts dressed in field gray aren't trying to blow my head off. The good news is that I'm not splashing ashore after sprinting down the ramp of an LST with a twenty-pound pack on my back. Instead, I'm strolling down the *Liberté*'s gangway with a travel satchel over my shoulder, holding V's hand.

We take the night train from Le Havre to Paris and get in just after dawn. Dovima, Dick Avedon's one-time muse, has moved in with the Chevalier de somebody or other and lent us her apartment in the Marais. We drop off our bags, and I wolf down a croissant and a cup of coffee as thick as mud before V drags me off to see Hubert de Givenchy, who's a friend of hers.

Hubert is a little stiff and formal, which is typical of a continental type, I guess, but he's not a bad egg. He takes us out to lunch at La

Coupole, where he orders me the *fricassée de rognons de veau*, which tastes as good as anything I've ever eaten despite being veal kidneys, something V only tells me later.

While I'm chowing down, Hubert and V chatter away. They're gossiping about Elsa Schiaparelli and Coco Chanel, about who Dorian Leigh is sleeping with, and what designers are showing at the Palais Royale next week. A couple of hours later, we're still sitting in the restaurant, which is another continental thing apparently, and I'm half in the bag after finishing off another bottle of the pricey Bordeaux Givenchy keeps ordering.

When the tab comes, I insist on paying despite the eye-popping price. I try to figure out how many francs there are to the dollar in my head, but I've never been much good at math, so I hand the waiter a fistful of bills and let him sort it out. When we finally leave, Givenchy kisses V's hand and shakes mine. After he takes off, we decide to take a stroll around town. V wants to walk off lunch, and I'm hoping the fresh air will sober me up.

"So, what did you think of him?" V wants to know. This is not an innocent question. It's part of a game she likes to play with me. Every time she introduces me to one of her haute couture male friends, she asks me some version of the same question with the same slightly snide inflection in her voice. That most of them are not guys you'd want to grab a beer with over at O'Doul's is supposed to get my goat, but it makes no difference to me. Besides, O'Doul's is a dump. They wouldn't be caught dead in the place under any circumstances, and I don't blame them. Actually, I have gone in there with Dick Avedon a couple of times. He didn't seem to mind hanging around the locals or the stink of dead cigarettes and stale beer. It looked to me like he was enjoying himself, but then maybe he was just trying to be polite.

"I liked Hubert," I say to V because I did and because V expects me to say something different. "Also, he's probably the best-dressed guy I've ever met in my life, but that pretty much comes with the territory, doesn't it?"

"He thought you were very handsome," V tells me, and I know what that grin on her face means.

"You afraid I'm gonna run off with him or something?"

"Jack Coffey in bed with a man. I'd pay to see that."

"Yeah? What makes you think I haven't been?" I haven't, but the momentary flicker of doubt that plays across V's face while she wonders whether I have is fun to watch.

A couple of weeks later, Dovima sends word that she and the Chevalier have decided to call it quits and she needs her place back, so V and I rent an apartment in the eleventh near the Place de la Bastille. It's a tiny month-to-month deal, but it suits us just fine, and after a few weeks we settle into a routine. In the morning I buy the *International Herald Tribune* at a kiosk on the Avenue Parmentier and grab breakfast at a little café nearby. In the afternoon I go for a run around the Tuileries or break a sweat in the gym Georges Carpentier owns, while V works a shoot for French *Vogue* or indulges in a long lunch with her model friends. She stops off at Les Halles or at one of the markets on the Rue de Buci on her way home to pick up something for dinner. It's usually something vaguely exotic, tripe or calf brains—the less I know about this, the better—but whatever V cooks up is always tasty. At night we listen to records on an old RCA Victrola I found in a secondhand shop, and after a shot of absinthe, we climb into bed and make love. We've been making love a lot since pitching our tent in Paris. Not that we didn't back in New York, but Paris turns out to be as romantic as everyone says it is, and we can't seem to get enough of each other. And at least a couple of times each week we go out to the clubs.

The first time we walk into the Tabou, Dizzy and his combo are on the bandstand, and I feel like I'm home. He does a comical double take when he spots me, then has a word in the manager's ear, and before we know it, V and I drinking for free. We stop in again the next night and the night after that, and pretty soon we're regulars. The Tabou's manager is named Boris, and he makes sure there's always a table reserved for us and our drinks are waiting before we sit down.

When Dizzy's two-week gig is up and he leaves town, Bud Powell takes his place, and after him, Sidney Bechet. I'm beginning to feel like I've died and gone to heaven.

In New York, if you walk into a jazz club with Victoria Hemming on your arm, it turns most everybody's head. The same holds true in the Tabou, especially among the artsy crowd and the crew of existentialists who happen to live in the neighborhood. Of course, I have no idea what an existentialist is or who they are, so when Boris, who doubles as a poet, ushers a hard-looking guy with a Gitane dangling from his lips over to our table and introduces him as Albert, I'm clueless.

But V isn't. She can't invite the guy to sit down fast enough, and the two start gabbing in French like they've known each other for years. By now, I've picked up a word or two and get that Albert is a writer and a famous one at that. Still, I'm beginning to feel like a third wheel, when he suddenly turns to me and asks in perfect English if this is my first time in Paris. I try to hide my surprise and tell him it isn't, but that the last time I was here, it was with the Eightieth Infantry on the day after liberation, and the perpetual French scowl on Albert's face disappears.

He was in the Resistance, he says, editing *Combat*, a Resistance newspaper. I've got to hand it to the guy. He was taking his life in his hands with no other way to fight back than with his pen. The Gestapo would have had him shot if they found him, and that's after torturing him in some dank basement for a few days.

Albert and I weren't more than fifty feet apart taking sniper fire on that August day in '44. It makes for a pretty amazing coincidence, and it isn't long before V feels like the third wheel while he and I get stinking drunk.

Naturally I'm curious about the guy, so the next day I wander over to Shakespeare and Company to pick up one of his books. The American college kid behind the counter finds a translation, and I take it home.

To say that *The Stranger* is dense is to give Albert too little credit, and I don't really understand the quote on the flyleaf. "In our society," it says, "any man who does not weep at his mother's funeral runs the risk of being sentenced to death." I've been thinking about what that means for days now, and to tell you the truth, I still don't get it.

CHAPTER TWENTY-NINE

Muffy Palmer is dead. The poor kid got caught up in something even I don't really understand and paid for it with her life. I know this because Janie Cantwell sent me a telegram, care of American Express in Paris, adding, "Call me as soon as you can."

I give my office number to the girl with the pixie cut behind the desk in the American Express office in the Place de l'Opéra and cool my heels in an airless phone kiosk for a good hour, waiting for her to connect my call. When she finally does and Janie comes on the line, it sounds like she's underwater.

"When did it happen?" I ask her, and she says that Muffy's body was discovered a couple of days ago.

"Where did they find her?"

"In an alley behind the Dalton School."

"Shot in the head?"

"How did you know that?"

"Who told you about it?"

"Bernie Rothstein came by the office looking for you."

Janie is smart enough *not* to let Bernie know where I am, but even at four thousand miles away, I can tell from the sound of her voice that she's rattled.

"And Jack, somebody broke into the office yesterday," she tells me, and my throat goes dry. I'm picturing Janie scared out of her wits hiding under her desk while some murderous thug ransacks my office looking for God-knows-what. "Lucky for me there was a white sale at Alexanders," she says. "I needed new sheets and pillowcases, so I wasn't here when it happened. But Nat was."

"Jesus, Janie. Is he all right?" If whoever that bastard is clipped Nat Bernstein, I'm on the next flight from Orly.

"Yeah, he's okay. You know how Nat's colitis has him running to the bathroom every five minutes. Whoever broke in spotted him zipping up his fly when he came out of the john and took a shot at him. I got back right after it happened and it looked bad, you know, lots of blood, and Nat was as pale as a ghost, but it didn't turn out to be very much. A bullet took a chunk out of his ear though, so I ran him over to St. Vincent's to get him patched up. The poor guy was scared half to death, but other than that, he's fine."

I tell Janie to lock up the office, go home, and not come in again until I let her know that it's safe. I've been gone for a few months now but kept paying her to look after things while I'm away. Nat must be laid up after his ordeal, so I wire Bernice and tell her to make sure that he stays home too. I feel bad about the whole business, bad and guilty like it's all my fault. Nat's an accountant for Christ's sake, not somebody you take a potshot at, not in his line of work. Janie signed on to take care of my filing and answer my phone. Risking her life while doing it wasn't part of the job description. I feel responsible for them both. He's a solid citizen and she's a great girl. I don't want to lose Janie, but I'm thinking it might be best if she looks for another job. Before I can tell her that, she wants to know when I'm coming back.

"Soon," I say. "Just stay home until I do. I'll have Nat send your check to your apartment."

"Forget it, Jack. You don't pay me to sit on my behind watching soaps all day long. You shouldn't anyway. And I'm not going to let some guy scare me off either. Look, I know you. I know you're worried about me and you're probably going to tell me to find another job, but I'm not doing it. Believe it or not, I like working for you. Okay, yesterday was a little more exciting than usual, but it's not like it's going to happen again. At least, I don't think it is. Anyway, how are you going to survive without me? Face it, Jack. You need me."

She's right. Janie runs the parts of my life that I'm either too inept or too bored to deal with myself.

"I'll have the locks changed and put the place back together, but you ought to stay in Paris for the time being—you know, so somebody doesn't blow a hole in your head too."

This is sound advice, and I love Janie for being brave and looking out for me, but I can't just hole up in Paris with V and swan around like some expat swell.

"I don't know what I'm going to do yet," I tell her, "but the one thing I do know is that the guy who broke into the office is a killer and I want you out of his line of fire. I don't care if the place looks like a bomb went off in it, just get out of there and stay out until I come back. Is that clear?"

"Yes, Master."

"And tell Nat to send his medical bills to me."

"Okay, but just out of curiosity, how are you going to pay them?"

"Nobody likes a wiseass, Janie."

"That's not true, Jack. You do."

I don't know how much of this I'm going to tell V. We're probably the happiest we've ever been here in Paris. She doesn't want to go home now, and she may not want to, ever. When we talked about it, V said that because she works everywhere, she can live anywhere. When I asked what I'm supposed to do to earn my keep while she's busy being beautiful, V tells me about a friend she has at the *Herald Trib*. She says that being a private detective, I have a good nose for secrets and scandal, and that as soon as I'm proficient enough in the language, her friend will take me on.

I have to admit that the idea of becoming a cub reporter appeals to me in a Ben Hecht/Charles McArthur sort of way, but my good nose for secrets and scandal also tells me that this offer isn't really on the up-and-up. Given who V is and what she looks like—and considering that her "friend" doesn't know me from Adam—I'm thinking that he might just have an ulterior motive.

I don't say this to V. Instead, I rub my chin like I'm intrigued. But even if the guy from the *Trib* is on the level, I'm not going to take the job. The business I left back in New York is not only unfinished, it's festering, and I have to do something to cauterize the wound.

But for the moment, I take Janie's advice and sit tight. Anyway, Monk is in town. I spot an item in *La Monde* saying he and his combo are playing two nights at Le Caveau in the Latin Quarter. Monk and Sidney Bechet are close, and I figure he's probably staying with Sidney in his flat in Montmartre.

I get hold of the number, call over there, and Monk seems tickled to hear from me. He's laughing when he comes on the line anyway and wants to know what a Hell's Kitchen semi-Jewboy like me is doing in the City of Lights. I promise to tell him over dinner, and V makes a reservation for the three of us at the Brassiere Lipp in Saint-Germaine.

Monk is holding court with a few of the locals by the time we get there. When he walks the streets of New York, nobody recognizes him. In Paris, Monk is a celebrity. It's not just that his embroidered skullcap and goatee are distinctive. Jazz is something of a secular religion over here, and Monk ranks as at least a cardinal, if not a candidate for pope in that hierarchy. He spots us when we walk in the door and waves us over to his table. He signs a few final autographs for his acolytes before gently shooing them away, and we sit down.

"As breathtaking as always, Victoria," he says to V, "but you look like the dog's dinner, boyo." I take the dig in the good-natured way that it's given, then kiss Monk on both of his cheeks because we're in France and because I know it's going to annoy him.

A couple of hours later, after we've stuffed ourselves, Monk tells me that before he left the city, he saw Louis Garrett with a covey of very young girls. He brought them into Minton's late one night, Monk says, and they were impossible to ignore.

This surprises me and not because Garrett is above parading jailbait around in public. I'm surprised because Teddy Hill, Minton's owner, is liable to lose his cabaret license if the liquor authority finds out that he's serving underage girls. I say this to Monk.

He shakes his head at me. "It probably costs Garrett a pretty penny, Jack, but even our friend Teddy can be bought." This is disappointing. I like to think of Teddy Hill as incorruptible in a pig-headed sort of way, but I suppose everybody really does have their price. More to the point, it means Bernie Rothstein hasn't been able to tag Garrett for abuse, or rape, or murder. Going out on the town with his schoolgirl harem is either an act of mindless bravado or evidence that Garrett isn't remotely worried about being pinched. I'd lay odds that it's the latter. It also means that whoever iced the Dugans and Muffy Palmer has gotten away with it—at least for now. This not only offends my sense of decency, but it means he's still out there looking for me, which gives me a very bad feeling in the pit of my stomach. And on top of all that, I still don't know what happened to Lucy Garrett.

"I do," Monk says, nipping the end off a Cohiba before dipping it into a snifter of cognac and striking a match. "I saw her."

"You saw her where?"

"At Minton's. Not the night her old man came in. A different night."

"Was she alone?"

"Alone? She don't get into the clubs alone. The girl was with a white cat, an older guy. And another thing. She has one in the oven. Looked like she was six or seven months gone."

Lucy's mother said that she was pregnant, but the woman isn't playing with a full deck so I wasn't sure whether to believe her. In fact, none of this is tracking for me. The last time I saw Lucy, she was passed out on V's bed on Beekman Place in a heroin-induced stupor. If she was expecting then, it didn't show, and now she's strutting around town big as life and pregnant without caring who knows it? She's on somebody's arm too. It's hard to know who that is, but seeing as Lucy seems able to twist men around her little finger, it could be almost anybody.

And I had thought that the Dugan brothers were killed because they got in the way when Lucy was snatched, but now I think maybe Lucy knew the shooter and was in cahoots with him. But what got Muffy Palmer killed? She must have known something that she shouldn't have, but what?

"So, when are we going home?" V and I are crossing the Pont Alexandre after our dinner with Monk, and she's reading my mind.

"I don't want you coming with me, V. The guy after me could take a crack at you too. I don't know how long it's going to take, but I have to wrap this thing up one way or another, and I'll rest a lot easier knowing you're safe over here."

"You still don't get it, do you, Jack?"

"Don't get what?"

V slips her arm through mine, smiles, and says, "I'll book us a flight in the morning."

CHAPTER THIRTY

Flying is old hat to V, but I hate it. Pan Am started flying jets across the Atlantic a few months ago, meaning that you can have lunch in Paris and dinner in New York, so everybody is anxious to give it a try.

The plane is packed, but we're in first class. V insists it's the only way to travel, and after taking a Miltown, she slips on an eye mask and dozes off. I, on the other hand, am as nervous as a cat. Every time the plane shudders or we hit an air pocket, my sphincter tightens. I order a drink from a passing stewardess, then another, throwing back a couple of those tiny bottles of scotch hoping they'll calm my nerves. They don't.

Six hours later, I let out a yelp when the pilot lowers the landing gear as we approach New York, which is about the time V wakes up from her nap, looking refreshed and fabulous. She smiles at me, asks if I enjoyed the flight, and doesn't seem to notice that I look like I've been on a weeklong bender.

We collect our luggage, grab a cab outside the Pan Am terminal at Idlewild, and take it into Manhattan. I don't want to risk going to my apartment on Perry Street or V's on Beekman Place. The shooter must know about them both and could be waiting at either one, so I have the cabbie drop us off at the Plaza, where we've booked a room.

It's a necessary precaution, but lying low with Victoria Hemming is a dicey affair. That face of hers couldn't be more recognizable, and if she hits any of her usual haunts or has lunch in someplace public, word is bound to get out that she's back in town. My problem is that V is pretty devil-may-care about the whole thing, and despite me telling her to be discreet, she isn't going to sit in a hotel room twiddling her thumbs while I try to put the Garrett case to bed.

Once we settle in at the Plaza, I walk over to Fifty-Eighth Street and call Bernie Rothstein from a pay phone. I don't want Jimmy Mullen overhearing us, so when Bernie comes on the line, I ask him if he's alone.

"Yeah, I'm alone. Where the hell have you been?"

"Meet me by the carousel in the park in an hour and don't tell Mullen where you're going."

"Okay, but why the cloak-and-dagger?"

"I'll tell you when you get there," I say and hang up.

Spring in Central Park is something to behold, particularly if you're a city kid like me. When I was in school, I'd cut class sometimes just to lie out in the Sheep Meadow and soak up the sun. I've got some time to kill before meeting Bernie, so I wander over to the zoo to check out the seals and Bobby the polar bear, whose once snow-white fur is now tinged a sort of nicotine brown from the soot of the city. I buy a hot dog smothered in mustard and sauerkraut from a street vendor, then amble over to the carousel, take a seat on a park bench, and wait for Rothstein to show. It isn't long before he does.

"Want a bite?" I ask, offering him my dog.

"Kraut gives me gas," he says. "Now, what am I doing here?"

"Do you have a line on who took out Muffy Palmer?"

"We've got our eyes on a couple of mooks, but I don't think either one of them is the guy."

"Why doesn't that surprise me?"

"Because it's the same shooter who came for you, isn't it, Jack?" This is why I trust Bernie. He has no tolerance for the usual games and gets right to the point.

"Probably," I say. "Where are you with Garrett?"

Rothstein doesn't answer. Instead he lights an unfiltered Lucky and exhales a stream of cigarette smoke.

"Did somebody chase you off?" I ask.

Bernie doesn't want to answer that question either, but he tends to get irritated when the department brass gets in the way of him doing his job, so I don't have to lean on him for more information. The two of us sit there without saying a word for a couple of minutes before Bernie opens up on his own.

He tells me that he paid Garrett a visit at the Beresford, a visit during which he made a show of being especially courteous so that Garrett didn't clam up and throw him out. Instead, he gently quizzed him about his daughter and asked where he had been the night the Dugans were murdered, as if his questions were just a matter of routine.

Garrett had an airtight alibi for the killings, one which I provided for him, and Burton, his butler, backed it up. As for Lucy? Well, that was a sad story. She ran away from home, he said, and not for the first time. But this time Garrett didn't hire a private detective to go out and fetch her—an oblique reference to me, I guess. Instead, he decided that Lucy should be left to "shift for herself," as he inelegantly put it. It was about time she found out just how the real world worked, he said, so he cut her off without a dime, which, given Lucy's expensive tastes, brought her home before too long. And when Bernie asked as if it was an afterthought whether Lucy was in the habit of having her girlfriends sleep over on school nights, a fairly sly and canny way of finding out about Garrett's penchant for young girls, he said that Lucy didn't have many friends and that to be honest, it worried him.

"Did you buy any of it?" I ask because I know that story is bullshit. Garrett didn't cut her off and make her shift for herself like he was a genuinely concerned parent. If Lucy really was home, that was because her father was holding her there against her will, keeping her close to control her. It's a hell of a lot more likely the kid is on the loose again, and Garrett's now desperate to corral her before she exposes him. I've been out of town so I don't have a clue as to where Lucy really is, but I'd lay odds she isn't in the Beresford.

Bernie snorts because he knows it's bullshit too and stubs out his cigarette. He says the next morning he got a call from Patrick Flynn, the deputy police commissioner, who was not at all pleased with his foray to the Beresford, no matter how diplomatically he handled it. Flynn wanted to know why Rothstein was bothering somebody like Garrett, somebody not only with friends in high places but an upright citizen who gave generously to the Police Athletic League and several other deserving municipal charities. He said that whatever the man's relationship was with his daughter, it was none of the department's business and told Bernie to lay off.

Bernie lied and promised that he would.

"Did Garrett claim Lucy was home while you were there talking to him?"

"That's the way he made it sound."

"Did he say anything about her being pregnant?"

"No. Why? Is she?"

"Yeah, and the kicker is that I think Garrett is the father."

I can tell from Bernie's reaction that as jaded as he is, he's having trouble wrapping his mind around this idea. I tell him what Monk told me at dinner in Paris, that Lucy was spotted in Minton's with an older white guy and that she was pregnant. I leave Monk's name out of the telling though. Given his history with the cops, there's no need to involve him, even if it's only peripherally. When Bernie asks if she wasn't at home, where do I think Lucy was, I tell him that I don't know and that I don't know the name of the older guy she was with in Minton's either. I don't know who killed the Dugans or Muffy Palmer, and I don't know whether the killer is still gunning for me.

One thing I do know, though, is that Louis Garrett is scared. He wouldn't have used his clout to try to back off Bernie if he wasn't. But exactly what is frightening him? Exposure—his own daughter exposing him, more precisely.

Lucy is his one real vulnerability. She's not only unpredictable but gets her kicks out of seeing him sweat. She knows about his girls and what he does to them. And if I'm right and her baby really is his, that alone is enough to send Garrett to jail. He has to shut her up and keep her shut up, but he isn't a psychopath. Despite the danger she poses to him, Lucy is his own flesh and blood, and Garrett's not going to have her hurt, much less have her killed—at least I don't think so. But it does explain why he committed her to the Hayden Institute. His wife has been safely locked away there for years. Why not his daughter?

"It's all about payback," I say to Bernie. That must be Lucy's motive in all this.

"Paying back her father for the abuse?"

"Garrett's screwed with her half her life, and now she's screwing him back."

"Which is pretty sick, if you ask me."

"Listen, here's the way we ought to play it." But Bernie shoots me a look, cutting me off before I can finish the thought.

"We? How do you get to 'we'? No offense, Jack, but as far as I'm concerned, you're still working the wrong side of the street. You've shot and killed at least three guys that I know about, and where I come from, that makes you one of the bad guys. The only thing that makes me think you aren't scum, I mean, besides the famous girlfriend, is that Jimmy Mullen wants you dead. That SOB is so deep in Garrett's pocket that wanting you out of the way almost makes me believe you're on the level. But I don't trust you. You play fast and loose with the truth and the law like neither of them matters, and I don't like that one bit."

"Fair enough, Bernie, but I don't see that you have much of a choice. You have to trust me. The department doesn't have your back, neither does Mullen. And Garrett is swinging his dick around like the big shot that he is. The only way to take him down is through his daughter, and the only way to get to Lucy is through me."

Rothstein may not like me or the way I operate, but he knows I'm right. And I'm thinking about telling him that I might not be as corrupt as he thinks, that having a reputation as a scumbag is good for business, but I don't want to push my luck.

"Okay," Bernie says, as if it's wildly against his better judgment. "You find the girl, but if you fuck with me, Jack, if you lie or connive or play both ends against the middle, I'll hand you over to Mullen and look the other way while he does whatever he wants with you. Is that clear?"

When I tell him it is and promise to be a good boy, Bernie says he expects me to check in with him every twenty-four hours or our deal is off. Then he shakes his head like he's just made the worst mistake of his life, gets to his feet, and walks away.

CHAPTER THIRTY-ONE

When I get back to the Plaza, V isn't there. My heart rattles around in my chest until I spot the note she left for me. In it, she says that she has gone to meet a friend, but not to worry. She's in disguise, she says, and nobody is going to recognize her. I'm not at all sure being "in disguise" means the same thing to V as it does to me. She probably thinks walking around incognito is only a matter of wearing a pair of dark sunglasses and a Gucci scarf wrapped over her head and tied under her chin.

But there's nothing I can do about that now. Now I have to figure out how to track down Lucy Garrett and find out who killed the Dugans and Muffy Palmer before whoever that is gets to V and me.

I'm going to start with Muffy's mother, Daphne. Being told that her daughter has been brutally murdered must have been devastating, and recovering from that terrible news nearly impossible. I'm going to have to be as gentle as I can.

I write Daphne a note on a sheet of V's sky-blue stationery telling her how sorry I am and saying that I know this must be a terrible time, but if she can spare me a few minutes, it might help me find Muffy's killer. I sign my name at the bottom, scribble down the Plaza's phone number, and rather than mailing the note, I hand it to the doorman at 998 Fifth and ask him to pass it along.

I wait a couple of days for a response, and when none comes, I walk over to the Met, sit down on the museum steps, and wait for Daphne to come out of her building, which is across the street. When she finally does, walking briskly down the sidewalk as if she's in a hurry, I get up and follow. She crosses Fifth Avenue, then walks across town until she reaches La Côte Basque on East Fifty-Fifth Street, where the maître d' greets her like an old friend and seats her at a table with three other stylish young matrons. La Côte is famous for catering to the well-to-do, and the maître d' is renowned for being an officious prick.

I walk into the restaurant like I've eaten there a hundred times before, wave to nobody in particular, and make a beeline for Daphne's table. But the maître d' makes for a pleb the instant he sees me and quickly moves to block my path.

"Is there something I can do for you?" he asks like the supercilious functionary that he is, and when I tell him I'm meeting Daphne Palmer for lunch, he flat out doesn't believe me.

When he says, "I'm afraid you're going to have to leave, sir," I have a few choices. I could try to slip the guy some cash to look the other way, but I have all of eleven dollars in my pocket and that won't be nearly enough. I could try to bull my way past him, but that's bound to cause a ruckus, and an embarrassed Daphne Palmer isn't going to give me the time of day. Or I could just show the guy my gun. Obviously, there's a not-so-implied threat in that, but if I tell him I'm a cop, a detective working undercover, and flash the fake NYPD ID I carry around, he might just find the idea thrilling enough to let me in.

I'm in luck. He buys this story but has a discreet word in my ear, asking me to keep his cooperation quiet because he has a reputation to maintain. His French accent suddenly disappears, replaced by a subtle but distinctly Bronx one, which probably explains why I'm getting away with this stunt.

I walk over to Daphne's table, but when I politely ask, "Excuse me, ladies, I wonder if I might have a word with Mrs. Palmer in private?" they all look at me like I've just descended from another planet. I figure that, given the slightly horrified looks on their faces, they might stand up and walk out, but they high-hat me instead and just stare.

Muffy's mother pretends not to know me. When I gently remind her of who I am and where we met, she snorts, "I don't remember that at all," and says that if I want to talk to her privately, I should make an appointment through her attorney.

I don't mind the brush-off, in fact I half-expected it, but still there's something about Daphne's attitude that seems odd. I'm not so memorable that it's impossible the woman doesn't recognize me, but what strikes me as off is that Daphne doesn't seem particularly upset. Her sixteen-year-old daughter has just been shot dead for no apparent reason and the police don't have a clue as to who did it or why, but she's carrying on with her life as if it didn't happen.

"I don't like to intrude like this," I say, "but I'm trying to find out who killed Muffy, and I really think you ought to talk to me." I'm sure that's going to get the woman's attention, but I'm wrong. Maybe she's putting on a brave face for the benefit of her friends, but her smug attitude makes that seem unlikely, so I lean on her. "Mrs. Palmer, somebody murdered your daughter and I'm sure you want to find out who it was. If you could just spare me a minute or two, I can help you with that."

Daphne doesn't say anything. Instead, ignoring me altogether, she primly refolds her napkin, returns it to her lap, and takes a sip from the glass of pinot she ordered with her lunch.

Then without actually looking at me, she says, "You wrote me that note, didn't you?" When I tell her that I did, she finally turns, looks me square in the eye, and says, "I don't know who you are or why they let you in here, but my poor Muffy's death is absolutely none of your business, and if you don't stop bothering me, I'll have the maître d' call the police."

I start to say, "Mrs. Palmer, I'm not looking for trouble—" but before I can even get that out of my mouth, Daphne raises her hand above her head, and snapping her fingers, calls out, "Phillipe!"

The guy's real name is probably Sal, but whatever it is, I don't want to get him in hot water, so when "Phillipe" approaches the table, I give him the high sign and move off before he's forced to throw me out.

Getting Daphne Palmer alone is going to be tricky. I'm going to have to track her movements and find a moment when I can box her in and make her talk. It comes as no surprise that her life is full in a petty and superficial way. She doesn't work. I suspect Daphne has never worked a day in her life, but she doesn't spend her time sitting alone in her luxury apartment either. She does sleep in most mornings though.

Cedella, the Palmers' maid, sees Muffy's ten-year-old brother off to school before Daphne gets out of bed. Daphne considers Jamaican-born Cedella a member of the family, which isn't the way Cedella sees it, but the pay is good, so she isn't about to disabuse her employer of that notion.

After Daphne's breakfast, which usually consists of Melba toast and a cup of black coffee, she dresses smartly and is driven over to the West Side, where five days a week she sees Dr. Leon Katz, her analyst, in his town house on West Sixty-Fifth Street. I can't imagine what the two of them have to talk about, but Daphne always has a spring in her step when she leaves his office.

The rest of her week is filled with hairdresser appointments, games of bridge and canasta, and lunch at La Côte, or the Colony, or Twenty-One with her girlfriends. In the evenings, there might be dinner with her husband, Harold, at Le Pavillon or someplace like it, then on to the theater or, on special occasions, the opera—that's if Harold isn't visiting his mistress in the apartment he keeps for her near the Museum of Natural History.

I'm not sure whether Daphne knows about her husband's longtime girlfriend—he's been keeping her in that apartment for more than a decade—or whether she's just willfully blind. Whatever the case, there are at least a couple of nights each week when Harold doesn't bother coming home, which probably explains why he and Daphne sleep in separate bedrooms. I manage to find out all of this because rich people aren't very good at keeping secrets, and neither are their help.

At precisely nine o'clock each night, Cedella takes the family schnauzer, Cookie, for a walk before riding the train home to Harlem. She and I have already come to an arrangement. I've slipped her a couple hundred bucks, and after assuring her I mean Daphne no harm, she gives me the keys to the apartment's back door and to the building's service entrance.

The rest is easy. I know Harold is off with his mistress, so I sneak in and take the freight elevator up to the apartment. Cedella tells me that Daphne doses herself with phenobarbital before going to bed every night, then watches *Gunsmoke* or whatever is playing on the *Million Dollar Movie* before turning out the light. I'm hoping the woman is so sedated that she won't have a heart attack when I suddenly appear, and that almost works.

In her barbiturate-induced haze, Daphne doesn't seem to notice that I'm there until I loudly clear my throat. Then much to my surprise, rather than screaming or demanding to know what I'm doing in her bedroom, she reaches under her pillow, produces a .38 Ruger, and aims it directly at my crotch.

"It was you, wasn't it?" she says, cocking her gun, and I stifle the impulse to ask, *What was me?* because when a woman is about to shoot your balls off, it's not smart to play dumb.

"I didn't kill Muffy, if that's what you mean."

"I could shoot you right where you stand, claim self-defense, and the police won't even bother arresting me."

"You could, Mrs. Palmer, but then Muffy's killer will still be running around loose, won't he?" My logic is inescapable, and apparently Daphne realizes it—that or she's simply decided that shooting me is more trouble than I'm worth—and she lowers her gun.

"Look," she says, switching on a bedside lamp, "why don't you just ask me whatever it is you're so anxious to know and then get the hell out of here before I really do call the police?"

"Did Muffy ever sleep over at Lucy Garrett's apartment?"

"No, and that wretched girl never spent the night here either. She may have lied to her father and said that she did, but she didn't. She did stop by a few times and try to lure Muffy into joining in on one of her tawdry sexcapades, but I wouldn't allow it."

"How do you know about those?"

"Because the girl showed up here dressed like a whore. It didn't take much imagination to figure out what she was up to."

"But Muffy never went with her?"

"I told you. I would not permit it."

When I was Muffy Palmer's age, I regularly slipped out of our apartment and spent the night listening to music in jazz clubs that shouldn't have let me in the door. When I met Muffy, she came off as naive and forlorn, but I don't believe for a second that a girl like Lucy Garrett couldn't entice her into defying her mother and sneaking out in the middle of the night. She must have jumped at the chance to go on an adventure with somebody like Lucy, but where did they go and what did they do when they got there?

"Who were Muffy's other friends? I mean, besides the Garrett girl. She must have had a best friend. Who was that?"

"There was no best friend," Daphne says. "Muffy wasn't very popular. She was sweet and eager to please, but I wouldn't have called her pretty or socially graceful. I tried to get her to do something about the way she looked and dressed, but Muffy was something of a mouse, I'm sorry to say."

If I didn't know better, I'd say Daphne Palmer is just as happy to be rid of Muffy. She wouldn't be the first Fifth Avenue matron to be disappointed in her daughter. Obviously, Muffy lived in Daphne's shadow, and the first time we met, she browbeat the kid almost to tears. She must have had high hopes of glittering coming-out parties, of cotillions and debutante balls. It wasn't Muffy's fault that she didn't live up to her mother's expectations, but I'll wager Daphne blamed her for it anyway.

"There was one girl," Daphne says suddenly. "Laura Watkins. Laura took an interest, you know, tried to make her over into someone the boys would like, but I'm afraid my Muffy was a lost cause."

"Was Laura a friend of Lucy Garrett's too?"

"You know, I think she was. I remember Muffy telling me that Laura spent almost every weekend at the Garretts'. But then that stopped. I don't know why."

"Where can I find Laura?"

"Oh, I'm sure the Watkins are in the book, Mr. Coffey. Now, if there's nothing more, you can leave the way you came in." Daphne leans over and turns out the bedroom light, and I make my way out.

CHAPTER THIRTY-TWO

It turns out that at the beginning of the winter semester, Laura Watkins's parents pulled her out of Dalton and sent her away to the all-girls Northfield School in Western Massachusetts. I'm curious to know what made them do that in the middle of the school year and whether it had anything to do with Lucy Garrett. It seems pretty obvious that Laura and Lucy didn't spend those weekends together at the Beresford playing jacks, so I figure it must.

I would have approached Austin and Emily Watkins directly about it, but Austin is a corporate titan, and he would have fobbed me off on some lowly assistant, who wouldn't have told me anything. Emily, a society doyenne and arbiter of Manhattan WASP tastes, wouldn't have deigned even to do that, leaving me no choice but to drive up north and talk my way into seeing their daughter.

This proves to be easier than I expect. I'm sure the Watkinses have tasked Northfield with keeping a close eye on Laura, but somehow she still manages to sneak off campus on weekends to meet a boy from the Mount Hermon School at a cheesy roadside motel.

I get this info from her roommate, Cornelia. I've convinced Laura's dorm mother that I'm her favorite uncle come to visit, but when they send someone up to fetch her, Cornelia comes down to the lobby instead. She's a friend and reluctant to give Laura away, but I use whatever charm I have to cajole the truth out of her. I hate to break in on Laura's little love nest, much less break it up, but I don't have a choice.

No one answers when I knock on their motel room door, but I hear muffled voices and Laura and her boyfriend skittering around, collecting their clothes. By the time she opens the door, Laura has already turned several shades of red and the boy is nowhere to be seen. Presumably, he's hiding in the bathroom.

Laura turns out to be a good kid, not the snotty brat I expect. I convince her to come with me to a diner down the road for a burger and fries. I offer to take her boyfriend along too, but he's even more embarrassed than Laura and stays back in the motel bathroom, behind a locked door.

She and I settle into a booth. Laura is ravenous for the obvious reason, I guess, and orders a double cheeseburger and an extra order of fries. When I ask about sleeping over at the Garretts', she goes red again and can't quite bring herself to look at me.

"Did something bad happen to you there?" I ask.

She swirls a fry around in a pool of ketchup before answering, "It was fun the first few times. Lucy's father was away so we did pretty much whatever we wanted, you know, stayed up real late watching TV and listening to music and stuff. Lucy had the key to Mr. Garrett's liquor cabinet so we got kind of drunk too, but don't tell anybody that, okay?"

"Were there guys there?"

"No, but Lucy always wanted to call boys from school and tell them to come over. She said she wasn't going to do anything with them, maybe just make out, but I didn't believe her. Lucy's sort of fast, you know? I mean, it's not like I'm a prude or anything. I guess you already know that after catching me with my boyfriend, but sometimes Lucy can be a real slut, so I didn't want any boys there. She sort of insisted, but I told her I was going home if they came."

"Okay, let me make sure I've got this straight. Are you saying that you and Lucy were always alone in the apartment, that Mr. Garrett was never there when you slept over?"

Instead of answering me, Laura stares out the diner window as if there's something fascinating going on in the parking lot.

"Did Mr. Garrett touch you, Laura?"

I know this is a question she really doesn't want to answer, but if I can get Laura Watkins to tell me that Garrett pawed her or did something worse, I might have an eyewitness willing to testify against him.

"I know how hard this must be, but you need to tell me if he did."

Laura takes a deep breath, then lets it out slowly. When a kid like her fights to hold back tears like she's doing now, it breaks my heart. And the idea that Garrett might have molested her makes me furious.

"He and his friend wanted to touch me," Laura says, then goes back to staring out the window.

"Who and his friend?"

"Mr. Garrett. He was with this other man, I don't know who he was. It's not like he introduced himself or anything. I wouldn't let them get near me though. I mean, it wasn't like they tried to force me. They were being nice, but they wouldn't stop staring at me."

"Was Lucy there with you?"

"She left the minute her father came into the room. I wanted to go with her, but he stopped me."

"So, it was just the three of you—Mr. Garrett, his friend, and you?"

"There was this other girl there too. I don't know who she was, but she kept whispering to me about how cool Lucy's father was, that he was, you know, really experienced and could teach me all these things. It was really creepy."

"All these things—meaning about sex?" I ask, and when I do, Laura's face collapses. Her shoulders begin to shake and her tears come on in a rush. I want to comfort her, but I'm not sure how. The last thing this kid needs is another grown-up laying a hand on her, even if it's to console her. Instead I offer her my napkin, which I admit is lame, but Laura takes it and dries her eyes.

"Just so I'm clear," I say when she catches her breath, "you never—"

"No!" Laura snaps. "But Mr. Garrett wouldn't leave me alone. And the other girl just sat on the edge of Lucy's bed, grinning like she was waiting to join in."

"You didn't know her?"

"No. She said she went to Dalton, but I would have known if she really did."

"It wasn't Muffy Palmer, was it?"

"God, no. Muffy isn't like that at all. The thing is, I really wanted to leave, so I told them that I was going to take a cab home. When I asked the girl if she wanted to come with me, she just smirked like I was really naive or something and said that she was staying. Do you think she was sleeping with Mr. Garrett and that other man?"

When I tell Laura that I'm pretty sure she was, Laura asks, "Then what did they want with me?"

I don't have the heart to tell her, but Laura's a smart girl and bound to figure it out on her own. That she can and will breaks my heart too. Meeting her teenage boyfriend for a tryst is perilous if they're not careful, but sweet and romantic in the way that it should be. Kids have been sneaking out and doing that sort of thing forever. And what underage kid hasn't used a phony driver's license to get loaded in a local bar, or told their parents some elaborate lie so they could stay out all night with their friends? Those kinds of antics can get you in trouble, but that's part of their attraction, and they usually end harmlessly. And even if the kid gets caught by their dad and gets a slap like I did when I was their age, they usually come out the other side of whatever adventure they've been on with their innocence intact. But when a guy like Louis Garrett gets ahold of a girl like Laura Watkins, seduces her, then uses her to feed his perverse habit, it can take a lifetime for her to get over it, that's if she's ever able to get over it at all.

The good news is that Laura had enough sense to leave before any of that happened to her. She isn't going to be the eyewitness I hoped she would be, but she has told me a few things that might help me take down Garrett. The first is that his girls aren't street urchins or runaways, desperate kids who he pays a few dollars to exploit and abuse. Street urchins don't go to the Dalton School or any place like it. The daughters of rich people do—meaning Garrett's penchant isn't just for young girls, but for rich young girls.

I thought Lucy might be procuring them for him. She seemed the only way Garrett had to get at private school girls like Laura, the only way he had to lure them up to his duplex. After what Laura told me about Lucy leaving the room the minute her father showed up, I'm not so sure, but whoever is recruiting for him must choose victims with care, getting close to girls who are damaged or unhappy, girls who are ignored by their parents or just tired of being told what they can or cannot do.

And despite what her mother and Laura Watkins told me, Muffy Palmer was one of those girls. Kimberly, the brunette I met with Rex Halsey in Minton's, must have been one too. She might have been on Rex's arm, but she was Garrett's type: spoiled, willful, and sexy in a petulant sort of way.

After we finish at the diner, I drive Laura back to school but pull the Rambler over to the side of the road a couple of blocks from the Northfield campus. Laura wants me to drop her off here so she can sneak back to her dorm without being seen.

"Do you know a girl named Kimberly?" I ask before she gets out of the car. "I don't know Kimberly's last name, but I think she might have been at Dalton when you were there."

"Kimberly Hutton?"

"I don't know. Maybe."

"Kimberly wasn't the girl I was telling you about, but she does have this really bad reputation. I mean, everybody at Dalton knows she puts out, so guys were always flirting with her, more than flirting really. I felt sorry for her though."

When I ask why, Laura tells me that Kimberly is a classic poor little rich girl caught up in the middle of an ugly divorce and custody battle. She was a freshman at Dalton when that began, and her classmates were less than kind about it. They teased her in that awful way kids sometimes do and seemed to enjoy making her cry. Kimberly's mother, Xenia, who'd mostly ignored her before the divorce and had virtually nothing to do with her after it, fought her ex-husband tooth and nail for custody. Wounded and confused, Kimberly began acting out, seeing guys like Rex Halsey to show her mother just how unhappy she was.

"She was a year behind me at Dalton," Laura says, "but Kimberly was sleeping with all these older boys—you know, seniors. Even some college guys, I think."

College guys were the least of it. Rex Halsey had to be at least thirty and Garrett is past fifty. I ask Laura whether Lucy ever introduced her to Rex, and she makes a face. "Lucy told me he was really handsome and that I'd like him, but I didn't like him at all. He took us out to one of the jazz clubs, you know, the ones on Fifty-Second Street? He said he knew a bunch of musicians, like that was supposed to impress me, but I don't really like jazz."

I like Laura even if she doesn't like my music. In fact, I'm feeling paternal toward her, so I wait until she safely hops the fence and is on her way back to her room before driving away.

CHAPTER THIRTY-THREE

A couple of days later, V has a hankering for a roast-beef hero with the works, and considering what a trooper she's been while I've been chasing after Louis Garrett, I offer to go out and pick up one for her.

I'm walking into the Carnegie Deli when I run into Bud. He's arm in arm with his latest, a girl named Rita who's an actress and a dancer. I recognize her from *The King and I*, a movie V dragged me off to see. Did I mention that Bud is married? To an actress named Anna Kashfi, whom I've never met and he never talks about. Judging by that and by Rita, I guess the marriage isn't going very well.

Bud wants to know how the Dugans are doing. He tells me he hasn't seen them at the gym in a while and wonders where they've been. I'd rather not tell him in front of Rita that the Dugan boys are dead, but Bud keeps at me about it.

When I tell him the brothers were murdered, shot dead no more than an hour or two after we left Beekman Place, his jaw drops.

Rita blanches too. She grips his arm a little tighter and wants to know if he's in any danger. To tell you the truth, I haven't really thought about that, though I probably should have.

I don't think whoever is targeting me knows that Bud tagged along that night, but I can't be sure. I don't want to scare him or Rita, and I figure the shooter can't want the publicity that knocking off a famous actor is bound to bring.

I tell Rita that, trying to reassure her, but I also tell her that it might be a good idea if Bud flies back to the coast and stays there for a while. It's hard to know how these things will turn out, I say, and I'd never forgive myself if anything happened to him.

But Bud isn't frightened, just the opposite. He likes the idea that somebody might be trying to kill him.

"It's all grist for the creative mill, buddy. Lee taught me that. To be a great artist, you need to be fearless," he says, which I don't get at all.

"Listen, it's not like I want to burst your artistic bubble or anything," I tell him, "but I don't think you'd enjoy having a loaded gun held to your head, no matter what your boy Strasberg has to say about it. I'll bet the closest that guy's ever come to being snuffed was crossing Forty-Fourth Street against traffic on his way to work."

"Lee's a genius, Jack."

"Yeah, okay, but do me a favor, will you, Bud? If you stay in town, keep on your toes. I'd hate to see you go from being a great artist to a dead one."

Rita doesn't like the turn this conversation has taken. I'm making her nervous, and she tugs at Bud's sleeve, anxious to leave.

But before they go, he has one last question. He wants to know my next move, what I intend to do to deal with Garrett, and whether he can lend a hand.

I could tell him about Kimberly Hutton and how I'm going to approach her to see if she's willing to give up Garrett, but I don't. I don't want Bud to get any deeper into this nightmare than he already is. I regret involving him in the first place, and the less he knows about it now, the better.

But Kimberly Hutton has vanished, Janie tells me. I told her to dig up Kimberly's details, where she lives, who she sees, whether she's still at Dalton or in school somewhere else, and where she sneaks off to when her mother isn't looking.

My first thought is that Kimberly might have met Muffy Palmer's fate, but unlike Muffy, whose body was discovered not more than a couple of hours after she was killed, no one has seen hide nor hair of Kimberly. Given what I already know about her, she could have taken off with some sleaze.

If that's what happened, I feel as sorry for her as Laura Watkins does. But if Garrett has gotten his hooks into her, I might be wrong. She might be lying dead somewhere. Judging by the way Kimberly behaved the night I met her, she could have mouthed off to Garrett or gotten out of line in some more serious way. Or maybe not. Maybe she's holed up with Garrett at the Beresford. If she isn't and she isn't dead, she might be anywhere—which brings me back to Lucy.

Lucy hasn't been seen in weeks. I asked Monk to tell the guys playing the clubs to keep an eye out for her, but nobody has seen her, not uptown at Minton's, not on Fifty-Second Street, and not downtown in the Village. It's possible that she's dead too, but I don't think so.

When Monk saw her at Minton's, she acted like she didn't have a care in the world. Rothstein hasn't pinched her for the Dugans not only because he can't find her but because he can't make a case. I'm not sure a killing that brutal is in her wheelhouse anyway. Monk said she was with an older guy, and it was an older guy who sprung her from the Hayden Institute. I just wish I knew who that was.

Or maybe she doesn't need anybody's help. She could be holding something over her father, something she can blackmail him with, something like those dirty movies the Baroness told me about.

"If Lucy turns the movies over to the police, her daddy goes to prison, doesn't he?" V says, snapping her suitcase shut in our hotel room at the Plaza. "I hope she does and they lock up that fuck forever."

A funny thing about V: she almost never curses. It might be her Southern Baptist upbringing, but she can't abide "a filthy mouth." Even I watch what I say around her. But Louis Garrett makes her blood boil, so she's more than willing to make an exception in his case.

"C'mon, we'll grab a cab and I'll ride out to the airport with you," I say, taking V's bag. She's flying down to the Bahamas tonight to work a shoot for Chanel.

"That's sweet, but they're sending a car."

Actually, I'm glad V's leaving town. She'll be safely stretched out on a beach in the Caribbean. We've been lying low at the Plaza for nearly a month now, and the close quarters are driving us both a little crazy. And we can't hide out here forever. The Plaza is costing us a small fortune, or I should say it's costing V a small fortune. At some point we're going to have to go back to Perry Street. I haven't told V this, but I've been making forays down there to check on the lay of the land. I'm going there again today after she leaves, but I don't tell her that either.

The limo Chanel sends is idling outside the hotel when we get downstairs, the driver standing by the back door like a sentry. I hand him V's suitcase, and he stows it in the trunk. We kiss before she slips into the back seat, a big wet, messy one, which is our way when we're going to be apart for a while.

Once V settles in the back seat, I shut the door and wave as the driver eases the limo into traffic.

"You still living off that broad, Coffey?"

I haven't clapped eyes on Iggy Ivanovich since he jumped me last winter. I thought he would be permanently curled up in the bottom of a bottle by now, not strolling down Fifth Avenue. And what's he doing in Midtown in the middle of the afternoon? Iggy usually spends his days lying in his own filth on the Bowery, usually spends his nights that way too.

"I don't have a lot of time, Iggy. What do you want?"

"Not trouble, Jack, I swear it. I mean, look at me. I'm a new man."

Iggy's bathed. Ordinarily I can smell him coming from a block away, but he's washed, shaved, and bought himself a new suit. It looks like something off the rack at Robert Hall, but it beats the BO-ridden rags he usually wears.

"So, I'm lying there in the gutter on Third Avenue with slush running down my pants the night you chucked me under that street sweeper," Iggy tells me, "and I'm thinking that maybe I got this wrong. Yeah, Sergei was my brother, but he was also a psycho and probably deserved what you gave him. You know, he was a piece of shit even when we were kids. I mean, he used to beat the crap out of me like once a week just for the hell of it. What was that all about?"

I don't know where this is coming from, but if I turn my back on him, I still think Iggy's liable to shove a shiv between my ribs.

"I know you don't believe me, Jack, and I don't blame you. You probably want to know how I knew you were here too."

"Yeah, Iggy, it had crossed my mind."

"I was having lunch with a customer in the Oak Room when I saw you put your girl into that car. I got a good job now, you know? Selling *schmates* for this outfit in the Garment District, if you can believe it. I had to lie to convince them to take me on, but I'm really good at it."

"Good at what? Lying?"

"Sales. Who had thunk it, right? Anyway, I wanted to return the favor. I mean you saving me from Sergei roughing me up whenever he felt like it, so here I am."

Now I'm really suspicious. What favor could Iggy Ivanovich possibly do for me?

"I don't know if you know it," he says, "but there are guys keeping an eye on your office."

"How do you know that?"

"I saw them a couple of times when I went by there—you know—before I cleaned myself up. I didn't recognize any of 'em, but there are two in the front and some big shot sitting in the back of a big car, like he's waiting on you."

"What makes you think it's me he's waiting on?"

"Oh, it's you all right. I saw that cute little secretary of yours leave the office, and the car followed her like she was gonna lead them right to you."

CHAPTER THIRTY-FOUR

After my office got tossed, I told Janie to stay away, but she didn't listen to me. She thinks that I can't do even the simplest things for myself, like clean up after somebody has ransacked the place, so she came in and did it. And she kept coming in, answering the phone, doing paperwork, looking after my life while I've been lying low. Now I wish she hadn't.

I'm not fifty feet from the office door when I spot a black Cadillac Fleetwood parked at the curb. A guy's in the back seat and two are in the front, just like Iggy said there would be. There's no point in trying to avoid them, so rather than walk on past like I'm oblivious, I open the Cadillac's back door and slide in next to Bob Carson.

I have to hand it to the guy. He doesn't look surprised. He doesn't even flinch.

"How was Paris?" he asks, like I've sent him a postcard from there, and relights his cigar, which has gone dead.

"What were you after, Bob?" I ask instead of answering, and he looks back at me with a blank expression like he has no idea what I'm talking about. "You know, when you had my office turned over," I remind him. "One of your boys shot my friend Nat while he was at it, which was kind of unnecessary, don't you think? It's not like he has anything to do with this. Nat's a CPA, for Christ's sake."

"Wasn't me, my friend," Carson says, and for some reason I believe him. It's not just because of the casual way he denies it but because

Carson is obsessed with Lucy Garrett, and if he thought I had something on her, he wouldn't have stopped at ransacking the office. He would have had the guys in the front seat pistol-whip me until I came clean.

"So what's the deal then? You got nothing better to do than hang out in front of my office?"

Carson considers his cigar for a moment, then says, "How much is it going to cost me, Jack?" When I answer with the same blank expression he showed me, he says, "How much is it going to cost me to make you go away?"

Now this game is beginning to interest me. There are people who are willing to pay me, even kill me, to forget about Lucy and her father, and since Bob Carson turns out to be one of them, I play along.

"Make me an offer," I say as if I'm ready to be bought.

"Give me a ballpark," he says.

When I tell him, "Fifty G's, take it or leave it," Carson thinks I'm serious.

"And I'll never see your face again?"

"You have her, don't you, Bob?" I ask, trying to coax him into telling me what he really knows. "You have Lucy." But he doesn't take the bait.

"Don't fuck me around, Jack. Do we have a deal or not?"

I'm tempted. Fifty thousand dollars is a lot of money. V has been trying to get me to drop the Garrett case almost from the beginning. If I took Carson's cash and walked away, we could go back to our old life without worrying that somebody is going to creep into the apartment in the middle of the night and slit our throats. And as much as I hate letting a guy like Garrett off the hook, is bringing him in really worth risking our lives? The smart answer is no, but I can't do it. I can't just walk away. The idea that he and Carson are rich and powerful enough to buy their way out of almost any jam not only offends me, it infuriates me. Maybe it's my dad's days as a Wobbly. Trying to stick it to the owners of the means of production was his favorite pastime. I guess the apple doesn't fall far from the tree. But as much as I'd like to tell Carson to his face what scum I think he is, this is no time to play self-righteous—not only because Carson doesn't care what I think but because the guys in the front seat are armed.

"And if I take your money, what happens?"

"You and Miss Hemming don't end up lying on a slab in the morgue."

I'm tired of guys trying to use V as a wedge against me. Threatening her makes me want to strangle Carson, but losing my temper now probably guarantees me an early grave.

"The big guy who came for me belonged to you, didn't he, Bob? And the hitter from Philly was yours too." Carson cracks a smile when I say this, like he did something clever. "What made you back off?"

"You mean and let you live? It was a simple business decision, Jack. I figure bribing you might be easier and cheaper than having you killed."

I don't find this remark very reassuring, but rather than say that, I tell Carson that I'll let him know about the money, and I get out of the car before I really do end up dead.

When I walk into my office, Janie is sitting at her desk, reading *Butterfield 8*. "Does your mother know you go in for that kind of trash?" I ask her, but she doesn't bother to look up.

"Madonnas and whores, that's what we all are to you, aren't we, Jack?"

"What's that supposed to mean?"

"Vicky is a Madonna because you're in love with her," she says, lowering her book. "I'm one because I'm young and cute, and maybe a little vulnerable, which makes you want to protect me. Lucy Garrett is a whore, even though she's only sixteen, because she puts it around. The same goes for the Hutton girl. And if you're asking yourself how I know about these things, it's not because I'm particularly insightful, it's because you guys are all so predictable." Going back to her book, she adds, "Bernie Rothstein called. He wants to meet—same place as last time. He said he'll be there by five, and it's twenty to now, so you better get moving."

I sit on the same Central Park bench I did the last time I met Bernie. After a couple of minutes, he sits down next to me. The poor guy looks exhausted: pasty skin, five-o'clock shadow, bags under his eyes like he hasn't slept in weeks. I hand him the cup of coffee I've been nursing.

He takes a sip, leans back against the bench, and says, "We found another one."

"Another girl? Where?"

"The Gowanus Canal. I'm on my way over there now. Do you want to come with?" he asks. And I jump at the chance.

The coroner's wagon is parked on the Carroll Street Bridge when we pull up, and Ed Riley, the Brooklyn coroner, is crouched over a corpse, doing a preliminary examination, a lit cigarette in the corner of his mouth.

Kimberly Hutton has been laid out on the bridge. Her body is bloated, her face a ghostly white, and the eels have gotten to her eyes, leaving them sockets.

"One to the back of the head," Riley says, getting to his feet before dissolving into a coughing fit, which he punctuates by spitting a bloody glob of phlegm onto the sidewalk. "I'd say she's been dead four, maybe five days, but I won't know for sure until I get her on a table."

Bernie takes off his hat and runs his fingers through his hair. "Just what I need. Another dead rich kid," he says.

"What's he doing here?" says Jimmy Mullen. I spotted him the minute we walked out on the bridge, and he isn't happy to see me.

"What shakes, Jimmy?" I ask, like we're still friends. "Remind me. When was the last time we saw each other?" The last time we saw each other was in the cottage in the Berkshires, where V nearly blew Mullen's head off. I'm pretty sure he doesn't need to be reminded, but I do it anyway.

"This is a crime scene, Coffey. You got no business being here. Now take a walk before I run you in."

"Leave him alone," Bernie says, and Mullen turns on him.

"What? He's a friend of yours all of a sudden?"

"I didn't say that. I said to leave him alone."

I get it. The battle lines between these two have been drawn. Bernie knows Jimmy's on the take. He's known it for a while and was willing to turn a blind eye until girls like Kimberly Hutton began turning up dead. Now Bernie is either fed up with Mullen being on Garrett's payroll, or he thinks Jimmy's involved in the killings.

"Coffey could be our guy, Bernie," Mullen says. "Did you ever think of that? He could be the shooter!" He's grasping at straws. There's nothing to implicate me. I was in Paris when Muffy Palmer was killed, so that won't fly. Bud and I were with the Dugan brothers just before they were murdered, and an alibi from a movie star is probably as good as it gets.

"I'm telling you," says Mullen, "he knows more than he's letting on. We ought to take him in and see what we can squeeze out of him."

This isn't going to fly either. It's considered bad form for a cop to give away his intentions in front of a suspect—that's assuming Jimmy actually intends on beating a confession out of me. I'm sure nothing would give him greater pleasure, but Bernie won't stand for it.

"You're reaching, Jimmy," he says. "Now, why don't you wrap things up here while I take Coffey home?"

I wish Bernie hadn't said that. Mullen is bound to report this conversation to Garrett, and I'd just as soon he didn't know that V and I are heading back to Perry Street.

Meanwhile, Jimmy is seething. If you're a cop on the grift and your partner is clean, you've got a problem. You can never be sure whether he's just biding his time before turning you over to Internal Affairs or letting your grift slide, which is what Bernie says to me when we get back in his car.

"Mullen's way over the line and I'm going to have to do something about it sooner than later, but he's the least of my problems."

"Meaning what?"

"Let me tell you what happens when a kid like that Hutton girl goes missing. Her daddy is worth a bundle, and he's got connections. He tells us his daughter hasn't come home in days, her mother is frantic, and when that doesn't get him any action, he puts in a call to the chief of d's or the commissioner, maybe even to Gracie Mansion. An hour later, my phone is ringing off the hook. 'Find her,' the boys downtown tell me. 'Do whatever you have to do but find her.'"

"And when she's found floating in the Gowanus Canal?"

"Then somebody has to pay. I just hope that somebody isn't me."

CHAPTER THIRTY-FIVE

I bought a new lock, one of those with a thick iron rod bolted to the floor on one end and to the apartment door on the other. It's a little extreme, but I feel better knowing it's there.

V doesn't like it. In fact, I don't think she likes me very much at the moment. She's been pretty quiet since getting back from the Bahamas, padding around the apartment and avoiding me if she can. It isn't easy. My place is small. I bought us a TV set a couple of years ago and put it in the bedroom. If we're staying in, we usually climb into bed, cuddle up, and watch an old movie, then make love before turning out the light. That isn't happening lately. V hasn't been in the mood to cuddle, and we haven't had sex since she came home.

She's been going out on her own too. I've warned her that it isn't safe, but she says that she won't be held prisoner in the apartment, even if somebody really is after her. We've argued about it a bit, but the truth is I can't really blame her. Anyway, I don't relish the idea of being V's jailer. It's a prescription for romantic disaster. Still, I worry every time she walks out the door.

Tonight, V is sitting in the living room reading. I'm in the bedroom listening to music, playing it low so it won't disturb her. I know there's a bottle of beer in the fridge, and after a while I haul myself off the bed to retrieve it. I have to pass through the living room to get to the kitchen, and I ask V if I can get her anything while I'm up.

"No, thanks," she says without taking her nose out of her book. It's a totally neutral remark, and ordinarily I'd think nothing of it, but V hasn't spoken more than two syllables to me all evening, and I'm getting a little fed up.

"Are you going to tell me what's going on with you or what?" I ask, and when V ignores the question, I snap, "V! I'm talking to you!"

She lays her book aside and takes a couple of seconds before telling me, "I gave up the apartment on Beekman Place."

"When did this happen?"

"A few days ago."

"Are you moving in here permanently?"

"No," she whispers so quietly that I can barely hear her, and that's when I realize she's been dreading having this conversation. "A two-bedroom opened up in Dick's building on York, and he arranged for me to take it."

This news is delivered in a sort of dispassionate monotone, and I feel my balls begin to shrivel. It's not because V has turned to Dick Avedon to help her find a new place. I'm sure he only did it because she asked him to. No, it's that I think V is about to tell me that she's leaving me.

I'm not too far from wrong.

"I don't know that I can do this anymore, Jack," she says. "I love you, but I can't spend my life in hiding or worrying that somebody is about to kill you."

I know she's right. I don't want to know it, but I do. I take a breath so that I don't say something I shouldn't, so that I don't shout or weep or lose my temper. Instead, I fold my arms across my chest and lean against the kitchen doorframe.

"Then you're moving out," I say, and because I can't help myself, I add, "That's great, V. That's just great."

"Don't take it like that, Jack. I'm not saying we're breaking up."

"Then what are you saying?" I'm being petulant. I know that too, but I'm hurt. I love V and I don't want her to leave, though behaving like a spoiled child isn't exactly an incentive for her to stay.

"I just need some time to be on my own," she says as gently as she can. "I'm suffocating here. It's not really your fault, but I'm bound to take it out on you sooner or later and I don't want to do that."

What I say now will probably determine whether we have a future. I like to think of myself as a pretty cool customer, able to control my emotions in a tight spot, but I'm not good at this. My head is buzzing, and I have an empty feeling in the pit of my stomach. But whatever I say is going to come out wrong and make things worse, so I grab my coat off the hook by the door and walk out of the apartment without uttering another word.

A few days later, V is gone. I kept away from the apartment as much as I could while she packed up. It would have been awkward if I didn't, and I would have seemed pathetic by hovering, not the last image of me I wanted V to have before she moved out.

When I finally screw up the courage to go back to the apartment, I find the place tidier than it has ever been. V is a bit of a slob, leaving her clothes strewn around the bedroom, dirty dishes in the kitchen sink, and the cap off the toothpaste in the bathroom. It irritates me, but whenever I say anything to her about it, she just smiles that crooked smile of hers without bothering to deny it. But she's made a point of cleaning and sweeping and dusting while I was out of her way, and I do appreciate that.

V also leaves me a note. It's in her looping, girlish hand and runs nearly five pages. The gist of it is that she still loves me and always will, which has the faint whiff of a kiss-off about it. But she also writes that we're not finished, that I'm not only her lover, but her best friend, that she can't imagine herself with another man, and that somehow we will survive this. I don't see it, but that may be my broken heart talking. Her note then gets a little gooey and a little explicit—meant to reassure me, I guess.

I once dated a woman named Dotty O'Brien. It was after I got out of the service, and we spent a year together before things between us went south. I don't know why they did, exactly. We were young, I suppose, and I was pretty traumatized after coming home from overseas.

There were a few other relationships, most of them brief. Those didn't end in high drama, but in low bathos with somebody saying that despite everything, we would always love each other—which is what I said to Dotty and why when V writes the same thing, I don't believe her.

Despite her telling me not to be sad and not to mope around the apartment, that's exactly what I do. For the better part of a week, I wander around the place in a torn undershirt, listening to Sinatra. I'm not that much of a fan really. I like this new kid Bennett better. He has a jazzier delivery and can make Berlin and Cole Porter sound like they were orchestrated by Billy Strayhorn. But Frank's "In the Wee Small Hours" fits my mood, and I play his version of Hoagy Carmichael's "I Get Along Without You Very Well" over and over again, hoping that it turns out to be true.

After a couple of days, V calls. The conversation starts off stilted, and I get annoyed when she asks if I'm all right for the third time. I ask how she likes her new apartment. She says she likes it fine and that she's gotten a cat. We go on like this for a while, filling each other in on the inane and mundane until I say, "You left a bunch of your stuff here. I can box it up and you can come by and collect it anytime you like."

"You don't have to do that," V says, and I hear a quiver in her voice. "I sort of left those things behind on purpose."

I'm not sure what to say to this, so I change the subject, but when we hang up a few minutes later, I feel better.

When the four walls finally begin to close in, I decide to go up to Minton's and see Monk and his combo. I take a table at the back and listen to them lay down their improvisational licks: brilliant as usual. By the end of their second set, I'm on my fourth Maker's Mark and more than a little worse for wear. The combo goes on a break, and Monk ambles through the crowd, taking a seat next to me.

"So she dumped you, huh?" he says like he can read the heartbreak on my face. When I tell him that he's right, Monk instantly contradicts me, "Nah, she'll be back. You've been pissing her off lately, but she's devoted to you, boyo."

"I'm not too sure about that."

"I am."

"Why?"

"Because she told me."

"When was that?"

"She came in by herself Saturday night. I bought her a drink and we had a little chat."

Despite the boozy haze clouding my brain, it occurs to me that if V appeared in Minton's on her own, it was with the express purpose of passing a message to me through Monk. She probably could tell that I didn't believe her when she said we weren't through. Or maybe she's breaking up with me by inches so I can get used to the idea before she administers the *coup de grâce*.

I test out this second theory on Monk, and he looks at me like I'm nuts. "You really are white, aren't you, Jack?" he says, and he doesn't mean it as a compliment. I might decide that I'm being paranoid when I sober up, but in the meantime I manage to convince myself that V is handling me. I say this to Monk like it makes perfect sense, but he rolls his eyes. "That's your wounded pride talking," he tells me, but I can't shake the feeling that I'm being indulged.

I don't see her coming, but I shouldn't be surprised. Lucy Garrett has a habit of turning up whenever I least expect her.

She says, "I knew I'd find you here," and lays a hand on my shoulder like we're old pals. "You really ought to think about being a little less conspicuous, though. I mean, if I know where you are . . ." Then, instead of finishing her sentence, Lucy kisses me on the top of my head.

She sits down uninvited, reaches across the table for my glass, and drains it without asking whether I mind. It's then that I notice she isn't pregnant, not anymore. She must have found some moonlighting doc to abort the kid, that or it was Hayden, or she's given birth and given the baby away.

There are any number of things I want to ask her, but because I'm in the bag and it's the obvious question I settle on, "Where the hell have you been?"

"Around," she says, like it isn't a cliché, and she giggles in an infuriatingly coquettish way. Then she says, "Daddy wants to talk to you."

Despite being loaded, I smell a rat. Why send the kid to deliver this message? And what does Daddy want from me now? What's she doing with her old man anyway? I figured Lucy was holed up with Bob Carson or the guy who took out the Dugan brothers.

"About what?" I ask, like I expect an honest answer.

Lucy grins and gets to her feet. "Ask him yourself. He's waiting outside in the car," she says and heads for the door like she's sure I'm going to follow, which, like an idiot, is exactly what I do.

CHAPTER THIRTY-SIX

I should have known better. It might have been the booze or the way curiosity can make you stupid. I should have sat tight, ordered another round, and let Lucy Garrett wander off into the night, but I didn't.

When we walk out of the club, I expect to see Garrett's limousine at the curb with his chauffeur behind the wheel. Instead, the only car idling in front of Minton's isn't a car at all, but a panel van.

"Okay, what's the deal?" I say to Lucy. "Where is he?"

"You'll find out," she says in a singsongy voice like she's a little kid.

But Lucy has some very grown-up friends. One of them brains me with a sap or something heavier like a baseball bat because my world goes atilt all of a sudden and then fades to black.

When I come to, I'm sitting on a cement floor in a dank warehouse that reeks of fuel oil and piss. There isn't much in the way of light, but I can hear water dripping somewhere and a compressor humming monotonously in the darkness. I'm also gagged, bound hand and foot, and Lucy Garrett is sitting in front of me in a lawn chair, holding a very large gun.

"Surprise!" she says with the same grin on her face she had in Minton's, and if I wasn't trussed up like a Christmas turkey and she wasn't armed, I'd strangle her with my bare hands. She gets to her feet, walks over to me, and pulls the rubber ball gag out of my mouth. I guess she wants to chat before finishing me off.

"You're cute when you're tied up like that, Jack," she says, enjoying my predicament. "Do you and Vicky play this game or does she like her sex straight?"

This is meant to provoke me, and it does, but I try not to let it show. "Here's what I don't get," I say instead because V is the last person on earth I want to discuss with this little psychopath. "Your old man gives you everything you could possibly need. You do what you want whenever you want. What's in all of this for you? Or is it only about payback?"

"It's fun," Lucy says, flipping her hair over her shoulder, flirting with me before she does me in. But there are still a few things I want to know.

"The Dugans, those nice guys watching over you while you were jonesing? You murdered them, didn't you?"

"Do you know what's really amazing?" she says. "What you guys will do if you think you're going to get your dick sucked. I mean, you should see the look of hope on your faces."

I can imagine Eddie Dugan making this mistake, but I thought Joe had more sense. Still, it does explain why, when I found Eddie, his pants were down around his ankles. I just can't believe Joe fell for the same gag.

But Lucy wasn't packing that night. Bud and I made sure of that before we deposited her in V's bedroom. And Eddie always had his gun on him. Lucy must have grabbed it while she had him otherwise engaged. In fact, I think that's Eddie's .45 she's holding on me now. Maybe she did the Dugans on her own.

"And Muffy Palmer? What sin did she commit?"

"You mean other than being annoying?" Lucy snorts. "You know, for a girl with braces and bad breath, you'd think Muffy would have learned to keep her mouth shut."

"Why? Who did she talk to?"

"You."

I didn't think she had it in her, but Lucy must have murdered Muffy. And Kimberly Hutton. And Rex Halsey too. Rex had been around the block more than once and should have seen her coming, but Lucy's right about guys and sex, particularly when blow jobs are on offer. Male brains can cease to function at the prospect—that, and I guess Rex hadn't realized that he'd outlived his usefulness.

"Five murders, Lucy," I say. "Five that I know about anyway. Did you do them all on your own or did somebody help out?"

"You know, I like you, Jack, I really do. I'll probably feel bad later, but I'll get over it. And just so you know. I didn't kill anybody."

"No? Then who did?"

Instead of answering, Lucy smirks at me like I'm supposed to guess.

"It's Carson, isn't it?" I say, plowing ahead. "He's not only sweet on you, but he's the only guy with pockets deep enough to go up against your father."

Lucy's smirk turns just pained enough for me to read it as phony. "Good old Uncle Bob," she says. "You know, he used to bounce me on his knee when I was little. I'd giggle and laugh and pretend he didn't have his hand up my dress. Uncle Bob was hard for me even then."

Judging by the expression on her face, I'm fairly sure Lucy is making this up, but whatever Carson did or didn't do, he isn't the big news. Garrett is. That bastard and a bunch of his well-heeled buddies are abusing underage girls, and they'll go to any length to make sure nobody finds out. Lucy isn't the femme fatale she makes herself out to be. It's a defense. She's as much a victim as any of those other girls. And she's telling the truth. Lucy Garrett didn't kill anyone.

"Who are we waiting for, Lucy?"

She decides to play coy. I wouldn't be surprised if Lucy started sucking her thumb.

"He's gonna make you the fall guy, you know?"

"Who: Daddy? No, he isn't. He wouldn't dare."

"Why's that?"

"Because I have his movies."

Of course she does.

"Do you know what I think? I think you ought to give those movies to me."

"Why would I do that?"

"Because I'm the only one who can get you out of this mess." Lucy thinks her father won't come for her, not for his own flesh and blood, at least not while she has those movies. I'm not so sure.

"When are they coming back for me?" I ask.

"Who's *they*?" she says, nipping at a hangnail. Lucy's making a show of pretending to be calm, but her knee's pumping up and down like a piston. It's not a reflex. She's scared.

"It's got to be soon. What do you say you untie me?"

Lucy smooths her skirt, then ties her hair back into a ponytail. "Okay, let's say you're right about Daddy blaming everything on me. But what am I supposed to do? Just let you go? I can't do that. Anyway, he's not going to hurt me. He loves me."

"I'll bet that's just what your mommy said right before your daddy put her away."

This seems to sink in. I don't lean on it any harder now because I feel sorry for the kid, besides its poor salesmanship.

"He made her have an operation, you know? Dr. Hayden did something to her brain. That's what Uncle Bob told me." Garrett must have paid Hayden to lobotomize his wife. It keeps her quiet and easier to warehouse. "I hardly remembered her, but she remembered me. I tried to be nice, I really did, but I didn't know what to say. You know, all she does all day in that awful place is eat stale cookies and stare out the window."

"That's exactly what your daddy has in store for you, you know? Maybe something even worse."

Lucy mulls this over for a moment, pouts, then says, "Why do you always have to be so mean?" before hauling herself out of her lawn chair and cutting me free.

CHAPTER THIRTY-SEVEN

I can hear the heart monitor whine when I begin to flatline. I can feel a guy pounding on my chest while another uses an Ambu bag to try to force air into my lungs. I can hear the two of them talking, judging the odds of making it to the hospital before I check out or whether they should call it then and there and let me go.

Luckily, I can also hear the tentative *bloop, bloop, bloop* of the monitor when my heart kicks back in and they realize it's not my time. I don't remember much else. Either I passed out in the ambulance or they shot me up with something because the next thing I know, V's sitting on the edge of my hospital bed with tears in her eyes and a smile on her face.

"You bastard, Jack"—which isn't the first thing I expect her to say. Still, I want to take her in my arms—not only because I'm glad she's there but because I'm relieved to be alive. I try to do just that, but a searing pain like somebody shoving a red-hot poker in my gut gets in the way. I also don't count on the maze of tubes running out of my nose and arms, which makes moving at all nearly impossible.

V takes pity on me. She leans forward, gently brushes her lips against mine, and says, "I never would have forgiven you, you know?"

"For what?" I'm not sure that voice is mine. It's thin and raspy, but I know it's me because my throat feels like it's on fire when I speak.

"For getting yourself killed. It would have been just like you, Jack Coffey, leaving me in the lurch when all I was trying to do by taking that apartment was teach you a lesson. I didn't leave you, you big dumb idiot. I love you."

I can't tell you how indescribably happy this makes me, though it's hard to show it given that I'm medicated within an inch of my life. Apparently, I've also been unconscious for a couple of days, so I'm groggy.

"For what it's worth, I wouldn't have forgiven you either." Janie is standing at the foot of my bed with her arms folded across her chest and an exasperated look on her face. "You owe me three-weeks' salary, and my rent is due tomorrow." Janie isn't the sentimental type, but her cheeks are wet too. "So, are you going to end the suspense and tell us what happened or what?" she says.

I wish I could, but the truth is I barely remember a thing.

I remember grabbing the gun out of Lucy's hand when three gunmen blew into the warehouse just as she untied me. I remember taking out two of them before a bullet spun me around and dropped me to the floor. I guess I got off a couple of more rounds before I blacked out because I'm still here and breathing—which wouldn't have been the case if I didn't. After that, it's anybody's guess. I don't have a clue.

"Is this your idea of taking it easy?" A doc walks into my hospital room with a stethoscope hanging from his neck. I recognize him. He's the guy who stitched up my scalp in the emergency room after the slab brained me. I never caught his name, but I'm guessing he saved my life when the ambulance brought me in. I took one in the chest that collapsed a lung and another in the side, so it must have been pretty touch and go. I make a mental note to send him a bottle of something nice so he knows how much I appreciate him.

"What can I say? I've always had a problem with authority," I croak and manage a grin in case the doc doesn't realize I'm joking.

"You know, you're down a kidney, Mr. Coffey. Fortunately, you have a spare, so you should be able to go home in a few days, but saving you was a close-run thing, so in the future do try to avoid getting hit over the head or shot again."

I spend most of the next week laid up in St. Vincent's. Despite the web of IVs, the hanging bottles of saline, antibiotics, and blood platelets, and having to piss in a bedpan, I'm having a pretty good time. It's against hospital rules, but V insists they set up a cot for her so she can sleep next to my bed, and whenever she's not working, she's by my side. Janie isn't quite as devoted—why should she be?—but she visits every afternoon. Bud puts in a couple of appearances, thrilling the nursing staff, who invent reasons to come in and take my temperature and blood pressure whenever he's around. Monk comes by with Miles Davis in tow, which is weird because I don't know Miles all that well. He doesn't say anything, just sits in a corner smoking reefer until the head nurse comes in and says the smell is bothering her other patients. Toots shows up one night after visiting hours, trailing a phalanx of waiters. They're carrying in trays laden with his best sirloin and baked potatoes with all the trimmings, and I don't have the heart to tell him that they're not letting me eat solid food. I can barely sit up and usually don't like being the center of attention, but everyone seems so happy I'm still alive, that I can't help but enjoy myself—that is, until Bernie Rothstein shows up.

Bernie shoos everyone out of the room, including V, closes the door, takes off his hat, pulls a up chair, and says, "Okay, smart guy, tell me what the fuck happened."

I go into my spiel about not remembering anything, but Bernie isn't buying it. "I don't mean who shot you, Jack. I already know that. We collected three stiffs in a warehouse over on Eleventh Avenue. What I want to know is how they got that way."

"I guess I'm a good shot."

"It's hard to miss when you're a foot away."

This makes no sense to me. None of the shooters got closer than twenty yards. "What are you talking about, Bernie?"

"Judging by the powder burns and the round one guy took to the back of his skull, I'd say the man was executed. You didn't do it?"

I want to tell Bernie that it wasn't me, but that would mean giving up Lucy Garrett, and for the moment I'd just as soon keep her out of it. Instead, I ask, "Were you able to make any of the stiffs?"

"Two guys from your neck of the woods," he tells me. Then after consulting his casebook, he says, "Patrick Healey and Ed O'Bannon. Do you know them?"

I didn't make them when they came at me, but I went to Cardinal Hayes with both of them. They were seniors when I was a freshman, so it wasn't like we were buddies, but everyone in Hell's Kitchen knows they run errands for Hughie Mulligan's Westies. It's supposed to be penny-ante stuff—collecting debts and shaking down shopkeepers, that sort of thing. I guess they graduated to attempted murder, namely attempting to murder me.

"We're still not sure about the third guy," Bernie says, putting his casebook back into his breast pocket. "He didn't have any identification on him, and he didn't look the part."

"Meaning what?"

"That he was a little too elegant for your run-of-the-mill hood."

"And he's the one who took a bullet to the back of the head?"

"Yeah, but if you didn't do it, who did?"

"Lucy Garrett," I say because if I don't, Bernie's going to think I did the killing no matter what I tell him.

"Explain that," he says, and I try my best.

I tell him about Lucy showing up at Minton's and luring me outside the club. I tell him that a couple of guys jumped me, guys who must have been Healey and O'Bannon. I tell Bernie they coldcocked me and shoved me into a panel van, then they must have taken me to that warehouse on Eleventh. After tying me up, they went to fetch the third guy, leaving me behind with Lucy. I convince her that her father doesn't care what happens to her and that he'll make sure she takes the fall if the cops begin to look at him, so she cuts me loose. Finally, I tell Bernie that the shoot-out couldn't have lasted very long, a couple of minutes tops, but that I really don't remember anything after I got hit.

"So, when the shooting stops, Lucy Garrett calmly walks up to the snappy dresser and blows his brains out? Is that your story?"

"If that's how he was done, yeah."

Lucy must have been furious when she realized that I was right, that the shooters were gunning for her as well as me. It had to be rage that gave her the stomach to put one of them down execution-style, that or she was proving a point to her daddy.

"She shouldn't have bothered. The guy's femoral artery was nicked when he got shot, so he would have bled out anyway. Finishing him off like that took nerve though. She must have been plenty pissed off."

Of course, Bernie wants to know where Lucy is now, and I tell him I don't know. She's in the wind again, as unpredictable as ever. Not only that, but now she's armed. Bernie takes all this in, then tells me to be where he can find me after they let me out of the hospital, and I promise him I will.

But when they release me from St. Vincent's, V drives me up to West Stockbridge without letting Bernie know. This is fine with me. I'm tired and as weak as a kitten, and the idea of V mothering me sounds better than good.

She got a couple of local high school kids to move our bed out onto the screened-in porch. It's cooler out there, the only place in the house to escape the summer heat, and V loves nothing more than to be lulled to sleep by the night birds calling to each other. She stopped by Perry Street before we left, grabbed a few of my favorite albums and the Victrola I picked up in Paris.

I spend the next few days flat on my back in the country, listening to music and sleeping. V bustles around, looking after me, making me tea and toast for breakfast, the clear chicken broth the doctor recommended for lunch, and something light for dinner. We listen to the radio in the evenings. We don't have a TV up here, which is hardly a sacrifice considering there are only two local stations and the reception is lousy. I'm in no condition to make love, as much as I might want to, so V and I snuggle and smooch before going to sleep. And each day, V dresses my wound. She's not squeamish about such things. In fact, she's fascinated, examining my stitches, making sure the wound is clean and free of infection, and gently, but expertly, changing my bandages. Life is idyllic and we're as happy as clams until the phone rings one afternoon.

"I thought I told you to be where I could find you," Bernie Rothstein says when I pick it up.

"You just did, Bernie. What's up?"

"What's up is I think we got an ID on the third guy, but I need you to come down to the morgue and see if you recognize him."

"When do you want me to do that?"

"How about right now?"

CHAPTER THIRTY-EIGHT

Burton the butler is lying on a stainless-steel table in the city morgue with the back of his head blown off and an exit wound in the middle of his forehead. He also has a through-and-through to his right thigh, which I guess is my handiwork.

"Know him?" Bernie asks me.

"Yeah. He works for Garrett. He used to anyway."

V and I waited twenty-four hours before driving back down to the city. I didn't feel up to going any sooner, and I didn't like the idea of being summoned, forced to drive a couple hundred miles because Bernie Rothstein commanded it.

"Do you think Garrett was behind the warehouse shootings? I mean, if this guy worked for him—"

"Probably, but Burton could have been freelancing. I don't think loyalty was his strong suit. But it does fit."

I'd had an inkling that he wasn't playing straight with his employer when I saw Burton with his feet up on Garrett's desk, smoking one of his cigars. It didn't exactly make for the image of a loyal family retainer, but it doesn't mean he turned on his boss either. More importantly, I tell Bernie about Garrett's movies. They not only implicate Garrett in sex trafficking and the abuse of minors but probably expose any number of other local bigwigs as well. And I tell him that Lucy is in possession of those movies and will use them against Garrett if she has to. Maybe even if she doesn't.

"This kid plans on blackmailing her own father?"

"If it suits her, sure."

"Are you two lovebirds enjoying yourselves?" The second Jimmy Mullen steps into the room, the tension gets very thick. "I heard you got plugged, Coffey, but lived to tell the tale. Can't have everything, I guess."

Bernie tells Mullen to give it a rest, but Jimmy isn't in the mood to play nice.

"Working the case with this scum now, are you, *partner*?" He hits the last word hard, so Rothstein doesn't miss his meaning. "It's a big mistake. I mean, a really big mistake."

Bernie isn't intimidated. He stands his ground, letting his coat fall open so Mullen can get a load of his service revolver.

"Just doing the job, Jimmy," he says with a smile, and I get the feeling these two are about to go for their guns, catching me in the cross fire.

I say, "Why don't you guys relax before somebody does something stupid?"

It takes a couple of fraught seconds, but they back off. Mullen then shoves his hands into his pockets and casually ambles over to where Burton is laid out.

"Who's this guy?" he asks as if he doesn't know. Jimmy's playing dumb on purpose.

But Bernie's on to him. Instead of answering his question, he slides past Mullen, pulls the sheet back over Burton's face, and asks, "Where's the girl, Jimmy?"

Mullen doesn't break character. "What girl?"

If I let this pantomime go on too much longer, somebody is going to end up on the slab next to Burton, so I take Bernie by the arm and whisper, "C'mon, let's take a walk." Like I said, Bernie isn't the type to back down, and I can see a vein throbbing in his neck, but ever so reluctantly he lets me ease him out the door.

"Don't ever do that to me again!" he snaps, wrenching his arm free when we hit the street. He's angry at me for dragging him out of the morgue, but he'll get over it.

Dealing with Mullen is a different story. I see now that Bernie is determined to take his partner down, but Jimmy isn't going without a fight. I have a rooting interest in seeing Bernie going a couple of rounds with Mullen, but to be honest, I'd just as soon he help me deal with Garrett before taking on his partner.

"Your timing is for shit, Jack—which, no offense, is pretty typical of you."

I'm having a late dinner with Carmine at Umbertos Clam House. He's inhaling a plate of the fettuccine carbonara, a napkin tucked under his chin so the sauce doesn't splash on his silk suit. I'm having the linguine because it's the Clam House's specialty.

"I thought you were through with that kid and her old man."

"I should be, but I'm not. I still got an issue with that fuck getting away with murder. It offends my sense of decorum."

"That issue put you in the hospital, didn't it?"

"How do you know about that?"

Carmine looks at me like I should know better, that there's nothing that goes on in the city he doesn't know about. Still, I fill him in on a few of the details in case he missed any. He hasn't.

"You iced a couple of guys, right? Healey and O'Bannon."

"Yeah. It was them or me, in case your bosses are annoyed."

"*Nah*. No big loss. Hughie Mulligan was done with those idiots anyway." After wiping his mouth with his napkin, he says, "I'll tell you what I'll do, Jack. There's a woman we know, calls herself Madam Alexa. She runs a house for us that caters to Wall Street types. Those guys get up to all sorts of stuff, not necessarily kids, but not just whips and chains either. Anyway, a lot of pillow talk goes on over there. I'll have Alexa find out if anybody knows anything about those movies or where to find the Garrett kid and let you know."

It's late, and V's already in bed by the time I get home from dinner with Carmine. She still rents an apartment in Dick Avedon's building but spends about as much time there as she did at Beekman Place. She switches on the light when I walk into the bedroom.

"You look terrible," she says, which I'm sure is true because it's the way I feel. I'm still reeling from being shot, and when I take off my jacket, blood is seeping through my shirt.

"Take that off too, so I can get a look," V tells me. I perch on the edge of the bed and slip out of my shirt. My bandage is soaked through.

V peels it back so she can see just how bad the damage is. "You busted open your stitches," she says, then gets out of bed and disappears into the bathroom to fetch gauze pads and a bottle of hydrogen peroxide. When she comes back, she cleans and rebandages the wound, then helps me into bed. I don't really need the help, but I'm enjoying being pampered.

"Does it hurt much?"

"Only when I laugh."

V groans and shakes her head. "How did I ever get myself involved with a doofus like you?" she asks, then climbs into bed next to me and turns out the light. I wrap my arm around her, and she rests her cheek against my chest.

"You're going to bust open those stitches again, you know?" V warns, but I don't care, and we make love for the first time in weeks.

CHAPTER THIRTY-NINE

A couple of days later, I hear back from Carmine. He says Madam Alexa might have a line on Lucy and it's okay if I go talk to her, but there are ground rules.

"Like I told you," Carmine says on the phone, "her joint caters to corporate hotshots and Hollywood types, so if you recognize anybody, you didn't. You get me? And it's gonna cost you, Jack. Nobody gets a freebie from Alexa no matter who you are."

When I ask how much, Carmine says a G at least.

A G at least is a lot of money to me, so it had better buy me some decent information or I'm liable to get irritated. "Listen, if this woman makes me for a mark and tries to con me, she's not going to like it when I make a stink in front of her customers."

"Fair enough," Carmine says, "but we got a guy who looks after the place for us. Frankie Guzzetta. I'll give him a heads-up so he knows you're coming, and if she tries to run a game, let Frankie know." I figure Guzzetta not only for a made guy, but for one of Carmine's *shtarkers*, so I go along with the plan. He gives me the address, a town house in the financial district. He also tells me that Alexa doesn't get in until after midnight so there's no point in showing up any earlier.

"Is that what you're wearing?"

I'm standing in front of the bedroom mirror tying my tie when

V asks me this. I've got my houndstooth on, which is my go-to jacket whenever I'm out on a job, along with slacks and a pair of brogans that could use a shine.

"Why? What's wrong with what I'm wearing?"

Instead of answering me, V goes to the closet and retrieves the only suit I own.

"I know the kind of men who go to places like Alexa's," she says, "and if the idea is to be inconspicuous, wear the suit." When it comes to these things, V knows what she's talking about, so I slip out of the houndstooth and into my three-piece Brioni.

From the outside, Alexa's three-story town house is nondescript, one of a row of them left over from the Gilded Age. I ring the bell, expecting a beefy guy to throw open a slat in the door and ask me for the password.

Instead, a pretty blond not much older than twenty ushers me in with a smile and a wave of her hand. I try to introduce myself, but she says, "I know who you are, Mr. Coffey. Madam Alexa is expecting you," and she leads me into a high-ceilinged Victorian-style parlor.

The furniture is plush, the drapes thick and heavy, and the art on the walls frankly pornographic. Young women, most of them stark naked, are draped over men in business suits, some of them twice the girls' ages. There's nothing particularly untoward going on, though. That must be reserved for the rooms upstairs.

I recognize a couple of the guys, not because they're famous, but because I've done work for them. Conrad Taylor, a minor member of the Whitney family, calls out, "Jack Coffey! As I live and breathe!" like he's shouting to me over the crowd noise at the Polo Grounds. This does not make me happy. I try to ignore him, but Taylor claps me on the back and says, "I'm surprised to see you here, fella," in his finest Locust Valley lockjaw. "I didn't think you people went in for this sort of thing."

I'm not entirely sure what he means by "you people." It could be a class thing or more likely because I'm a half-Jew. In other circumstances a crack like that would earn Taylor the back of my hand, but tonight I let it slide.

"You're right, Conrad," I say. "I don't go in for this sort of thing."

"Then what are you doing here?"

"Mr. Coffey is here on business," says Madam Alexa. She appears from out of nowhere and slips her arm through mine. "Now, if you'll excuse us, Jack and I have things to discuss," she says, leading me away.

I follow Alexa up three flights of stairs and into what once must have been the attic. She has converted it into an office. It's tidy and businesslike: a solid oak desk with paperwork neatly piled on top of it, a telephone with flashing buttons, filing cabinets, and a chintz couch for visitors like myself.

Alexa takes a seat behind the desk. "I understand you're interested in purchasing information."

I'm trying to judge her age, but it isn't easy. She looks to be about forty but could be a decade older. She's attractive and I suspect was once an expensive pro herself.

"You're looking for Lucy Garrett," she says. "I've known her father for years, you know?"

"Do you know where Lucy is?"

"Shall we settle my fee first?"

Like any experienced professional, Alexa wants her money up front, and I oblige her. I pull a wad of cash out of my pocket and peel off a thousand dollars in crisp tens and twenties. She carefully counts it and slips the cash into the top drawer of her desk. "I want to show you something," Alexa says and leads me down a flight of stairs into a dark room.

Stag films. Grainy black-and-white 16 mm movies of three people having sex. I've seen these things before, and they're chilling and depressing. Judging by the vacant look in their eyes, the two girls are either junkies earning their next fix or street waifs desperate for cash. The guy is middle-aged, fat, balding, and covered in body hair. The flickering images are explicit and revolting, but they aren't the reason Madam Alexa has brought me in here. I know this because she switches on the lights to the groans of a half-dozen guys sprawled on chaises with their hands down their pants.

Alexa shoos them all out of the room, then hands another reel of film over to the girl working the projector. She tells me to take a seat, something I'm a little reluctant to do considering what the previous occupants have been up to, but I take my chances.

"I don't see what this has to do with Lucy Garrett," I say.

"You will." And Alexa turns out the lights.

It takes a couple of seconds for my eyes to adjust, and at first I don't see the difference between this movie and the stag film that preceded it until I spot Louis Garrett. A young girl in a baby-doll dress with her hair in pigtails is sitting in his lap, sucking on a lollipop. The tableau is so clichéd and comical that I almost burst out laughing—that is, until Garrett forces the girl to her knees and unzips his fly. Mercifully, the film is a snippet and ends before he does something truly disgusting.

When Alexa turns the lights back on, I ask, "Where did you get it?"

She says that it was delivered to her by courier the week before, but that she's fairly certain it came from Lucy. "I'm sure she hopes I'll show it to her father," Alexa says, fitting an unfiltered Chesterfield into a black enamel cigarette holder.

"Have you?" I ask.

"Shown it to Garrett? No, not yet." Alexa lights her cigarette and exhales a stream of smoke through her nostrils. "But I will if he pays my price."

"How much is that?"

"A great deal more than I'm charging you, Jack," she says and smiles.

That Louis Garrett frequents Madam Alexa's whorehouse is hardly shocking. That Lucy knows he does isn't a shock either, but using Alexa against her father is a novel ploy. Alexa is the soul of self-interest and sure to use the snippet to extort money from Garrett. It's a dangerous game, but she's no novice. She'll calmly threaten to expose him unless he pays up and use the mob in the guise of Frankie Guzzetta as protection if he tries to move against her. Lucy must have had the snippet delivered because it lets her old man know that whatever he pays Alexa to keep quiet, she still has more and could drop a dime on him at any time. If she does, Garrett's ruined and on his way to jail for statutory rape and possibly murder. I don't say any of this to Alexa, but I tell her to be careful. Garrett is capable of almost anything, but I suspect she already knows that.

Before I leave, Alexa asks if I want to indulge in any of her establishment's many delights, but I decline.

"Are you sure I can't tempt you?" she says, and as if on cue, the blond who opened the front door reappears, wearing nothing but a smile.

There was a time when I might have taken the plunge, a time when I was young enough, a time before V, a time when I was too naive to realize Alexa is trying to lure me into a trap. If I take her up on her offer, there are sure to be lurid photographs taken by a camera hidden behind a peephole in the wall. I don't know what Alexa would do with them exactly—threaten to show them to V, I guess—but fortunately, I'm not naive, not anymore.

When I tell her that I'm not interested, Alexa loses interest in me. She stubs out her cigarette in a cut-glass ashtray, and calls out, "Frank!" like she's summoning a servant.

Frankie Guzzetta appears in the doorway with a sad-sack look on his face. Doing Alexa's bidding is a lousy job, and I can't help but feel sorry for the guy as he escorts me out of the room and back out onto the street.

CHAPTER FORTY

Bernie Rothstein has been told to stand down, taken off the case of the dead girls. He tells me this while scarfing down a pastrami-on-rye with the works in a deli on Columbus Avenue. I can't tell whether he's pissed off or relieved.

"Downtown sends this captain to see me," Bernie says, washing down his pastrami with a gulp of cream soda. "I don't know the guy, but I know the look. He gives me this song and dance about how the chief of d's wants me to work a mob hit, a guy they found floating off Pier Fifty-Two, and that Jimmy Mullen's gonna take over Muffy Palmer and the rest."

"Garrett got to somebody," I say.

"He must have leaned on downtown pretty hard or had somebody do it for him. I make the commissioner for a straight shooter. It's not like him to stick his nose in an ongoing investigation, but that's not even the kicker."

"What is?" I ask, reaching for Bernie's pickle. He snatches it away before I can get to it and says, "Jimmy told the higher-ups that Burton did the killings, and with Burton in the morgue, they're ready to drop the whole business."

"Meaning Garrett walks away from all of it."

"Unless another dead girl turns up, I guess so."

Part of me wants to break every dish on the table, but instead I study

Bernie's face for his reaction. He's pretending not to care, but I can tell it's an act—and not a very good one at that.

"Then what's our next move?" I say. I don't expect Bernie to jump at the chance to help me out—it's not his style—but I'm pretty sure he'll come around if I keep at him.

"I'm coming up on my twenty, you know?" he says. "What I should do is keep my head down, and when the time comes, take my pension and pack it in. My father-in-law owns a construction business over in Jersey and he's offered to let me buy in. There's still a lot of housing going up out there and I'd make a pretty penny."

"You'd be bored out of your mind."

"Yeah. Well, there is that." Bernie drains the rest of his soda and wipes his mouth with a paper napkin. "But I could lose my pension and everything that goes with it if we go for Garrett and miss."

"We won't," I say, but Bernie isn't impressed by my bravado.

"You got an answer for everything, don't you, Coffey? It's what I always hated about you. You strut around town with that stunner of a girlfriend on your arm like nothing can get to you, like you're the luckiest duck in the world."

"That's true as long as you don't count being knocked unconscious with a length of lead pipe, snatched off the street by a couple of thugs, tied up by a psychopathic teenager, and nearly getting shot to death. Yeah, I'm lucky as fuck."

Bernie lights a White Owl and smiles. He shapes the ash of his cigar on the edge of his plate, then says, "I probably should have my head examined for this, but if I go along with you, our next move would be to get hold of those movies."

"For that we need to track down Lucy Garrett," I say, but Bernie has other ideas.

"Not necessarily. Madam Alexa might have been holding out on you, letting you get a taste of what she has on Lucy's old man just to see your reaction. But she won't cross your friend Carmine, so why don't you see what he has to say?"

"How do you know about me and Carmine?"

"I'm a detective, remember? Anyway, Rizzo's bosses won't like it if he's seen anywhere near me, but he'll talk to you."

Bernie's probably right. It's like Alexa to play all the angles, and it will get back to Carmine if she's up to something. Unfortunately for me, Carmine is nowhere to be found. He's not dead, not yet anyway, but a couple of The Chin's boys were shot down on Linden Boulevard in Brooklyn a few days ago and I know that Carmine's lying low. The hit was splashed all over the front pages. I'm assuming it was payback for the crack Gigante took at Frank Costello, Luciano's consigliere. That sort of thing just isn't done, not without permission. Everybody has rules, even the Mafia.

And somebody is keeping an eye on me again.

A week later, Bud and I are coming up out of the Eighth Street subway station when I spot him, a plainclothes cop in a trench and a fedora. As always, his shoes give him away. We're heading over to the White Horse for a beer after working out at Stillman's, and he falls into step a half block behind us.

I'm pretty sure Mullen sent him but figure the worst he can do out on the street is pinch us. Arresting me for no reason is a move Jimmy would make without worrying about the consequences, but if he picks up Bud, it'll make the papers. Still, I decide it's best to give Brando a heads-up, so I ask, "How much cash do you have on you?"

"I don't know. A couple hundred maybe. Why?"

"It really does pay to be a movie star, doesn't it?"

"You know, Jack, if you need money, I'm always good for it."

"I think we both might need it."

"For what?"

"Bail."

I expect the idea of being locked up to make Bud nervous. What I don't expect is for him to go head-to-head with a cop. It's a gutsy move and not something I'd try, but then I'm not a famous actor. Bud walks right up to the poor schlub and gets in his face.

"You got a problem with me, Mac?" he says and rises to the balls of his feet like he's ready to slug the guy. If he was just a civilian, the cop might have rousted him for a remark like that, but he recognizes Bud and it flusters him some.

"You know what I don't like?" Bud barks at him, getting close enough so the guy can smell his breath. "I don't like it when some two-bit bull thinks he can make a monkey out of me by tailing me in public."

The cop goes meek and compliant. He calls Bud "Mr. Brando" a half-dozen times and apologizes for bothering him, but Bud's not through. He threatens to sue the cop and the department for harassment, then tells the guy to get lost, which, to my surprise, he does. It's a bravura performance, and when Bud ambles back over to me, he's got a grin on his face like he's just gotten away with something. I don't have the heart to tell him that his act is liable to come back and bite me on the ass one day and instead let him enjoy the moment. But I do say, "You're lucky he didn't take you in."

"It wouldn't be the first time," Bud says, and we stroll over to the White Horse to while away the rest of the afternoon with some of the local West Village riffraff.

It's after dark by the time I get home. When I do, I spot the same plainclothes cop Bud went after, lurking outside my building. I consider going up against him myself, but I'm worse for the afternoon's wear and I don't feel like spending the night in a holding cell in the Tombs.

V is waiting for me in the apartment when I walk in, and she's annoyed. I'm not much of a drinker and rarely stumble home loaded, although tonight is an exception. It's something V has done more than once herself, so I know that can't be what's bothering her. But she's drumming her fingers on the kitchen table with a scowl on her face, so it has to be something.

"What?" I ask when I sit down, but instead of answering me, she tosses a manila envelope on the table.

"That girl dropped it off an hour ago," V says, then leans back and folds her arms across her chest. I don't know who "that girl" is until I tear open the envelope and dump out a reel of eight-millimeter film.

"Lucy Garrett was here?"

"In the flesh," V says before getting to her feet and leaving the room.

CHAPTER FORTY-ONE

It's worse than I thought. I'm prepared to see Garrett cavorting with girls his daughter's age, but he must be behind the camera. Instead, a sweaty, overweight guy in his sixties with a florid face and a bulbous nose is raping a girl who can't be older than fifteen. I recognize him too. Josiah Sloane is a New York State Supreme Court justice. He's known without affection as "Hanging Joe" and has a reputation for dishing out death sentences with relish. Hypocrisy is a coin of the realm in the upper echelons of the city, but I thought even a scumbag like Judge Sloane would draw the line at something like this.

The girl is screaming, "No! Please stop! I don't want this!" but Sloane doesn't care. He flips her onto her back, takes her that way, and when he's through, walks out of the room, leaving the poor kid staring blankly at the ceiling and that's how the film ends.

I sit in the dark for a few minutes, horrified and angry. I want to tell the world what a sick perverted pig Sloane is and realize that's precisely Garrett's point. If he slips a copy of the film to a reporter for one of the tabloids or exposes it in some other way, Sloane is ruined. I'm sure Garrett told him as much, probably even let him have a peek at the movie. Garrett owns Sloane now, and I'll bet Hanging Joe isn't the only one he owns. He isn't above indulging in the same disgusting behavior himself, but that's not Garrett's real game. Blackmail is. Lucy knows that it is too. She's been feeding me the films selectively not only to tell me what her father's up to but what she's up against. And she's holding back the bulk of the films until she judges the time is right to get her own back and finally make her old man pay.

V comes into the room. She flips on the light and flops down onto the couch next to me. "Are you all right?"

I'm not all right. In my line of work, sometimes I see the absolute worst in people. It's supposed to make me hard and cynical, but that's just a Hollywood fantasy. I'd have to be dead inside not to let something like this get to me. I must look pretty grim too because V changes her position on the couch, lays my head in her lap, and strokes my hair. Her touch is cool and comforting, and we stay that way without another word.

After a while, V dozes off, but I'm still wide awake. It's past three in the morning now, and the last thing I expect is another knock at my door. Burton's dead, but whoever this is can't be anyone I want to see. I get to my feet, careful not to wake V, grab my gun, go to the door, and call out, "Who is it?"

"We need to talk, Jack." That's Jimmy Mullen.

"About what, Jimmy?"

"C'mon, Jack, it's late and I'm tired. Don't leave me standing out here in the hall."

I move to the side of the door in case Mullen decides to bull-rush me when I open it and raise my gun to what I judge to be level with his temples. I slide back the door's deadbolt, and when Jimmy crosses my threshold, I press the barrel of my gun against the side of his head.

"There's no need for that," he says, raising his hands. But I'm not so sure. I reach into his jacket, take his service revolver out of his shoulder holster, and grab the .32 strapped to his ankle.

The commotion wakes V, and when I walk Mullen into the room at gunpoint, she sits up and says, "Officer Mullen. We've been here before, haven't we?"

Jimmy spits, "Detective Mullen," at V like it makes any difference to her, and when I point to a chair, he sits.

I stay on my feet and hold my gun on him in a casual way that still lets him know I'll use it if I have to. He takes a pack of Luckys out of his jacket pocket and asks whether we mind if he smokes.

V tells him that she does, just to annoy him, but Mullen lights up anyway and asks, "How much will it take for you to drop the whole business, Jack—the movies, the girl, all of it?"

"You know, you're not the first person to ask me that, Jimmy."

"How about a hundred grand?" he says. "A hundred on the condition you help me find the kid and bring her and the movies back to her old man."

"Then what happens?"

"Then what happens is none of your business."

"The answer is no," V barks at him. Mullen could have offered me ten times as much and she would have shouted the same thing, but he ignores her. My impulse is to back up V and tell Mullen to go to hell, but if I'm going to stop Garrett and guys like Judge Sloane from molesting children, the smart thing to do now is see where this game leads.

But the look on my face must give away how I really feel because Mullen says, "What? You're too offended to take the man's money? Plenty of other guys do the same sick shit he does, which you already know, so spare me the 'I'm shocked and appalled' act."

V expects me to unload on Mullen for the crack, but I don't. This isn't about staking a claim to the moral high ground. It's about cat and mouse. Garrett might let me walk away with his money in exchange for Lucy and his movies, or he might have Mullen put me in the ground once I've delivered them. I have no intention of swapping either one with Garrett, but Mullen doesn't have to know that. More importantly, I'm not sure how I'm going to work what Mullen's telling me to my advantage yet, so I stall for time.

"Let me think about it, Jimmy," I tell him, but I must not sound too convincing.

"How about I give you ten seconds to give me an answer?"

Mullen can get as chesty with me as he likes, but I've got his guns, so it doesn't much matter. I suppose the plainclothes cop I spotted in the street could be out in the hall waiting to see if Mullen needs him, but he'd have to take out V along with me, and Garrett can't want that. The tabloids would have the same field day they would if he iced Bud. They and city hall would lean hard on the department to find out who did it and bring them in in a hurry. It's a headache Garrett doesn't need, but Mullen might not be smart enough to realize that, so I say, "I know you think your boy outside the door evens the odds, Jimmy, but if I hear so much as a floorboard creak out there, the first thing I'm going to do is put a bullet in your head."

Mullen's trying to decide whether I'm serious. He is a cop, and if I shoot him, the department will come down on me like a ton of bricks. But he did bust into my apartment in the middle of the night, so self-defense is a pretty solid plea. And if the guy out in the hall hears the shot and blows through the door, I should be able to take him out before he gets too far.

Jimmy must be figuring the same thing because he says, "Okay, I'll play it your way. But if I don't hear back from you soon, soon like by tomorrow, end of day, I'm gonna make what's left of your life a misery." He gets to his feet.

I take a step back but keep my gun on him as he moves toward the door.

"To hell with this guy," he calls to the cop in the hall, "let's get out of here." A few seconds later, Mullen and his pal are gone.

"Jimmy Mullen is on Garrett's payroll, that we know, but it goes up a lot higher than him," Bernie tells me. We're meeting at the Cloisters in Fort Tryon Park late the next afternoon. I've decided to take my chances and ignore Mullen's deadline. I don't figure he's bluffing, but Jimmy's pretty clumsy and I'm betting I can see him coming if he guns for me. Anyway, I don't have either Lucy or her daddy's dirty movies, and I don't know where they are.

The Cloisters is an odd sort of place, a museum meant to look medieval. It features sculptures, paintings, and tapestries dating back to that time, and not the sort of place thugs or cops on the take are likely to hang out. We're sitting on a stone bench in one of the museum's gardens. There are a couple of other people around, tourists most likely, but otherwise we're alone.

"How high is higher?" I ask Bernie.

"There's a commander downtown who owns a horse farm upstate that he can't possibly afford. And another with a place in Westchester and a beach house down the Jersey Shore. They may not be the only ones in Garrett's pocket, but they're enough to make sure nobody looks at him too closely."

"So, what are you saying, he's untouchable?"

"No. I'm not saying that. But we'd better come up with something rock solid—I'm talking indisputable evidence—or they'll make sure he walks away."

I tell Bernie about the film Lucy dropped off at my apartment, but Garrett doesn't actually appear in it, so it proves nothing. I could use the film to send Josiah Sloane to the penitentiary, which would do my heart good, but he's not who I'm really after, not at the moment anyway.

"You're not going to like hearing this," Bernie says, staring at his shoes, "but I think we're way in over our heads, Jack. Unless we catch Garrett in the act, you know, with his pants down and his *shvantz* out doing a kid, we're never going to be able to put him away."

I suspect that's what Lucy has on film, but I don't know for sure. But whatever does come next, I don't think Bernie wants to be a part of it.

"Is this your way of telling me I'm on my own?"

"Don't get me wrong, Jack. There's nothing I'd like better than to see Garrett in cuffs, but I just don't think that's going to happen. Even if his kid has him on film, he'll put in the fix somehow, come away clean, and we'll be left standing around with our dicks in our hands."

I can't blame Bernie. He's got a wife and kids, and he's right about his pension being on the line. He's already crossed Jimmy Mullen, and that's bound to cause him trouble. Anyway, he doesn't really have a dog in this hunt. I guess I don't really either, but I'm not about to back down now, not after what I've seen. I don't have a family to protect, but there is V. That face of hers is as recognizable as can be, but that doesn't make her immune. I guess I could get hold of Dick Avedon and ask him to get her out of town on some pretext. It's a favor he'd probably do for me even if I told him that I couldn't explain why I needed him to.

"I get it," I tell Bernie. "And no hard feelings. I appreciate everything you've done."

"I hate leaving you high and dry like this, Jack, but I don't see another way."

Bernie may be a pain in the ass, but he's a solid citizen. I've given him a lot of grief in the past and enjoyed doing it, but he's a stand-up guy. And he probably wouldn't bail on me if I asked him not to, but that's not right either. We get to our feet, shake hands, and Bernie wishes me luck before moving off and leaving me alone.

CHAPTER FORTY-TWO

I don't know how the kid does it. Lucy either knows my routine like the back of her hand or she's paying someone to follow me. I grab a bialy and a black coffee at my usual place on Varick, then start to make my way into the office. Before I know it, Lucy Garrett is walking alongside me, like it's the most natural thing in the world.

"So, what did you think?" she asks.

I assume she's talking about the movie she left at my apartment, but somehow I don't think she's really interested in a review.

"You know everybody and their brother is out looking for you?" Of course, I've been looking for her too, but that seems obvious and hardly worth mentioning.

"It's nice to be popular," she says with a smile. Lucy's under the impression that she's untouchable. She's wrong, which could be fatal. But I envy her: I wish I could walk through life that obliviously.

"I don't think you're very popular with your father just at the moment."

"No, I suppose not. He wants you dead, you know?"

"And you left me for dead in that warehouse. Wishing me gone must run in the family."

"That's not true. I untied you, and who do you think called the ambulance when you were all bloody and unconscious? Plus, I shot Burton—I did it for you, you know? Anyway, he deserved it."

It's hard to argue the morality of blowing Burton the butler's head off when it was done to save your life.

"You know, now that I think about it, you owe me, Jack."

She's right. I'm beginning to like this kid, despite her nutsy antics. But the thing I need Lucy to do now is hand over the rest of those movies so I can take them to the DA and put away her father. And as if she's reading my mind, she reaches into her purse and hands me another film canister.

"I think you're really going to like this one," she says, then steps into the street and hails a cab.

"Lucy, wait!" I yell after her, but she doesn't.

Instead, she grins at me and blows me a kiss from the back seat of the cab as it drives off.

It doesn't seem possible, but this one is worse than the last. It features two middle-aged guys gang-raping Muffy Palmer. Again, I recognize one of them. Gino Carlucci is a city councilman from Brooklyn and a bigwig at Tammany Hall. The other guy looks like a well-heeled WASP. He probably has a manse up in Scarsdale or one of those lily-white towns on the North Shore. Poor Muffy is hysterical and writhing around, trying to break free, but they're holding her fast and won't let her go.

"For God's sake, turn it off, Jack," Janie pleads with me.

She borrowed an old Bell and Howell projector from Nat, and we're watching the film together in my office. I tried to warn her beforehand, saying that what she was about to see might be too much for her, but Janie said that after working for me, nothing much shocks her.

But this movie did, and I've had enough of it too, so I switch off the projector.

The phone rings. Janie is too upset to answer, so I reach for it. It's Bernie Rothstein.

"I thought you were content to ride your desk until you put in your twenty," I say, meaning it as a good-natured dig, but Bernie's got something serious on his mind.

"Meet me at the Long Island Rail Road station in Jamaica, Queens. There's something I want to show you."

"It's Jimmy Mullen," I say when Bernie peels back the blood-soaked sheet covering a corpse.

"A transit worker found him at the mouth of a tunnel leading to Penn Station. And he didn't get this way being hit by a train, not while he was alive anyway. Somebody put one in the back of his skull, then dumped him here."

If a cop is murdered in this city, even a dirty one like Jimmy Mullen, the department will move heaven and earth to find out who did it and bring him in. They're not going to be gentle about it either. They'll tune him up within an inch of his life and claim he walked into a door when they haul his ass into court for arraignment. The judge will turn a blind eye and whoever the poor bastard is will be lucky to survive long enough to get the chair.

As if to prove my point, a dozen squad cars are parked at the scene with their lights flashing, an expanded forensic unit is dusting for prints and searching for clues, and a team of detectives is interviewing possible witnesses. I assume they've brought Bernie in because he and Mullen were partners, and I'm sure Bernie and I have the same thought: this must be connected to Garrett.

But Mullen was Garrett's boy, so he probably didn't order the hit.

"Who then?" Bernie wants to know, and so do I.

"Unless Jimmy crossed his boss, I don't have a clue."

"What about the girl?"

Lucy is reckless and arrogant, but she didn't murder Jimmy Mullen. Burton was a one-off. She did him to protect me.

"No. It can't be Lucy," I tell Bernie. "Jimmy was a big guy, six feet and two hundred pounds at least. Lucy Garrett is a slip of a girl. She couldn't drag his dead weight ten feet, much less haul it into a train tunnel and leave it on the tracks so the seven fifteen from Manhasset could cut it to ribbons."

"Maybe there's another player we don't know about," Bernie says.

"I mean, you've gotta have big brass ones to hit a New York City homicide detective."

"And deep pockets too. Something like this has got to cost what? Fifty grand?"

"More than that," Bernie says.

"Maybe Garrett hasn't been sharing the wealth with the boys from Delancey Street," I say.

"Delancey Street? I don't get it."

I haven't filled him in on Garrett's connection to Meyer, Bugsy, and the rest of the boys, but I do now. He's trying not to show it, but I can tell Bernie's surprised. Like me when I first met him, he thought Garrett was old money, not a murderous delinquent born in a tenement on the Lower East Side.

"So, let me get this straight. You think Garrett's in bed with Lansky?"

"There isn't a shady financial pie Meyer doesn't have his fingers in, so I'd say yes."

"Then why hit Mullen?"

I don't have an answer. The hit could be meant as an object lesson— that or a warning. It would have been a lot easier just to kill Garrett if he's been stealing, but Meyer's sentimental.

It wasn't that long ago that Luciano wanted Ben Siegel dead. Meyer protected him until Bugsy skimmed so much mob money building the Flamingo in Vegas that he had to be taught a lesson. I'm sure Garrett remembers that, and if he doesn't, Mullen's corpse is a powerful reminder. I'd ask Carmine if that's what really happened if I knew where the hell Carmine was.

"I know I told you I was through with this business," Bernie says to me in case I'm wondering, "and I meant it. But the brass wants me to take the lead on Mullen, which puts me in a tough spot. If I try to beg off, the boys downtown will want an explanation, a convincing one too considering Jimmy was my partner, and I don't want to open that can of worms by telling them the truth. IAB will get involved if I do, meaning everybody in the department will want to hang my ass out to dry, and I don't need that kind of tsores."

"Then how do you want to play it?"

"I already talked to the chief of d's, but it's gonna be an all-hands-on-deck kind of deal with downtown looking over my shoulder, so let me worry about who did it. You find out why."

With Carmine in the wind, that's not going to be easy. There is somebody who might know, but the idea of spending even five minutes with the guy turns my stomach.

Walter Winchell is a gossip columnist, a radio and television personality, and a lying, red-baiting piece of garbage. In his heyday he ruined any number of people by insinuating they were Communists or homosexual, or just because they looked at him cockeyed. The good news is his heyday is just about over, but he's still holding court at his usual table in the Cub Room over at the Stork Club.

Also, Winchell still has impeccable mob connections. Back in the thirties, he was a bosom buddy of Owney Madden's, a murderous Irish gangster and later he was the one who turned Louis "Lepke" Buchalter, once an upstanding member of Murder, Inc., over to J. Edgar Hoover and the FBI.

I know this scumbag because he leches after V whenever he sees her. Neither of us can stand him, but V gets all dolled up, I put on my suit, and we go over to the Stork to see if we can get him to spill what he knows.

Naturally, heads turn when V walks into the room, and Winchell jumps to his feet the second he sees us coming. He goes all courtly, kissing V's hand and ushering her into a seat. He ignores me completely, but that's all right because V and I have agreed that she should do most of the talking. If Winchell really does know anything, he's likely to show off by blabbing it to her.

V flatters him shamelessly, telling Winchell how young and virile he looks. This is a bald-faced lie. The guy's face is beet red and glistening with sweat. He's morbidly obese, has hair sprouting out of his ears, and looks like he's about to keel over. But Winchell is such a buffoon that he believes every word of it, and he keeps putting his hand on V's knee as if pawing her is going to get him laid.

I don't know how she puts up with it. I'm ready to punch the guy in the face, but pretty soon V's got him telling stories about the mobsters he's known, and when she steers the conversation around to Meyer and Garrett, Winchell can't stop mouthing off.

"I've known Meyer since he was a *pisher*," he says to V. "I'm talking back in the days of the Purple Gang. Hell, I knew Lansky and Ben Siegel were gonna hit the Mustache Petes for Lucky even before it happened, but I kept my mouth shut. Not because I was afraid, you understand. They're my *landsman*, you know what I'm saying?" V smiles but has no idea what Winchell is talking about. "*Landsman!* Jews!" he bellows, then lowers his voice like he's conspiring with V, "Let me tell you something, sweetheart, I'd have sooner let out a fart in synagogue on Yom Kippur, the holiest of all days, than let the Feds in on what I knew."

Cut through the idiot bravado and this is still a lie. Luciano would have opened Lansky's throat if he told Winchell about those hits before they happened. He would have opened Winchell's too, but the asshat is enjoying himself, so instead of busting his lie, I let it go.

"Now, let me tell you something about Abie Gotbaum, a.k.a. Lou Garrett," he says to V. "His business looks legit, but it's a front. Meyer launders his millions through it and has been for years. Abie takes his cut and everyone goes home happy."

When V gently suggests that maybe that's changed, that maybe Garrett has his hand in Meyer's till, Winchell is horrified, or at least pretends to be.

"I'm sorry, but you don't know what you're talking about, sweetheart, you really don't. Abie Gotbaum and Meyer Lansky go back too far to pick each other's pockets." Then he adds, "Honor amongst thieves, lover," and grins.

V has enough self-control not to retch at being called "sweetheart" and "lover," and I don't vomit because Winchell has just told me something that I didn't know. If Lansky and Garrett really are in business together, the implications go way beyond Lucy Garrett's issues with her father.

"Did you hear about the cop they found dead over in Queens?" I say, deciding it's time we get around to the point of the evening.

"Did I hear about it!" Winchell shouts at me like I'm from out of town. "Don't you read my column? I got the details straight from the horse's mouth!"

When V asks him who that horse might be, he tells her that no self-respecting reporter reveals his sources. "A self-respecting reporter" is the last thing in the world that Walter Winchell is, which makes me think he might be full of shit. But if he isn't, there's a lot more going on here than Louis Garrett using homemade pornographic movies to blackmail the local aristocracy, more even than sex abuse. He's in thick with Lansky and the mob, which just made this case even more complicated.

CHAPTER FORTY-THREE

If there's one thing I learned growing up in Hell's Kitchen, it's that you don't get between hard guys who hate each other, particularly when they're armed. What you do is go home, eat the stuffed cabbage your mother made you for dinner, listen to the radio or maybe read a book, and wait for the smoke to clear. I say this to V over drinks in the Oak Room. We've walked over here after our encounter with Winchell and are holding a postmortem at a table in a corner of the bar.

"You know, Jack, if Garrett really is stealing from Lansky," V says, "we could just wait until Meyer—"

"Has somebody put a bullet in his brain?" Actually, this isn't necessarily a bad idea. It takes care of one problem, namely what to do about Garrett, and probably gets us out of harm's way. It's an idea with flaws, though. For one thing, I don't know whether Garrett really is stealing from Lansky. It was a guess when I said it to Bernie, and as much as I hate to admit it, Winchell might be right. The two of them may go back too far for Garrett to pull a stunt like that.

"Okay. Let's say Garrett's laundering Lansky's cash for a percentage of the action," I tell V. "And let's say the vig is three or four points. That comes to a hell of a lot of money, V, eight figures at least."

"Then why steal from him?"

"Maybe he isn't. Maybe he's playing it straight with Meyer. Maybe blackmail is a sideline, a way for Garrett to make the Harvard club types eat a little dirt while he makes a lot of money off of them. Guys with those kinds of pedigrees would treat little Abie Gotbaum from Delancey Street like he doesn't exist, so he pretends to be somebody he isn't to get back at them. He lures them upstairs in the Beresford with the promise of some twisted fun, and the next thing they know, they're captured on film and paying Garrett through the nose to keep him quiet."

"Then who killed Jimmy Mullen?"

"I don't know, but I don't think it was a mob hit."

That night, after we get home and turn in, I dream about a guy I knew in the service. He joined our unit in Belgium, and despite being a cracker from Louisiana, we got along pretty well, though my being a half-Jew threw him a bit. He said they told him in church back home that Jews had horns. He even had a picture of a guy with a long beard and a hook nose who had goat horns sprouting out of his forehead. I told him that's what the guys with the swastikas thought, and I even let him get a good feel of my scalp to prove that it wasn't true.

He and the rest of us are slogging our way through the Hürtgen Forest when a round from a German mortar blows the guy's head clean off. He's standing not ten feet away from me when it happens, splattering me with his brains.

I've never gotten over it. It still shakes me, and I pour sweat whenever I dream about it, which is pretty often. It scares poor V half to death when I wake up howling, and she tries her best to comfort me, but I'm not any good to her the next day and sometimes for longer than that.

Anyway, I'm dreaming about the guy again when the phone rings and blasts me awake. It's Carmine, who I haven't heard from in over a month, and he doesn't sound happy.

"The Chin wants to see you, Jack," he says. "You'd better get over here as soon as you can." By over here, I assume he means the Triangle. I guess the mob bosses have come to an agreement to end their little spat and Carmine has come up for air.

"It's three in the morning, Carmine. Tell him I'll stop in tomorrow."

"No, now, Jack. And do us both a favor. Behave yourself," he says before hanging up the phone.

Two of Gigante's boys meet me at the Triangle's door and pat me down. They don't go easy on me either. Ordinarily, I'd be packing when summoned like this, but I could tell by Carmine's tone that I'd better play it cool. They lead me to the back of the club where The Chin is sipping a double espresso and smoking a Winston. I pass by Carmine on the way, who doesn't say a word but shoots me a look that tells me this is serious and I'd better not screw around.

Gigante doesn't look up when his boys shove me into a seat, and I know enough to keep my mouth shut until he decides to speak.

"What's your beef with Garrett, asshole?" he says finally. I'm not called an asshole by a lot of guys, and sometimes it annoys me enough to do something about it. This, however, will not be the case with The Chin, mostly because if I do, I'm liable to end up dead.

"The guy molests kids," I say flatly. No further explanation seems necessary.

"So what?" The Chin says. Carmine did warn me that Gigante enjoys something close to the same thing, so I shut up again and wait to see what he'll say next. "Lay off him," Gigante says. "You get what I'm saying?"

I get exactly what he's saying, but I've been working this case too hard for too long to drop it just because some mobster orders me to. "I can't do that," I tell him.

Gigante looks at me like he can't believe what's just come out of my mouth. "You got a death wish or something, Coffey?"

"Look, Vincent"—I call him Vincent because calling him The Chin is liable to get me shot on the spot, and calling him Mr. Gigante would sound so obsequious that I can't bring myself to do it—"I get where this is coming from, and it's not like me to ignore a threat from a made guy like you, but Garrett has been doing some pretty despicable things to girls too young to understand what's happening to them and putting them in the ground if they make the mistake of getting in the way. I can't walk away from that."

"Then leave the kid out of it."

"Which kid?"

"Garrett's kid. She's all right, you know? Okay, she's got a screw loose, but you would too if you grew up with an old man like hers."

I didn't expect this. Omertà is the only ethical construct guys like The Chin normally abide by. I thought incest and child molestation were sins they were just as happy to forgive.

"I don't know nothin' about those other girls, but I do know Garrett's kid," Gigante says to me. "That bastard has been doing her since she was little, I'm talkin' five, six years old. Can you believe it? Her own father. That's enough to make anybody nuts, so leave her out of it."

He's absolutely right and I can't believe that it's taken Vincent "The Chin" Gigante to make me feel like a louse for ever treating Lucy Garrett like she's some kind of psycho teenage seductress. She told me her father was molesting her the first time I met her, but I'm such a schmuck that I thought it was just another part of her sex kitten act. I've been around the block more than once, but child abuse is something I haven't really run into before, so I was skeptical—a pathetic excuse. But V saw it almost right away because it's happened to her. I should have seen it too. Lucy playing at being shameless is just so much compensation. The kid is broken, maybe broken beyond repair, but for too long all I could see was a selfish young girl determined to get her own way. I'm not sure how I can forgive myself for that.

And what about her baby? When Monk spotted her, Lucy was close to her time. Garrett must have wanted her to get rid of it, and he has the money and connections to force her to, but she must have balked. I didn't think Lucy wanted the kid and was taking it to term as just another way to defy her father, but that take suddenly seems far too cold and cynical. She might have been traumatized by Garrett, permanently damaged and acting out behind it, but that doesn't mean she isn't capable of loving her own child. And someone must have helped her when her time did come, someone who's probably helping now.

"Listen to me, Coffey," Gigante says, but I'm so wrapped up in thinking about how badly I misjudged Lucy that I almost forget he's there. "It's not that I like Garrett. The shit he gets up to just doesn't go, not even with us. But word's come up from Miami Beach. You leave him alone until our friend down there decides what he wants to do. We clear on that?"

This is not an easy pill to swallow, but I tell The Chin that I get it and that I'll steer clear of Garrett until Meyer decides how he wants to handle him.

I stop in at an all-night coffee shop on Mulberry Street, order a cornetto and a cappuccino, and consider the irony. I started out on this job over a year ago looking for what I thought was a pillar of the city's financial community's errant daughter. Now, I'm thinking that I need to protect that daughter from her mobbed-up pedophile father. Of course, nobody is paying me to do that, and I could just step back and let Lansky deal with Garrett. My problem is that I'm not at all sure he's going to do anything more than give the guy a stern talking-to.

I promised The Chin that I'd leave Garrett alone and breaking that promise isn't a good idea. But he didn't say anything about looking for Lucy while Meyer makes up his mind.

CHAPTER FORTY-FOUR

Bob Carson has summoned me. The first time I met him, I thought he was a glad-handing toad. His concern for Lucy sounded phony and made me suspicious. When V and I ran into him and his wife at Toots Shor's, it was supposed to be a coincidence, but it didn't feel like one. He sat at our table without being invited and made a show of saying how impressed Garrett was with me, implying that I was about to become a rich man. I thought that was just so much grandstanding, and I was right. And again, he made a point of telling me how fond he was of Lucy, how they had been close since she was a little girl, but I didn't believe that either. Still, Carson was the first one to tell me Garrett was abusing his daughter, and that turned out to be true, so it's hard to tell whose side he's really on. I'm soaking in the tub with V, and when I say all of this to her, she says, "Wasn't he the one who tried to have you killed—twice?"

This is a good point. Carson just about admitted as much to me and laughed about it when he did. He said bribing me was easier than killing me and offered what I assume was going to be a ton of cash to step away from the case. I told him that I'd get back to him about the money, but I didn't, and I never heard about it from him again. The truth is I still don't really know what his angle is in all of this.

"Maybe he thought he was protecting Lucy when he sent those men after you," V says. "I mean, you were working for Garrett then and he seems to be the only one who genuinely cares about her."

Another good point. Lucy told me that she was sleeping with "Uncle Bob" and made him sound pathetic, like screwing him was a mercy, but that may just be a tale she likes to tell.

When I say this to V, she says, "Yeah, I think she was making it up. I think Lucy was showing off when she told you that."

"Then they weren't really having sex?"

"You mean was Carson really *molesting* Lucy? I think the answer is no. You know, Jack, to survive what happened to her, Lucy had to build a really hard defense, a shield that protects her from reliving that nightmare and makes the whole horrible thing bearable. She had to invent a story to tell herself, one that made sense to her or she was going to fall apart. I did the same thing. I told myself that I was strong enough not to let abuse ruin my life, that what happened to me wasn't my fault, that my father was a complete bastard, and that I would never speak to him again. Lucy's story is her father's abuse taught her sex is power and that she can twist any man around her little finger with just the promise of it. And do you know why she told herself that, what that gave back to her?"

"Control."

"That's right, control. Because along with her innocence and any feeling of security she might have had, that's what her father took away from her, control over her own life."

I'm walking down Eighth Avenue with V's words ringing in my ears. She knew there was more to Lucy than I did. I took her at face value. I should have known better.

I'm about to jump on the subway at Fourteenth Street when I hear somebody call my name. It's Richie Costello. The monsignor is waving me over from the back seat of a stretch limousine.

"Need a lift?" he says with a grin. I peek through the limo window and see His Eminence Cardinal Francis Joseph Spellman, the archbishop of New York, sitting next to Richie.

I don't like being ambushed, so I say, "Thanks, but I'd rather take the train," which I'm sure will annoy Costello, and it does.

"Just get in the car, Jack," Richie snaps at me, but I hesitate for a second or two because I'm enjoying seeing Costello sweat in front of his ecclesiastical boss.

The cardinal doesn't say anything when I finally climb into the limo. Instead, he holds out his ring for me to kiss. I just let his hand dangle there not only because I'm only half-Catholic and not a believer but because I know this is really a power move and I don't feel like giving in to it.

Spellman is a formidable guy, a big gruff Irishman who must have mixed it up some when he was a kid in Boston, but he's not a kid anymore. Now, he's not only risen to the top of the church's hierarchy but gone in for the finer things in life. The coat and scarf he's wearing are cashmere, and his cassock, complete with scarlet piping and sash, is expertly tailored. I can just picture a bevy of nuns losing their eyesight stitching it together.

"His Eminence has concerns," Richie says, like Spellman isn't going to deign to speak to somebody as lowly as me. "I asked you to do a favor for him, and it was good of you to oblige. While the cardinal is appreciative, he now feels that the matter is closed and that you should no longer pursue it."

"We're talking about Garrett, right?" I say this directly to Spellman because we both speak English and don't need Costello to translate.

"Mr. Garrett has asked me to intercede with you on his behalf," Spellman says in his best deadpan.

"So, what's the deal? Are you going to offer me eternal life if I back off?"

"Your sarcasm isn't appreciated, Mr. Coffey," says Spellman.

"You do know what Louis Garrett has been up to, don't you?"

"No, and I don't wish to know either."

This is perfect. The spiritual leader of six million Catholics in the greater metropolitan area is willing to ignore the fact that one of his major patrons is a serial pedophile and blackmailer as long as he continues to cross the cardinal's palm with silver.

"You know, I recently had a guy say the same thing to me," I tell Spellman. "Of course, he's a murderer and a career criminal, but maybe the difference between the two of you is just a matter of semantics."

The cardinal's face, which was florid when I got into the limousine, has now gone from beet red to vermilion. I don't think anybody has said anything that audacious to him in a long time, and it's gotten his Irish up.

"You know, I can make life quite difficult for you, Mr. Coffey."

"I'm sure you can, but you're not the first person to say that to me either, and the last guy who did was holding a gun on me at the time, so my answer is no dice." Spellman would smack me across the face for being insolent if he wasn't a man of the cloth. He might smack me anyway, but I decide I've had enough fun at his expense.

I tell him, "Look, Your Eminence, you've said what you needed to say. I'm sure you find this whole business as distasteful as I do. Why don't we just agree to disagree and leave it at that?"

"Then you're not going to let Mr. Garrett be?"

It's a question that doesn't deserve an answer, so I just smile, open the car door, and step back into the street.

I duck into the subway and take the train downtown to see Carson. I was surprised when he called, surprised that he didn't have one of his boys just show up, grab me by the collar, and haul me off. He said that he wanted to treat me to lunch in the private dining room adjacent to his office and that his chef will fix me anything that I like. I balk. I don't trust the guy, and if I'm going to break bread with him, it's going to be in someplace neutral and public. I told him to book a table at Fraunces Tavern on Pearl Street and hung up before he had a chance to give me an argument.

Fraunces Tavern has been around since before the Revolutionary War. It's the oldest restaurant in New York and was once George Washington's military headquarters. Now it's an expensive white-linen eatery on the corner of Pearl and Broad Streets, frequented by bankers, financiers, and other such fat cats. I don't think Carson is still interested in seeing me dead, but if he is, Fraunces Tavern is about the last place on earth he would have his boys carry out a hit.

Despite the time I wasted with the cardinal, I still get to the restaurant early and take a seat at the table Carson reserved with my back to the wall. The move is something of a cliché, but a useful one. I can't be taken unaware this way, as unlikely as that might be. Still, to be on the safe side, I steer clear of the windows in case somebody wants to take a crack at me from the street.

The maître d' fawns on Carson when he walks in. He slips the guy a twenty and claps him on the back like they're old friends. Carson has got a grin on his face as he approaches the table. He's also carrying a large bulky leather satchel. I don't stand, but I do shake his hand before he sits.

"Aren't we drinking?" he asks jovially, then motioning over a waiter, he orders a martini very cold and very dry like he's describing an ex-wife.

I order a Maker's Mark neat, and after the waiter takes off, I say, "Why am I here?" I don't feel like indulging Carson's fraudulent bonhomie a moment longer than I have to.

"I have something for you," he says and plunks the satchel down in the middle of the table. He holds it open so I can see that it contains canisters of 16 mm film. "I assume you'll take them to the DA," he says, pushing the satchel over to me. "That's been your plan all along, hasn't it?"

To say this strikes me as convenient is a rather large understatement. And I have questions. Assuming these are the dirty movies Garrett is using as blackmail, how did Carson get hold of them? Did Lucy give them to him, or did he take them from her? Loyalty is a fungible commodity with this crowd—meaning Lucy could have decided to throw in with Carson, but that doesn't seem too likely. If she wanted to take down her old man, she could have just given me the movies or brought them to the DA herself. Why use Bob as a middleman?

"What's in this for you, exactly?" I ask. Carson wouldn't be handing me Garrett on a platter if he didn't think he benefited somehow.

"I told you. I have a soft spot for the kid."

"Aren't you in business with Garrett?"

"There are some things more important than business, don't you think, Jack?"

"You mean like incest and child molestation?"

"You know, years ago when Lucy told me her father was touching her, I wasn't sure whether to believe her. The girl is precocious and likes to shock."

"But you believe her now."

Carson nods at the satchel, then, getting to his feet, adds, "When you speak to the District Attorney, I'd appreciate it if you'd keep my name out of it."

"Not a problem," I say. Of course, I'm lying, something I'm sure Carson knows.

"Good. And order anything you like. I've already taken care of the bill." And with that, he turns and heads for the door.

CHAPTER FORTY-FIVE

I feel like I'm being played. I don't know why; I got what I wanted. Now it's just a matter of turning Garrett's movies over to the DA and getting on with my life. That's what I'm thinking sitting on the subway with Carson's satchel at my feet, but instead of getting off when the train stops at Fourteenth Street, I ride it up to Midtown.

I'm pretty soggy from lunch—more than one Maker's Mark will do that to you—but I'm going to kill another hour or two with Kevin O'Doul. I stop by his joint every once in a while, touching base with him and the old neighborhood when something has gotten under my skin. It isn't that the folks who still live in Hell's Kitchen are the salt of the earth because they're not. Mostly they're poor and lumpen with any number of liars, thieves, and sociopaths thrown in for good measure. Still, it's a place where I can get my bearings, so despite it being the time in the afternoon when any self-respecting working stiff is back on the job, I stop in at O'Doul's.

The usual rummies are in evidence, lingering over the one shot of rye they can afford. The ball game is blaring from the TV Kevin mounted above the bar. The Giants and Dodgers left town last year, which caused a lot of garment rending out in the boroughs, but nobody here gives a rat's ass. They all root for the Yankees.

Mel Allen is hawking Ballantine beer between innings, which is Kevin's cue to turn around and see who came in his door. When it turns out to be me, he grins and asks, "Maker's, right?"

I appreciate that he knows my poison of choice, but I'm still reeling from lunch, so I tell him a bottle of seltzer and grab a handful of beer nuts from a wooden bowl on the bar.

He pops open the bottle with a church key and plunks it down in front of me. "What do you got in the bag?" he asks, meaning the satchel.

"Dirty movies," I tell him, but he doesn't believe me, so rather than explain, I change the subject. "Do you ever hear from Bridget Moran?"

"Dead," Kevin says like he's swatting a fly, and when I ask how it happened, he says, "Smack," just as plainly. "She passed six months ago. I let Jerry hold the wake here. I mean, it's not like he could afford a funeral home, and I ponied up for the burial too."

"That was real good of you, Kev."

"The decent thing to do, Jack. I've known Bridget since she was a kid. I wasn't going to let her go to that great beyond without a send-off." This is what I like about Kevin, what I've always liked about him. Taking over his father's bar might not have been what he had in mind for himself when he graduated from Cardinal Hayes, but now that he's here, he goes out of his way to look after the locals, does it as best he can anyway. And to tell you the truth, I'm a little ashamed of myself. I left Bridget out on the street last winter. I knew she was hurting, but besides giving her a few dollars, I didn't really do anything to help her out.

I feel bad about it now, and I'm about to tell Kevin when he says, "Bridget had this really big crush on you, you know?"

I remember Bridget following me around when we were kids. She was a buddy's little sister so I was nice, but I also remember shooing her away when she got on my nerves. Now that I think about it, it a was pretty lousy thing to do. Bridget's ma wasn't the only rummy in the family. Her old man was a drunk too and a mean one. And Jerry wasn't the only one he knocked around. Sometimes, Bridget would turn up with a shiner or a split lip. How that happened was no mystery. He might have been molesting her too, but I never said anything, which is probably why what's happening to Lucy Garrett has gotten so deep under my skin.

"Bridge thought the biggest mistake she ever made was not getting you to knock her up," Kevin tells me. "She said it would've changed her life."

It would have changed mine too, though not in the way she thought. I always liked Bridget, but I couldn't have saved her, not from herself.

The bell above the bar door sounds. Kevin and I turn, and I just about fall off my barstool when V walks in.

"There you are," she says like I'm a lost kid. "She called."

"Who?"

"Lucy Garrett, and she sounded terrified."

She didn't leave V a number, just a time and a place to meet. V could tell she was in trouble, but Lucy wouldn't say what the trouble was over the phone. V scribbled down the address on a scrap of paper and, handing it to me now, says, "She wants you to meet her there at midnight and said to make sure you're not late. She doesn't feel safe out on the street alone."

This smells rotten to me. Either she was putting on an act for V's benefit or Lucy really is frightened of something—more likely of somebody.

V wants to know what I'm going to do, and when I tell her that I don't know, I mean it. I have the evidence I need to put Garrett away and that should be enough to put the whole business to rest. And as much as I sympathize, I'm not sure Lucy can be trusted. Playing at being her white knight is plenty dangerous, but I have a nasty habit of listening to my better angels and I'm genuinely curious. There are people who would be happy to see her dead, maybe including her own father. And after what Kevin just told me about Bridget Moran, I'm not sure I could forgive myself if I did nothing and Lucy shared the same fate.

"Lucy she said she wants you to bring them with you. I don't know what that meant, but she was pretty insistent."

She meant Garrett's movies.

"Listen," I say to V, "there are a couple of things I need to do before I meet her, so why don't you go on home and wait for me there?"

"No. I'm not going to sit in the apartment like some mousy little housewife and worry that you're lying dead somewhere." V sets her jaw when she says this, letting me know that she won't brook an argument, that nothing I say is going to change her mind, but I try anyway. I tell her the meet is liable to turn murderous, that I don't know what Lucy wants or what the lay of the land is, and that the whole thing might be a setup.

V isn't buying any of it, so I put my foot down.

"You're not coming with me, V, and that's the end of it."

"Listen, Ace"—V calls me Ace whenever she's furious with me—"I don't need you to look after me. I can take care of myself."

"No, you can't, and I'm not going to let you get killed just to prove I'm right."

"Do you know what, Jack? Fuck you. I mean it. Fuck you!" And V gives me the finger for good measure before storming out of the bar.

When she's gone, Kevin whistles and says, "She's really something, isn't she?" and I have to agree.

I walk over and take a look at the address on West Fifty-Sixth Street Lucy gave V. I recognize the building. It's an old tenement that was packed five to a room when I was a kid. It was dilapidated even then, and after evicting their tenants, the owners hired Tommy O'Connor, a local firebug, to torch the place for the insurance money. Nobody has lived there since, and the building is still burned out and looks about to collapse. There are any number of places to hide both inside and out, and I decide I need more firepower before meeting Lucy.

I head over to Carmine's apartment in Brooklyn to see if he can help out, but he's not home. His wife, Estelle, tells me Carmine is where he always is on warm spring nights, fishing off the Sheepshead Bay Pier, so I hoof it over there.

"Catch anything?" I call out, and without turning around, Carmine takes a striped bass the size of a small dog out of a bucket and holds it up for me to see. "It's yours if you want it. I got a ton of them in the freezer. Estelle'll have my head if I bring another one home."

"Fish gives me hives," I say and lean up against the pier railing like I'm taking in the view.

Before I get a chance to tell Carmine why I'm here, he says, "The answer is no."

"You don't know the question yet."

"Yeah, I do. You want to know whether we've heard from our friend in Florida, and like I said, the answer is no. Meyer takes his time about these things, so you're just gonna have to wait." I don't say anything, but it doesn't take Carmine long to figure out what I'm up to. "You're gonna blow him off and turn Garrett over to the cops, aren't you, Jack? In my personal opinion, this is a bad idea."

"You're probably right, but I'm going to do it anyway."

"Then why don't you just tell me what you want."

"C'mon, Carmine, work with me here. You know how this kind of thing goes."

"We're talking guns."

"We're definitely talking guns, and something a lot heavier than the automatic I'm packing."

Carmine thinks this over for a second or two, then says, "Yeah, okay. But do me a favor, will ya, buddy? When this is over, forget you know me."

Carmine owns a half-dozen semidetached houses in Bay Ridge and rents all but one of them out. The one he keeps for himself is used for a host of nefarious purposes. It's got a panoramic view of the street, so it must have been where Carmine and the boys holed up during the recent mob unpleasantness. It's also a handy place to keep a stiff on ice until it's safe to dump it out in the Meadowlands. And it serves as a low-rent love nest when Carmine is in the mood for a quick *schtup*, but I don't think that happens much anymore. Prostate problems apparently. Carmine told me he hasn't taken a decent piss in years.

The garage is around the back, and the inside looks like an armory. Weapons of all sorts and calibers are mounted on the walls or packed in grease in their original crates. There are M5s and M15s, .50-cal machine guns, military-grade sidearms, a box of fragmentation grenades, even a bazooka.

"What're you looking for?" Carmine asks, like he's running a sale and I have to think about it. If somebody comes for me, they'll be carrying something like a Thompson, so I take a Browning automatic rifle down from one of the racks.

"You're gonna want these too," Carmine says, handing me a couple of thirty-round banana clips. I also grab a military-style .45 modified to full auto and jam it into my waistband.

"You sure you want to do this?" Carmine asks. "If Garrett's sending people after you, they're gonna be good."

I tell him that I'm sure. I tell him that Lucy wants the movies back so she can return them to her father. Otherwise, Garrett's going to kill her.

"Her own father?"

"I can't let that happen, Carmine. I can't let him hurt his kid, not again."

"Yeah. Okay. I get it. Your funeral, Jack." When I glare at him, he adds, "It's a figure of speech," and rolls down the garage door.

CHAPTER FORTY-SIX

I've been standing in the doorway of an abandoned shoe repair shop since a quarter to eleven. I'm watching the tenement where I'm supposed to meet Lucy from across the street, but no one has gone in or out of the building, not as far as I can tell anyway. It's obvious the idea to meet here wasn't hers, which doesn't mean she isn't in on whatever comes next. I'm not new to this game, so I'm going to stay right where I am until I see if she or anyone else turns up.

I don't have to wait long. Around eleven thirty Garrett's limo cruises down Fifty-Sixth Street, followed by the panel van that spirited me off a few weeks ago. The two cars make a left onto Tenth Avenue.

Bob Carson's Cadillac Fleetwood appears a few minutes later and pulls to the curb in front of the tenement. He also has help. His guys spill out of a Chevy station wagon, and along with Carson and his driver, they all disappear into the building.

The odds of me surviving an encounter with these hitters are exceedingly long, so I stay put. And it doesn't take but a minute or two before Garrett's boys steal around the corner and creep up on the tenement. They have guns drawn—handguns, sawed-off shotguns, and just as I suspected, two of them are carrying Thompson submachine guns.

I can't be the object of all of this. I'm pretty good at what I do, but it doesn't require a small army to take me down. And whoever leaned on

Lucy to arrange this meet can't possibly believe that I'm stupid enough to bring Garrett's movies with me to an abandoned tenement in the middle of the night. No, I'm just the icing on the cake. This is about Garrett and Carson having it out once and for all.

I feel like I have a ringside seat on what's about to happen, so I'm content to stand in the shadows and wait for the action to unfold. What I don't count on is Lucy Garrett's sudden appearance.

Even before I see her, I can hear her high heels clacking against the sidewalk as she hustles down Fifty-Sixth Street. I didn't think she'd actually show, despite her call to V, but here she is: nervous, walking fast, and constantly glancing behind her to see if anyone is following.

"Lucy!" I hiss as loud as I dare, but she doesn't hear me. Instead, she makes a beeline for the tenement, and I have no choice. I unstrap the Browning, snatch the .45 I cadged from Carmine's garage out of my waistband, and dash out into the street.

"Lucy," I hiss louder this time.

When she spots me, she shouts, "There you are!"

I can't have much time, so I grab her by the arm, bark, "C'mon let's go," and try to hustle her off the street before the shooting starts, but she doesn't make it easy.

She rips her arm free and bellows, "I want those movies, Jack!" She pulls a .22 Ruger out of her purse and aims it at my head in case I miss her point.

Not only is Lucy armed, but her voice is echoing off the tenement, and she's standing in a pool of light from a streetlamp.

"You've got to let me handle this, Lucy."

"I mean it, Jack. I want those movies. He's going to kill me if I don't give them back!" She cocks the Ruger's hammer.

"Okay, but I'll tell you what. Come down to the Village with me and I'll give them to you there. How does that sound?"

"No! I want them right now!"

"I don't have them on me, Lucy. Just come downtown with me and I'll hand them over. I promise."

I still half-expect her to take a shot at me, but instead she sits in a cross-legged heap on the pavement and buries her face in her hands. She's a pretty good little actress, but those tears are real, so I squat down next to her and lay a hand on her knee.

"I know I've been really bad," she confesses, "but it's not my fault. And now everything's ruined. What am I going to do? What's going to happen to me?" Lucy's shoulders begin to shake, and when I put my arm around her, her tears come on.

"I'm going to make your father burn for what he did to you," I tell her, and I mean it. "I'm going to make sure they lock him up and throw away the key, but what we need to do right now is get out of here. You were right when you told V you weren't safe. Neither of us are. So for now forget about the movies. Forget about your old man and the terrible things he did. Forget about all of it and just come with me."

Lucy wipes at her tears with the heel of her hand and she's letting me help her to her feet when I hear V call out, "Lucy? Lucy, is that you?" and my heart sinks.

She comes striding down the street big as life, ignoring the warning I gave her in O'Doul's and oblivious to the danger.

"V, get off the street!" I shout, but she walks right past me and takes Lucy in her arms.

The kid sags against her. They're both victims, both scarred by their fathers' abuse and still suffering from it, but as horrible as that is, this is no time to commiserate. This is the time to run, and as if to prove my point, gunfire crackles from the tenement.

I heave V to the pavement, throw myself on top of her, and return fire. Tracers from the Browning light up the tenement's entryway, and whoever's shooting at us ducks for cover.

"Are you okay?"

Ever the smart-ass, V says, "I will be as soon as you get off me," and I'm about to ask Lucy the same thing, but she's far from okay.

She's taken three in the chest, there's blood everywhere, and now V is crouching over her with a ghastly look on her face, desperately trying to stanch the bleeding with her bare hands.

It's pointless. Lucy's gone.

I lose it. My brain begins to sizzle and bile rises in my throat. I wheel and open fire again, emptying a thirty-round banana clip. I see two guys go down and what I really want to do is reload, charge over there, and make sure they're both dead, but I don't. I catch my breath, and my head clears enough to realize that V and I are still easy targets.

"C'mon, we've got to go," I shout at V.

But V's frozen, too undone to move. I have to do something or we're both dead, so I snatch her off her feet and carry her off the street just as gunfire erupts again.

But this barrage isn't coming in our direction. Muzzle flashes light up the tenement windows. Garrett's and Carson's guys are going at it, which gives me enough time to dart down the alley between the tenement and the building next to it.

I sprint out onto a garbage-strewn vacant lot and put V down as gently as I can. We're crouched behind the rusting hulk of an abandoned car. V is trembling and her blood-soaked hands are shaking.

"She's dead, Jack," she says as if she can't believe it, and when I don't answer, she throws her arms around me.

Every cell in my body is screaming at me to do whatever I have to do to make V safe, but I can't—not now. "V. I need you to listen to me. Do you think you can do that?" When V manages to nod, I say, "Okay, here's what you're going to do. You're going to sit tight here until the shooting stops. When it does, you'll make your way up to Ninth Avenue. There's a phone booth on the corner of Fifty-Fifth and Ninth. If you haven't heard sirens by then, call the cops. Do you think you can do that?"

She doesn't answer.

"V!"

"Yes, okay. But what are you going to do?"

"I'm going in after them."

"You can't, Jack! They'll kill you!"

"I don't have a choice, V," I say as calmly as I can. "If I don't end this here and now, whoever survives will come for us next and they'll keep coming until they run us down. I can't put you through that, so stay here until the shooting stops, then make that call." I tell V I love her, kiss her, then dash into the tenement through a back door.

I check the Browning's ammo. I've got about fifteen rounds left in my clip, but I'm holding the other two Carmine gave me. They should be enough to give me a fighting chance.

The tenement is a rabbit warren, full of dark corners to hide in and lie in wait. All of the apartments are abandoned, their doors off their hinges, their interiors dark and shadowy. The hallways are strewn with garbage and stink of urine and feces. I'm feeling my way along when a burst of gunfire coming from the floor above me sends me into a crouch. It's so dark that I can't see a thing—which is an advantage. If I can't see them, they can't see me. That's what I'm hoping anyway. And I'm moving again, trying to be as quiet as I can, but I manage only a few steps before stumbling over something.

It's a body. I can't make out who it is, but I smell the blood. I feel for a carotid pulse, but there isn't one. The guy has taken a round clean through the throat, and my hand comes away thick with his blood.

I hear two guys whispering. Beams from their flashlights dance across the hallway walls. They're bound to spot me, so I drop into a prone firing position before they do and let loose a burst from the Browning. They take the fire full-on and are catapulted backward. More voices now. Shouts. Footsteps coming my way. I duck into one of the empty apartments just as two more guys come hurtling down the hall. I let them get past me, then come up from behind, shout, and when they turn, fire.

I've been lucky so far. I've held the element of surprise, but now that's gone. I've got to keep moving, trying to outflank whoever comes for me next. I grab a flashlight out of the hand of one of the guys I've just shot and search for a stairwell, a way to get to the high ground, a way to the roof.

There's carnage in the stairwell. Three bodies are sprawled there, and four more are lying in the hallway of the floor above. I shine the flashlight on their faces, looking to see if they are Garrett or Carson or both, but they're not here.

I make my way to the top of the stairs and try to push open the door to the roof, but something's blocking it. It takes effort, but I manage to shove it open and find still another body. It's Carson's driver, shot through the heart, his automatic still in his outstretched hand.

"I'm over here," Carson calls out.

This is probably a trap, so I'm cautious. I ease my way out onto the roof, around a corner, and find Carson propped up against the iron base of a rooftop water tank. He's been hit and it's bad.

"We just don't know when to leave well enough alone, do we, Jack?"

"Occupational hazard in my line, Bob. You're bleeding, you know? You should probably see somebody about that."

"A little too late, don't you think?"

"I guess so."

"Is the kid okay?"

"You mean Lucy? Lucy's dead." My delivery is pretty brutal, and Carson takes the news like he's been slapped.

"Then I've got something of hers for you. It's in the back seat of the Caddy. If you make it out of here alive, look after it for me, will you?"

"Where's Garrett, Bob?"

"I'm right here, Jack." Garrett appears from behind me. He's heard every word, and before I can even turn around, he shoots Carson, killing him.

Garrett then levels his gun at me. "Where are they, Jack?"

I'm not sure what good stalling for time is going to do me, but it's the only thing I can think of. "Are we talking about your home movies, Abie?"

If calling him Abie annoys him, he doesn't show it. "You didn't bring them?"

"What do you think?"

"That's a shame," Garrett says, jacking another round into the chamber of his gun. "It really is."

"Listen, before you do something you'll regret," I say, vamping as fast as I can. "You should know that your friend in Florida isn't exactly pleased with you. He thinks you've been up to business even he and the boys find pretty appalling, and from what I hear, he's not going to put up with it."

"Yeah? How do you know that?"

"If you walk away right now, he might let you live. If not, well, you know what Meyer's like once he makes up his mind."

If this threat worries Garrett, he doesn't let it show. Instead, he says, "If you don't have the movies, Jack, I guess I'll have to get them from your girlfriend."

"I don't have them either," V says, stepping out of the shadow of the water tank, and without a moment's hesitation, she puts three bullets in Garrett.

He's dead before he hits the ground.

I guess I knew V still had the gun she showed me on our way back from Miami, but to tell you the truth, I thought of it more as a fashion accessory than a deadly weapon. But it turns out V has been carrying it in her purse since the day she bought it, which is a lucky thing for me. If she hadn't, someone would be saying Kaddish over me—that and the *Our Father* just to keep my funeral appropriately ecumenical. Anyway, I'm so grateful to V for saving my life and so amazed by the way she coolly dispatched Garrett that I nearly forget that Carson said he left something for me in the back seat of his Cadillac.

But before I get a chance to find out what it is, I have to answer to the cops. The tenement is swarming with them, at least two dozen in uniform. On the street, three meat wagons from the coroner's office are being loaded up with the dead.

A homicide detective from Midtown North has got me sitting on the curb outside the tenement, and he's grilling me. He isn't giving me the third degree exactly, but he's leaning in pretty hard, wanting to know the who, when, and why of it all. I'm reluctant to say anything, and he's ready to take me downtown, thinking the trip might get me to talk, when Bernie Rothstein steps in.

Bernie pulls rank, shoos the guy away, sits down on the curb next to me, and says, "This is going to take a hell of a lot of explaining, Jack."

"Yeah. I figured that."

"Did you do Garrett?"

"Nope."

"Who then?"

"You really don't want to know the answer to that question, Bernie. Let's just say he was dead when I found him." Rothstein must know there's more to the story than I'm telling, but he's willing to let it go. His life is simpler that way.

"I'll have somebody take your statement, then you can go home." He pats me on the knee before getting to his feet and moving off.

When I find V, she's peering into the back seat of Carson's Cadillac.

"What did he leave me?" I ask.

She turns around and says, "You're not going to believe it."

She's bundled in a blanket with a tiny knit cap on her head and the tip of her thumb in her mouth. Somehow she's slept through all the commotion, and careful not to wake her, I gently lift an infant off the back seat.

"She's beautiful, Jack."

You might think that I'm the last person on earth to be moved by holding a child in my arms, but when that little girl opens her eyes and smiles up at me, I'm hit by a surge of joy so unadulterated that I nearly begin to cry.

"She must be Lucy's," V says. "What are we going to do with her?"

"I don't know, but we're sure as hell not leaving her here."

CHAPTER FORTY-SEVEN

After we get the baby home, I promise V that I'll find a good family for her, a good home where she can grow up safe and happy. The law says that I should turn her over to Child Services, but I'm not about to do that. She'll be shuffled from foster home to foster home, and God only knows what will happen to her then.

V is more than patient and helps out whenever and wherever she can. She buys the baby most everything she needs: diapers, baby clothes, a bassinet, a little stuffed rabbit to hold while she sleeps, even a mobile of stars and half moons to hang over her crib. V even picks up a copy of Dr. Spock's *Baby and Child Care* and laughs when I spend hours poring over it, trying to do everything the good doctor recommends. She cuddles and plays with the baby and volunteers to get up with me for her 3:00 a.m. feeding, even on nights when she has shoots in the morning.

I've been calling her Mouse because she's about as small and as cute as one, but V says I might scar her for life by calling her that and she names her Sarah after my mother.

But as wonderful as she is, Victoria Hemming is not really cut out to be a mother. She tries her best, but motherhood doesn't come naturally to her. Maybe it's her father's abuse or because Sarah isn't really hers, or maybe she's just one of those women who doesn't want children. V doesn't say that in words—she never would—but as sweet and helpful as she is, I can tell her heart isn't in it.

My heart is. I'm supposed to be this hard guy, but that little girl makes my life worth living in ways that I never could have imagined, which surprises the hell out of me. I might have felt guilty for keeping her if Lucy was still alive, or if her father was, but who was that exactly?

As disturbing as I find the idea, it might have been Bob Carson, but there was something avuncular about his affection for Lucy and I wouldn't be surprised if he never touched her. It could have been Rex Halsey, but I hope not. I don't much like the idea of Sarah swimming around in his sleazy gene pool. And it might even have been Garrett. Or maybe it was somebody else entirely, somebody I don't know and never heard of. I don't care really.

Bernie Rothstein calls a few days later and says he wants to stop by the apartment to talk. The last thing I want is Bernie asking me what we're doing with an infant in a crib in our bedroom, who the infant is, and what we intend on doing with her, so I tell him I'll meet him downtown. When he wants to know how I got myself in the middle of the tenement shoot-out, I tell him the truth—most of it, anyway. I leave out my trip to Carmine's arsenal in Bay Ridge, and I don't say a word about Sarah, but I tell him most of the rest.

When I finish, he says, "You know, Jack, the deal wasn't what we thought it was."

"How do you know that?"

"Lillian Crouse told me."

Bernie managed to flip Lillian. She was a loyal family retainer, but she was also a good Catholic girl. When she realized what her boss had been up to, she was appalled, but the job paid too well to leave it and there was her mother to support, so she turned a blind eye for as long as she could. Bernie approached her in much the same way that I did, but he's a cop so he didn't have to resort to subterfuge. He just knocked on her door. And he didn't have to threaten Lillian with arrest or incarceration to get her to cooperate. Catholic guilt took care of that, and she volunteered to be his informant. When Garrett turned up dead, Lillian was out of a job, but at least she didn't have him to worry about anymore.

"Carson knew Garrett was laundering money for Lansky and wanted a piece of his action," Bernie tells me. "When Garrett refused, he had Lucy steal those movies to blackmail him. It was all about money. It always is."

"No, it wasn't, Bernie. Not really. It was all about the kid."

As the months go by, I keep telling V—keep telling myself, for that matter—that I'll find someone I like and trust enough to take the baby and raise her, but the truth is I can't bring myself to let Sarah go. V knows this and feels for me, but like I said, she isn't really cut out to be a mother and the strain is showing. I don't think it's really Sarah that's our undoing though. I'm not sure what is exactly. All the usual clichés probably apply. It's not something I can really put my finger on, not something as simple as someone coming between us. All sorts of guys still chase after V, most of them rich, some of them famous, but monogamy is in her DNA. I'm pretty sure the thought of cheating never crosses her mind. It never crosses mine either. But we're going sour.

One afternoon when Sarah is about eighteen months old, we're pushing her stroller across Sheridan Square. The silence between us is fraught, and it's past time to say what needs to be said. We agree that if we're going to break up, we ought to do it before Sarah gets any older. It's bound to be confusing and hurtful if we don't, and neither of us wants that. We're both pretty sad, despite knowing we're doing the right thing. V slips her arm through mine, and we promise always to be a family. But it's a promise we don't keep.

Years later, I tell Sarah about all of this. She's a grown woman, pregnant with a child of her own when I finally find the courage to tell her that I'm not really her father and that I don't know who really is. I meant to tell her sooner, as soon as she was old enough to understand, but I kept putting it off, afraid of how she might react. Now I feel like I owe her the truth.

To my enormous relief, she isn't shocked or horrified. She isn't even angry. Instead, she kisses me on the forehead, says that none of it matters, that I'm her father whatever genetics might have to say, and that she loves me. When she gives me a hug and a big kiss to prove it, I embarrass myself by bawling like a baby. A month later Sarah gives birth to a little girl, and then two more girls after that, and they all grow up to be as beautiful as their grandmother, which strikes me as utterly unbelievable. For me Lucy Garrett will be forever sixteen.

I saw Bernie's obit in the *Daily News*. It was just a blurb really. We got off on the wrong foot, but I liked Bernie. I hope he felt the same way about me. Sadly, he was pretty much persona non grata with the NYPD after all of that happened. In those days there were more crooked cops in the department than you could shake a stick at, and straight ones like Bernie made even the police brass nervous. He put in his twenty, bought a farm upstate, and retired.

I lost touch with Bud too after a while. It was inevitable, I guess. Fame is corrosive, and as much as he liked to pretend he was just another guy from Nebraska, it ate at him and finally ate him up. He didn't come into town as much as he used to. Instead, he holed up in Tahiti or Bora Bora like that would protect him. It didn't. Like everybody else I followed him in the papers and the gossip columns. I tried giving him a call after I saw *The Godfather*, but the number I had for him wasn't any good. No surprise there. It probably hadn't been for years.

Monk and I never lost touch. His combo played on at Minton's, which survived acid rock, heavy metal, punk, and everything else that came before, between, and after. He recorded some of his best work in the sixties. *Monk's Dream*, *Criss-Cross*, and *Underground* are all classics, but by the end of the decade, his mind was beginning to go. Too many drugs and too much alcohol, I guess.

Al McKibbon told me that on his final tour, Monk didn't say more than two words: "Not good morning, not good night. Nothing." He got so bad that Nellie had to have him hospitalized. I went to visit him a couple of times, but he was too far gone to recognize me. She and the Baroness nursed him through those last few years until a stroke finally took him. I went to his funeral over at St. Pete's. Gerry Mulligan played "Ruby, My Dear," Sheila Jordan sang "'Round Midnight," and

Max Roach, Charlie Rouse, and Tommy Flanagan sent Monk off to his eternal rest in style.

Carmine passed in his sleep at ninety, which surprised almost everyone who knew him. Most made guys end up getting whacked for one reason or another, or they spend their last days rotting in Dannemora or a supermax like Joliet. Even The Chin died in prison. But somehow Carmine avoided getting arrested when the Feds took down Gigante's crew. He might have turned on The Chin in exchange for a free pass, but I don't know that for sure. What I do know is that he and Estelle stayed married for more than fifty years, had a passel of kids and grandkids, and that Carmine happily fished off the pier at Sheepshead Bay until the day the good Lord called him home.

Dick Avedon became world-famous for his photography. He never quite left fashion behind, but his portraits were considered art, and for good reason.

And I finally went to a Giants game with him. In '62, he called me out of the blue and said he had an extra ticket to the championship game. It was freezing cold when I met him up at the stadium, the Giants lost, and we got loaded in P.J. Clarke's after the game. I saw Dick once or twice after that, but the worlds we ran in couldn't have been more different. It was big news when he passed. I sent a note to his widow. I didn't really know her, but it seemed like the stand-up thing to do.

And V? V and I drifted apart, which was inevitable, I guess. About a year after we broke up, she met Leo Randall. He was a downtown artist with a trust fund, but I didn't hold that against him. Leo was a decent guy, more than decent really. When V introduced him to me and Sarah, it was obvious that they were in love, and I tried to be happy for her. They married, and we didn't see much of each other after that.

I'd read about her and Leo going to charity openings at the Modern or the Whitney, or the papers would run a picture of the two of them at the Fire and Ice Ball. I felt a twinge of jealousy then, but it didn't last long. I had met Tracy, and we fell into a different kind of love, one that was solid and built to last.

Tracy couldn't have kids and embraced Sarah like she was her own.

It wasn't long before the three of us settled into a comfortable if slightly boring routine, and we were happy together.

Around the time Sarah turned sixteen, V was killed in a car crash out on the island. It was late, the weather was bad, and she was driving too fast when she lost control of the wheel. I was pretty broken up about it, despite not having seen or spoken to her in a long time, which was why I was surprised when I got a call from her lawyer.

He asked if Sarah and I wouldn't mind coming over to his office for the reading of V's will. It seemed like a strange request, and I asked him why he wanted us there, but he wouldn't tell me over the phone.

Leo was waiting when we arrived, and he looked haggard and grief-stricken. We hugged in that awkward way men do when they share a tragedy. I reintroduced him to Sarah, and we took seats for the reading.

It seemed pretty boilerplate at first. V had made a lot of money in her time and, naturally, left most of it to Leo.

It all seemed perfectly straightforward, and I wondered what Sarah and I were doing there until the lawyer came to a codicil in the will. To my astonishment, V bequeathed one million dollars in trust to Sarah so that she could get "a good start in life. A better start than mine." V said that she was sure Tracy and I had raised her right, with the right values and sense of herself, and that she was investing in Sarah's future.

And then she wrote, "I'm leaving the cottage to you, Jack. I know how much you loved it there and it makes me happy to think of you sitting in that overstuffed chair by the fireplace, listening to Monk, and maybe even thinking about me."

I lost it then. We all did. Leo and I hugged each other again, and this time we meant it. Sarah hugged him too and kissed him on the cheek, and we promised to stay in close touch. We did, too, until Leo passed. I could see why V loved him. He was a sweet and generous man.

My hearing may be almost gone, but that's Sarah and her girls pulling into my driveway. They're closing up the cottage for the winter, bundling me up, and driving me back down to the city. I'm still on Perry Street, upstairs in a bigger apartment. I'm long past being able to climb the stairs, but they put an elevator in the building a few years ago, so I'm still able to manage. And I finally let Sarah hire a minder for me, a stout Honduran woman who cooks, cleans, and generally looks after me.

When she comes through the door, Sarah calls out, "Dad?"

"I'm in here." Her girls stream into the house, throwing their arms around me and kissing me on the top of my head. They busy themselves collecting my gear. I try to help out as best I can, but that doesn't amount to very much these days. They load up the car, and pretty soon we're on the Taconic Parkway headed back into town.

I've been pretty lucky, you know? Very lucky really. If that luck holds, I'll be back at the cottage again in the spring forever, grateful for Tracy, God rest her, and for Sarah and her girls, and remembering that I was once in love with Victoria Hemming.

I still think about her, you know? I think about her most every night before I drift off to sleep. Somehow, I'm sure V knows that I do.

ACKNOWLEDGMENTS

I'm grateful to the late Richard Coffey for encouraging me to become a writer when everyone around me thought it was a foolish notion. I'm equally grateful to Jack Rapke, the last of the gentlemen Hollywood agents, for launching my career and helping it prosper. I'm forever in Adam Chromy's debt for his persistence and his belief in me as a novelist. And I want to thank Dana Isaacson for his invaluable advice in crafting and focusing this novel.